Arnold Zable is a highly acclaimed novelist, storyteller and educator. His books include *Jewels and Ashes*, *The Fig Tree*, *Cafe Scheherazade* and *Scraps of Heaven*. Zable was born in Wellington, New Zealand, in 1947. He lives in Melbourne with his wife and son.

SEA *of* MANY RETURNS

Arnold Zable

Text Publishing Melbourne Australia

The paper in this book is manufactured only from wood grown in sustainable regrowth forests.

The Text Publishing Company
Swann House
22 William St
Melbourne Victoria 3000
Australia
textpublishing.com.au

First published by The Text Publishing Company, 2008
This edition printed in 2010

Cover and page design by Susan Miller
Typeset by J&M Typesetters
Printed and bound in Australia by Griffin Press

National Library of Australia
Cataloguing-in-Publication data:
Zable, Arnold.
Sea of many returns / author, Arnold Zable.
Melbourne : The Text Publishing Company, 2008.
ISBN 9781921520389 (pbk.)
A823.3

This project has been assisted by the Commonwealth Government through the Australia Council, its arts and advisory body.

To the people of Ithaca, and my travelling companions, Dora and Alexander.

And now, speak and tell us truly: where have you been in your wanderings? Which parts of the inhabited world have you visited? What lovely cities did you see, what people in them? Did you meet hostile tribes with no sense of right and wrong, or did you fall in with hospitable and god fearing people?

THE ODYSSEY, BOOK VIII

CHORUS
Ti na kanoume
Ti na kanoume
What can we do?
What can we do?
Ola ine tikhe
Ola ine tikhe
All is luck
All is fate.

Family Tree

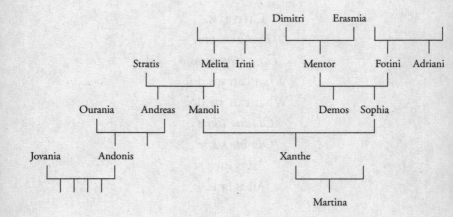

BOOK I
PROLOGUE

A boat called Brotherly Love

ITHACA 1928–1939

BEWARE dear reader. The story you are about to be told is a fairy-tale, a romance. There will be time enough later to tear it to shreds. In the meantime sit back and become a child again. Is there not enough darkness in the world? Come. Sit by the fire. Allow the voice of the storyteller to soothe you while you gaze at the flames. Perhaps it is an uncle, a grandmother, perhaps a lifelong friend. The day has drawn to an end. Your work is done. Outside, a storm is brewing. The wind is rising. It mocks the seas and rattles the shutters, but inside, the fire is burning. And the fire loves you. *Arkhe tou para-mythiou.* The fairytale begins. *Kalispera sas.* Good evening to you.

———

On the day they launched *Brotherly Love*, the whole village accompanied them on the long descent to the bay. At the head of the procession, a step ahead of his two sons walked Stratis. Behind them swayed the boat, balanced on a horse-drawn cart. Roosters crowed, goats stared from the mountainsides, a band of children tagged along, and villagers waved from the balconies of homes that lined the way.

The brothers had built the boat in the *katoi*, the storeroom beneath the house. Andreas was seventeen years old, Manoli fifteen. They cut the cypress on full-moon nights, for this, according to their mentors, was when the sap was most alive. They watched the boat-builders of Vathy and returned to the *katoi* to emulate what they had seen.

They sawed the logs into submission and laid the keel the length of the *katoi*. They carved the ribs and beams with tools that had been used by generations past, crafted the masts from cypress beams, and cut the sails from hand-woven cloth. They clad the hull and deck with planks of pine and caulked the gaps between them. And when the work was done, as if awakening from a dream, they saw that the boat was wider than the entrance to the *katoi*.

The men of the village laughed at their folly. The brothers gritted their teeth and cut the entrance until it was wide enough to release their prize. So it was a caesarean birth that enabled the boat to emerge into the light of day, and it was the priest who named it *Brotherly Love* for he had observed the close bond between the two boys. Andreas and Manoli were inseparable. While the villagers tended their fields and groves, the boys hovered on the periphery among the cypresses on the rocky heights, locked in conversation. 'How can two boys have so much to say to each other?' the villagers asked.

The men of the island were leaving, lured by tales of distant riches. They dreamt of returning to their impoverished villages, their trunks laden with spoils. As it turned out, many did not return and some disappeared without trace. But Stratis had returned, at long last, from the Great Southern Land. He reappeared suddenly, as if cast back by the same sea that had claimed him fifteen years earlier, but too late to see his wife Melita, who had died in his absence.

He unloaded trunks crowded with books: encyclopaedias of animal husbandry, dictionaries of medicine, illustrated discourses on the maritime arts, a seven-year collection of *National Geographic*, navigators' manuals charting the currents of the seven oceans, and the memoirs of mariners' journeys long past.

'These volumes are worth more than gold,' he declared, as he ran his fingers over the pages. 'Just to smell them is an education.' He studied them late at night at the living room table while his boys lay asleep in the adjoining room. But he had grown remote. His hair was a premature grey, and his face knitted into the permanent frown of a preoccupied man. He walked the village paths with an abstract air. He held secrets, so it seemed, and knowledge that had been gained at the expense of nights in the bare-boned rooms of boarding houses in distant lands.

Within months of his return he became the most sought-after man in the village. Whenever a problem arose, medical, domestic or maritime, it was Stratis who was consulted. He would turn to his books and from them draw remedies for common ailments, plans for more effective cisterns, designs for better goat houses and diagrams pinpointing the location of dwellings buried deep in the earth. He became part physician, part counsellor, part master mariner and world-weary sage.

Or was he merely a dilettante? This is what plagued him. This is why a frown remained creased on his brow. He saw himself as a fraud. He lay awake for hours tormented by the thought that he had wasted his life. He had never fully applied himself, and abandoned too many ventures. He had become a shadow of his youthful self and his sons had been raised in his absence. He saw that instead of love, he seemed to inspire wariness. He saw how free-spirited they had become except when they were in his presence.

Nevertheless, he walked proudly at the head of the procession that autumn morning. The path curved beneath the Marmakas Range or, it seemed, the range curved above the path, so that at one point it rose behind them and at another, reappeared in front. This is how it is on the island. Mountain, valley and sea stand in close proximity, so that by the time the procession unwound itself on the cusp of the bay, the hills were behind them, and all that could be seen were the boats lining the waterfront.

The crowd toasted the fledgling seamen, the priest raised his arms in blessing, and *Brotherly Love* was away, accompanied by a fleet of fishing caiques. Stratis watched until it was out of sight, and at that moment he knew that his sons would forsake him, as he had forsaken them. The sea coursed through their veins. *Thalassa. Thalassa*, it whispered. This was their ancestral calling. *Thalassa. Thalassa*, it hummed. It was their Sirens' song. *Thalassa. Thalassa*, it demanded, for this was their reality and living myth, inscribed in the verses of blind Homer, and embedded in the tales of Ithacan seamen long past.

Stratis was an Ithacan, a stoic, able to ride out any storm, and able to conceal his feelings. He turned, proud in bearing, in his wide-lapelled jacket and matching trousers, to trudge back to the white-stone house in the Village of the Forty Saints.

———————

As for Andreas and Manoli, their journeying had just begun. As they moved beyond the causeway, they knew why they had laboured to build the boat. It was the moment of their liberation and their imprisonment. They were cursed with a craving for departures and arrivals, condemned to live for the sight of islands receding and horizons beckoning.

It was the night-sea that sealed the brothers' addiction. At night they sensed the solitude that would outlive them, the sounds not known by day: the groan of pressured beams, the dialects of lapping waters, the murmur of restrained talk. Andreas and Manoli courted this solitude. They would leave the house at night and set out for the bay. They walked the familiar route beyond the last shadows of the village, past the shelter that housed the olive press, and homes that stood like petrified ghosts in the lower hamlets.

They knew each cypress on the way. The cypress was a tree of the night, a reflector of the moon. They approached the outskirts of Frikes and looked up at balconies that cast forlorn shadows over their path. The final windmill, perched on an outcrop of rock, marked the way, and beyond it, past one last row of darkened homes, the path petered out by the wharf.

The boat awaited them like a faithful mule straining at the ropes. They loaded their supplies and readied the nets. They untied the ropes, lifted anchor, and moved past the breakwater to the open sea. As soon as the winds allowed it, they cut the engine and hoisted sail. At the fishing grounds they lowered the anchor and spread the nets. The Marmakas Range disturbed the sky with the black outlines of its peaks.

As the nets settled, the brothers lay back on the boards and rested their heads on their arms. Only the bare planks separated them from water. Remove those planks and all that remained was sky and sea, and two brothers in between. Andreas and Manoli drifted towards manhood in silence. To talk now was a desecration, a scar upon the night. They returned before dawn, left the nets to dry, and began the long walk home with their catch.

As they ascended the sea ascended with them; they retained its presence in their skin and clothes. The air exhaled the scent of pruned olive branches burnt during the day. It was an unspoken secret, this love of movement through the dark. It was their joint venture, a passion that bound them together. They loved both the casting off and the return, the sight of the village receding and reappearing still covered in night. And years later, when out at sea at opposite ends of the earth, each brother would feel the absence of the other as acutely as a missing limb.

———

Though self-proclaimed atheists, Andreas and Manoli could not completely abandon the old ways. They nailed an icon of Saint Nicholas, patron of harbours and fishermen, to the wheelhouse wall. Whether Nicholas, wild Poseidon, or Aeolus, lord of the winds, the impulse to call on a higher power would rear with the first intimations of a gale.

The brothers came to know the winds because their lives depended on them. They had been taught to know them by an uncle, a fisherman, an Ionian seaman, a family friend. Each wind was a living force, identifiable, capable of being understood. There was a west wind that brought rain, and a west wind that thrived under clear skies. There were hot winds that brought storms and winds that trailed rainbows in their wakes.

Every point of the compass was accounted for, and each wind possessed a personal name. *Pounentes* was a summer wind that blew from the west. *Levantes*, the east wind, bore the echoes of an Ottoman past. From the northwest, the winter *Maistros* stirred savage seas on its flanks. The *Sirocco* conveyed the sands of African deserts and scalded the eyes. *Garbi* was a southwesterly that spawned sudden squalls. While below them surged the Ionian, besieged by swells and currents, and pacified by deceptive calms.

For days on end the calms persisted, until broken by an outbreak of chaos. White squalls, the seamen called them. They swooped down from the summits spurred on by winds that had swept away the sun. Within minutes, clouds blanketed mountain and sea. The brothers would return to the deep to ride out the storm, or if close enough to land, they would lower the sails, start the motor, and head for the safety of the nearest cove.

Ithaca was the epicentre of their world. A map of the island was glued to the cabin wall. From Agios Ioannis in the north, to Andri in the south, the island measures twenty-nine kilometres. The two halves, north and south, are joined by an isthmus, barely eight hundred metres wide at its narrowest. The boys did not need the map to navigate its shores. They knew each pebbled beach and treacherous rock, each inlet and harbour.

The brothers graduated to bigger boats, and ferried passengers and freight to ever-distant ports. They voyaged where ships confined by timetables could not. They crossed the narrow strait to neighbouring Kefallonia where prized robola wines were lowered to them by rope down steep slopes. They journeyed east to the coastal town of Zaverda and returned with contraband tobacco and brides for Ithacan men. They crowded the decks with potatoes and wild horta, gathered from the uninhabited hills of smaller isles.

They voyaged east to the mainland port of Patras and berthed between ships from all corners of the globe. Ocean liners lounged against the wharves like stranded whales. Freighters strained at their leashes, their bulwarks almost touching. The brothers walked the esplanade lined with warehouses and the offices of shipping lines. They sat in coffee houses with seamen who spent hours eyeing the heavens while dealing cards to pass the time.

It was always the first approach, the virgin voyage on an unknown stretch of sea that quickened the heart. It was late afternoon when they first approached Zakynthos. Andreas and Manoli made out the full sweep of the bay, the outlines of baroque mansions and shaded arcades. They walked the streets at night, crossed the cobbled square of St Mark, and paused at the doors of the opera house while the perfumed audience filed out.

They sailed north within a breath of the mountains of Albania. Corfu appeared on the horizon beneath a halo of subdued light. They rounded the old citadel into the main harbour and eased the caique towards the waterfront. The stucco-clad buildings were fading to ochre facades. Above the city an anvil-shaped cloud billowed into a darkening sky: the moment of perfection before the onset of a squall.

———

Twice a year, in October and August, on the feast days of Gerasimos, patron saint of Kefallonia, the brothers were called on to ferry the insane and their desperate kin. The caique set out in the darkness with its cargo of the distressed. It sailed the length of the east coast, rounded the southern cape and continued west, across the strait to the port of Sami. The insane, restrained in straitjackets, howled like lost spirits in search of a way home. The brothers watched as they were led off the boat like tethered goats.

For want of something better to do they accompanied them to the Omala Valley, home of the saint. Cypress and firs glittered in the sun as they descended the path from the road. Pilgrims lined the avenue that ran from the church of Gerasimos to the plane tree the saint was said to have planted four centuries ago. The procession moved from the church led by three boys dressed in white. A file of priests accompanied the bier bearing the mummified remains. Mothers clutched sick babies, and teenage daughters supported their crippled elders. Children stared at the shrivelled corpse and wondered what the fuss was about.

The possessed and the pious, the lame and the troubled, flung themselves on the road so that Gerasimos would cure them by passing over. And as if in defiance of the brothers' scepticism, when the boat cast off for the return the change was palpable. Madness had been subdued into tranquillity. The insane stood on the deck and gazed at the sea with the awe of infants. It rarely lasted, of course. Within days, perhaps hours, the burden returned, but this interlude of quiet homecoming was ample reward for the journey to the saint.

For twelve years Andreas and Manoli plied the Ionian. In time, the movement took hold, an eternal orbit of casting off and return. The brothers came to know the veil that falls as one island recedes and the next is yet to appear. In calmer weather they surrendered to the drift and savoured their moments of respite; the labour of departure behind them, the labour of arrival yet to come.

At night the caique sailed through a protean world. Shadows took fleeting form before giving way to darkness. Chapels and monasteries on deserted heights appeared abruptly, and dissolved like pallid ghosts. Phantom-like figures could be seen moving on mountain paths. Hamlets twinkled with the promise of warm hearths. Come, the Ionian whispered. Come and know the Ionian light, the stark contrast between whitewashed days and becalmed nights.

It was Manoli, the younger brother, who began to long for other worlds. He scanned the horizon with a gnawing restlessness. He was lured to oceans bigger than the confined sea on which he sailed. He envied those islanders who had set out on voyages to the Americas, Africa, Asia and *Afstralia,* the Great Southern Land. After all, his father had made the journey and, Manoli reasoned, unlike Stratis he would be away for a restricted time.

He would return pockets bloated with cash, and enough wealth to place the finest marble on his mother's grave. He would return wealthier than his father and build a home overlooking Afales. He would ply the Ionian, and establish trading routes by way of the Adriatic to Venice. He would build bigger boats and run them to the Black Sea and through the mouth of the Danube. He would replicate the Ithacan shipping dynasties of centuries past, and construct a fleet of liners and freighters. He pictured the day of his return, his arrival back in the village, the children chasing him, chanting: Manoli is back! Manoli is back!

No matter how hard Andreas tried to dissuade him, Manoli clung to his plans. Andreas ferried his younger brother, as they had both ferried many others on the first leg of their journeys. For the final time the brothers descended from the Village of the Forty

Saints. They were silent as they walked, and remained silent as they moved away from the port of Frikes to sail south, within sight of the east coast.

Manoli did not allow himself to dwell on the landscape. He did not register the three windmills on the headlands of Kioni Bay. He did not glance up at towering Mount Neriton as they spiralled into the Gulf of Molos. He remained detached as the boat bent past Mount Aetos into Vathy Bay. He avoided his brother's eyes as Andreas helped him deposit his suitcases on the waterfront. He did not look back when he stepped aboard the larger boat.

Andreas untied the ropes and set out for the journey home. For the first time, he sailed the caique alone, and he could not dispel the words that recurred, unbidden. 'He has turned his back on the island.' No matter how hard he tried to erase them, the words pursued him on the voyage home: 'He has turned his back on the island.'

———

The sun was barely on the ascent as Manoli stood on the deck, bound for Patras, the mainland port. His mind teemed with grandiose plans. He was oblivious to the island's receding presence. The first to wane were the sharper colours, the ochres on the upper slopes. He lost sight of the windmills and Kathara monastery, perched on the Mount Neriton heights. The peaks sank under the horizon; the island was completely shrouded within itself.

Only then did he realise that he had cast off without the prospect of imminent return. He had not counted on this. He was seized by a sense of panic, the first suggestion of a nagging doubt. Perhaps nothing would become of him. He tossed in his bunk at night, and paced the decks, consumed by conflicting thoughts. There were no familiar harbours within reach, nor familiar seas to ferry him home.

No matter how much he tried to ignore them, he was plagued by images of his caique moving homewards, huddled against wind and rain, lit by rising suns. And in the cabin, the smell of tobacco, the map of the Ionian, a pot of basil, and the ancient amphorae they had pulled from the sea.

He dwelt on the homecoming ritual: the dropping anchor, the flinging of ropes, stepping ashore to gut and clean the night's catch, spreading the nets to dry. And the village madman, limping towards them, chanting his habitual refrain: 'Ah. You are back from the sea. Did you bring any fish?'

Weeks later, as the ship moved over the equator, Manoli's doubts sharpened. One thought, above others, repeated itself. It grew more incessant with each kilometre. It resonated as he sighted the white sands of the west coast and moved towards the port of Fremantle. It persisted as he sailed east from Albany along a deserted coast. It pursued him through the entrance of Port Phillip Bay, the final landfall. Would he ever see Ithaca again? Would he ever see his Ithaca again?

BOOK II

Return to Ithaca

IT IS a long flight from Melbourne to Athens. I sit beside my daughter Martina and watch the lights of the city vanish. We stop for several hours in Singapore and wander the shopping arcades. We no longer know what time it is, but we know it is night and we are tired and disoriented, and seduced into purchasing goods we do not need. Passengers cheer when the plane lands in Athens, and release the grip on their worry beads.

We haul our luggage aboard the bus to the city, timed to arrive as the working day begins. Snarled in the early morning traffic, we crawl through suburbs littered with scrap metal yards, advertising hoardings, foundries and junkyards, crushed beside apartment blocks that rise from the lower slopes like asthmatics gasping for air. After ten years, I am back in a Levantine city, trapped in an infernal battle with heat and decay.

Even at this hour the city veers between fatigue and defiance. Grit settles on cracked facades. Streaks of rust triumph over walls recently painted white. Antennae and airconditioning units sprout from roofs and walls. There are leafier suburbs with luxurious homes tucked away elsewhere, but for the most part, Athens, as I have come to know it, is a chaos of commerce tempered by apartments spawning balconies that vie for a glimpse of neighbourhood square, a sliver of sky. A city of a thousand villages coalesced into one sprawl that strives to live like the one village that started it all.

Yet at the core there is something else. I see it from the bus as it nears the final stop. The Acropolis rises above the chaos; on its plateau I glimpse the Parthenon and Temple of Nike, the symmetries of a more ancient past. Even after the long journey, weighed down by weariness, I am elated. I know now, as I always do at this moment, that regardless of what follows, I am glad to have embarked on the journey.

As soon as I have found a room, I set out with Martina for the climb. I am struck by the resemblances between Martina and my mother, Sophia, and for a moment my regret returns, a regret known only to daughters whose mothers have died before the birth of their first child.

On the descent we pause to sit on a perimeter wall. Viewed from the heights Athens is a maze of rectangular white shapes, softened by distance and fading light. This climb to and from the summit of the Acropolis has become a private ritual born out of previous journeys and, in this moment, poised above the city, the ritual conveys me, as it always has, to a sense of calm.

The ritual is not complete. The following morning we walk from the *pension* through the streets of the Plaka to the Agora, where the citizens of the ancient polis gathered to gossip and conduct their affairs. I bypass the excavated remains of stellae, pediments and colonnades, and make my way to the assumed site of the state prison.

All that can be seen are fragments of wall overgrown by wild grasses and clovers. Shards of ceramic are embedded in the paths. A dog wanders by in search of shade; emaciated cats nestle against moss-grown rocks. The wind rustles through olives and pines. It is an ideal place to contemplate what took place here over two millennia ago.

In 399 BCE, surrounded by disciples and friends, Socrates swallowed a goblet of hemlock as directed by those who had condemned him to death. He was not the first, and certainly not the last, to be murdered for the subversive act of asking questions.

Martina is eight years old. I tell her that it is not so much the fact that Socrates may have died on this site that brings me here, but that he was an independent thinker, a lover of knowledge.

'It is sad that he died,' she says.

A tortoise diverts her attention. The carapace is barely visible, all but camouflaged in the ruins.

'Is the tortoise dead?' Martina asks.

She reaches out for the carapace, but before she can touch it the head darts out and the tortoise shuffles off to a safer retreat.

Martina has eyes for tortoises. And cats. And there are many. They slip between the stones of the Agora, slink down alleys, hide and seek among rubbish bins, crouch in derelict buildings, and scavenge at the tables of pavement cafes. The cats are an underclass unto themselves, mangy foragers who eke out an existence in the netherworlds. Whenever we eat out, Martina forsakes half her meal to feed them.

'Watch out, they are carriers of disease,' says a passer-by.

'Mind your own business,' snaps Martina, and tries to corner one. The cats of Athens are survivors, adept at eluding any grasp.

There are other beings, apart from cats, that move discretely. The streets of Athens may be paved with dust, but in the eyes of the new beholders the dust glints with the promise of gold. They flit like shadows, the newcomers, from Africa, Asia and impoverished corners of Europe, clutching sacks slung over their shoulders. The sacks are filled with belts, shoes, bras, watches, handbags, jackets and socks. Occasionally one stops on a patch of pavement, spreads a blanket, upends the sacks, and sets up shop. With the approach of the police, he hastily packs and vanishes like an elusive breeze.

Each group has staked its modest claim. Pakistanis labour alongside Albanians on building sites. A Bulgarian housemaid cleans the rooms of our *pension*. Nigerians spread out woodcarvings and snakeskin drums, and stalk the pavements with pirated CDs. Romanians on accordions and fiddles serenade diners, with the ill-humoured grins of reluctant performers. A young man from Bangladesh moves between cafe tables, selling roses. Disappointment skitters over his face when he is rebuffed. He moves on, trailing the bitter taste of humiliation.

A gypsy girl plays a mouth organ and holds out her free hand for cash. She has no energy, nor desire to smile. Chinese hawkers ferry imported goods from warehouses into cars, and set out for the port of Piraeus to sell them through the islands. Late at night, prostitutes from Eastern Europe circle Omonia Square, while their pimps keep a watchful eye for the police from the shadows. Greece is no longer a land of emigrants.

———·———

In the evening I open the shutters onto a direct view of the Acropolis. Jutting out from one of the flanks is a solitary palm. In the distance behind it, a hint of mountains and reddening skies, and in the foreground, the Plaka, a congregation of buildings that rise as far as the lower slopes. Not one leaf is moving on the rooftop gardens. No sign remains of the late night revelry. All is still, everything at rest. The ritual is complete. I have retrieved the rhythm of travel, a sense of detached movement, of the journey unfolding. Tomorrow I will return to the island.

———·———

The balcony of the *patriko,* the patriarchal house, overlooks the tiled roofs of Ageii Saranda, the Village of the Forty Saints. Two metres to the left, the open shutters of the bedroom windows are clipped to the white-stone wall. Whenever I am on the island I sleep in the bed in which Manoli, my father, was born. Martina now sleeps with me. On the first night she was afraid of the gnawing rats trying to forge a way into the room. Now that we have slept here several nights, she feels at ease.

We awake to the premature boast of a rooster, and the tinkling of sheep bells. The sheep are being driven past the house. Costas, the village shepherd, walks beside them, staff in hand. He strides the mountain like a colossus. He knows the lairs of trap-door spiders, and where the vipers burrow for their hibernation. He knows who lights the lamps in remote chapels and for whom the death bell tolls.

We step out on the balcony. Sit here long enough, as I did with Uncle Andreas, Manoli's brother, and you will see the entire island go by. A millennium has drawn to a close and the village is changing before our eyes. Two homes have been bought and restored by Germans, a derelict house acquired by Italians. In the lower reaches lives an English woman whose house is locked and boarded in the winter. She returns in spring, flings open the shutters, expels the dust, stocks the larder and, once the work is done, heads, towel in hand, to the pebbled beach of Afales.

Houses long abandoned have been restored by Ithacans who have returned to the island after years of toil in foreign lands. On the lower fringe of the village, an Athenian icon painter has transformed the husk of a cottage into a studio. An Albanian family has for the past decade rented a house nearby. Now that their fortunes are rising they are building a villa of their own. On the verge of the hairpin bend by the lower end of the village, they have erected a stone where one of their kin was killed when his motorcycle careered off the road. A plaque bears his ghostly photograph.

At siesta time the Albanians are still at work unloading sand and gravel, laying concrete, drilling and bulldozing, hammering, sawing, charged with the energy of those who, after years of oppression, have seized an unexpected opportunity to begin life anew. In the thousands they have crossed: from the Albanian mainland to Corfu, and south over the Ionian Islands. I have seen them in past journeys, mainly single men on the move, standing about in town squares, on street corners, stomping their feet to keep warm on cold mornings, stoic, in search of work.

Yet some things remain the same. Families of gypsies still pass through. They arrive on the ferry in the port of Frikes, and I hear them from the balcony proclaiming their wares over speakers as they ascend the northern roads. They journey like the carpet sellers of old, entire families, from grandmothers in white kerchiefs to babies swaddled in woollen clothes. One van is crammed with household utensils, plastic buckets, crockery, aprons and shirts. Another van follows, full of shoes.

And there are those who still wait for the call, and rely on agents in Piraeus to provide them with work on the boats. Cousin Andonis, Andreas' son, would like nothing more than to stay on the island and fish, but he must take his caique ever further from the coast. The seas are being fished out. Illicit dynamite and poachers have wiped out entire species.

Andonis lives in the lower village, near Frikes, where his fishing caique is moored. He lifts Martina up and greets her eye to eye. His fifty-year-old body radiates a physical energy that seems to burst beyond his taut confines. He is a tough muscular nugget who speaks with a bemused smile. He has children to support and must rely on his skills as a ship's engineer on oil tankers. His assignments take him from Argentina to Newfoundland, the Indonesian archipelago to San Francisco, from the icy waters of Vladivostok to the sapping heat of tropical ports.

'Once the agents would come looking for us,' he says. 'Now we have to go to them cap in hand.' All this for months at sea in the wombs of corroded hulks, fine-tuning the motors of tankers while choking on diesel fumes.

The living room of the *patriko* too is as it was when I saw it on my first visit two decades ago. A walnut table occupies the centre.

A chest of drawers, a worn divan, and glass-panelled cupboard lean against the walls. The room is governed by a framed photo of Stratis, my grandfather, beside his wife Melita. His head and shoulders are visible above his two sons, Andreas and Manoli, aged twelve and ten.

Look closely and you will notice that Stratis is not truly present. He was in Australia at the time. His image has been skilfully inserted, but no amount of skill can hide his distracted gaze. His thoughts are elsewhere. He is a disembodied presence, a white haired patriarch lost to other worlds. And, missing in the photo entirely is my grand aunt, Irini, Melita's younger sister, who took care of the boys after she died.

The house is two hundred years old, or more. No one knows exactly how old. Andreas and Manoli added a kitchen when they were fourteen and twelve, so the story goes. Stratis was still absent, the boys had to make do. Their kitchen was demolished six years ago. I appreciate the convenience of the spacious kitchen that replaced it, but miss what has gone.

Imagine a Chagall painting of a crooked room. The brothers built the kitchen without planning or forethought. They whitewashed the walls, painted the shutters green, and the perimeter of the fireplace black. They did not see, until it was too late, that they had fashioned the room to their own height. The angles were not quite right, the walls tilted, but the size did not deter visitors.

It became the most lived-in room of the house. Aunt Ourania, Andreas' wife of fifty years, would sit at the table by the open window and observe the neighbours as they moved past. On cooler nights, long after she had retired, Andreas and I remained by the kitchen fire. 'The fire is burning,' he would say. 'And the fire loves us.'

One evening I was mesmerised by a burning log crowded with ants. They had retreated in the thousands to the edge of the log. As the flames moved closer, the ants began to scurry about. Some darted into the flames. Others fell into the smouldering coals. I tried to herd them from the flames with a stick, but to no avail. They had lost their bearings. Perhaps they no longer cared to live with the loss of their queen. Unaware of their presence, Andreas leaned over, grabbed the edge of the log, and shoved it into the fire.

On warmer nights we sat on the balcony. It was here that Andreas first told me the tale of the boat called *Brotherly Love*, and he embellished it in the kitchen, and as we walked about the village. In his ageing he was a restless man. I would come across him leaning against the cast-iron balustrade, and soon after, seated on the veranda outside the kitchen. Then he would be gone, and I would catch him standing below the balcony, gazing at the mountains.

'We are born to die,' he said, 'all of us, except the mountains. They only get smaller.' An hour later, I would come across him sitting in a neighbour's courtyard, gesticulating in his rapid fire Greek. Then he'd be gone, and would reappear on the road, hunched over his walking stick, in search of a way to whittle away the hours.

Uncle's walking stick had a life of its own. It had nine lives. I once saw it almost fall into the fire. I saw it all but crushed by a donkey. I saw it fall over the road into the path of a swerving car. At times it seemed abandoned, a solitary stick at rest against the bedroom door, but mostly it remained in the hands of its master.

Andreas would clutch it, twirl it, lean on it and, when seated, rest his head against it. It bore the full weight of his arms and upper body in the town square when he stood and talked to a friend he had not seen in a while. I saw it on cliff tops supporting an old man gazing at the waters he had once plied. And many times I saw it in the distance, in the hands of a bow-legged sailor and rider of donkeys, limping to the old *kafeneion* in Stavros, the largest village on Ithaca's northern heights.

———

To this day I prefer the old *kafeneion* to the bars and cafes that have sprouted on the main street, but there have been changes since I was last here. The floors are tiled, and the counter is marble, as fitting for a modern bar. Yet the old men still gather each morning, and they return, post siesta. A single light bulb still sheds a glow over each table, and the cards fall upon the green felt late into the night.

'A big wind today,' says one of the players, a former seaman, absent-mindedly. The men lift their heads and glance at the tourist bus that arrives mid-morning. The tourists are on the island for a day, and in Stavros, barely an hour. They roam the streets, cameras in hand, enter the cafes for a quick bite, and crowd around the bust of Odysseus on a pedestal in the village square. They study the map that tracks his journeys, photograph the bust, and are gone without a trace.

As the wind rises we retreat from the cafe terrace. The church clock, on the opposite side of the square, strikes eleven. The clouds have buried the mountains. They regroup, fall apart, and leave unexpected clearings of blue.

'How long will the winds blow?' I ask.

'Don't ask me, ask him,' replies one of the players, pointing at the sky.

Shadows slant over the mountains with the lengthening rays of the sun. We are returning from Stavros, a forty-minute walk from the Village of the Forty Saints. A kid bleats. Sheep pause to eat by the verge. Martina digresses to chase ill-fed cats. Below us, the last donkey of the north stands by a path, braying at the skies.

Late afternoon we are back on the balcony. Sunlight falls on the chapel, a white enclave high on the slopes, shaded by a cluster of trees. It is the eye of the mountain, I tell Martina, the guardian of the northern heights. Every time I have entered it, I have found a candle burning. Who makes the steep trek to light it?

The chapel is dedicated to John the Baptist. His eyes stare from an icon on the wall opposite the entrance. He holds a platter on which a replica of his head lies severed in a pool of blood. I feel a chill every time I see it, and I am reminded of my father's rage.

———

We have been on the island a week and our daily routine has been secured. We make our way to Stavros where we are invited to a gathering in Polis Bay to mark the first catch of the whitebait season. The boats have been out since early morning and have long returned. For the fishermen Ithaca is a constant presence, always within sight. I envy them their good fortune. They possess it all: the sea and the harbour, the departure and the return.

Old seamen jump like agile goats on and off the boats. They have dragged ashore the nets, secured the ropes, fastened the hatches and hosed down the decks. Several hundred guests are seated at tables beneath the plane trees, metres from the quay. The aroma of frying fish drifts from the kiosk door. Fishermen deliver plates heaped with olives, feta and whitebait.

A priest walks the quay with an assistant, blessing the fleet. The guests are too busy eating to take much interest. Vassili points to the crowded tables and claims there are over thirty retired sea captains seated among the guests. 'There are more captains and first mates than ordinary seamen,' he tells me. 'We are an island of captains; how can it be otherwise for a people who do not like being ordered about?'

Vassili, a retired public servant, cannot help but speak his mind. He reveres the Homeric myths, but loves nothing more than to deflate them. He had received threats in recent days for writing an article in an Ithacan newspaper that challenged the conventional view of Penelope. She had not waited faithfully for Odysseus to return, according to his version, but had slept with all the suitors. As a result she had borne a child, Vassili had written, and called him Pan, because no one could know who, among the suitors, was the father.

'Those that threaten me claim I have insulted the myth of their chaste Penelope, but it was not I who said this,' argues Vassili, 'but ancient Greek philosophers, like Duris of Samos, for pity's sake.' This is how it is on the island: true believers and sceptics live out their days side by side.

Uncle Andreas was a sceptic. Like many self-taught men, his philosophy was a homespun fusion drawn from his years at sea, countless conversations in waterfront cafes while holed up in Ionian ports, his endurance of the Occupation, and the books that randomly came his way. 'He would still be reading when the cocks crowed,' Ourania complained.

'I am a citizen of the world,' his hapless brother Manoli proclaimed on the other side of the globe, his legs firmly planted on the ground, his chest puffed out, the veins on his forehead pulsating. His aloneness was palpable when he made his claim. 'All men are created equal and should not starve,' he added. My father was a man of noble sentiments, but as a child I lived with his dark moods, his anger. And I was afraid.

———

Though he was an atheist, Manoli would have found common cause with Dionyssios, the priest. I see him from the balcony at the wheel of his utility careering by. He stops at the all-purpose corner store for a round of drinks, to add to the considerable quantity he has consumed in cafes on the way. *'Exo ftokhia, ke kali cardia,'* he says, 'out with poverty and in with good heart,' signalling yet another round.

His greying hair is thick and tied in a ponytail. He walks with quick steps propelled by a nervous energy and a robust smile. He had worked as a stonemason before studying for the priesthood, and to prove he still possesses great strength, he shakes hands with a vice-like grip.

Once, while giving me a lift from Vathy to the village, he asked: 'Why haven't you had a child?' I was sitting beside him in his utility while my partner sat, out of hearing, on the tray.

'You are thirty years old and time is running out,' he said without waiting for an answer. 'Your husband should do as I did. After years of trying, my wife had not conceived. I went to Doctor Kouvaras, who knew how to treat problems with remedies far more affective than potions and pills.

'The doctor instructed me to climb beyond Kathara monastery, to the wooded peak of Mount Neriton. "Put your builder's hands to good use," he said. "Make a hut out of branches and deck it out with cypress leaves, and on the next full moon take your wife to the monastery. Do not tell her where you are going. Lead her by the hand to the hut and, as soon as you enter, take her with passion." I followed his advice to the letter, and my wife conceived. That is why I have a daughter, and grandchildren to keep me company in my old age,' he chuckles.

I have caught the Ithacan disease. I digress and chatter about this and that, but I want to slow the story, as the island has slowed me, and convey its rhythms, the ebb of its silences. There will be time enough for the storm. I wish to begin with gentler times. I have come, yet again, in autumn. The summer chaos is over, the holiday crowds gone. Motorcycles that tear through the villages like a plague of mosquitoes in July and August, are far fewer in number. They call it the little summer of St Dimitri, this October interlude, weeks of clarity and warmth that herald the descent into winter.

———

It was October when Andreas would leave the island for Athens. His restlessness would increase as the day of departure drew nearer. I would hear him swearing late at night from his bedroom. Perhaps he was dreaming of old enemies, taking stock of unfinished business. Perhaps fuming at the inevitable passing of his days.

Thinking back on that time, I tell Martina the tale of the almond tree. We are sitting in the renovated kitchen, which has absorbed Andreas' old bedroom. 'There is a saying,' I begin, '"I said to the almond tree, speak to me of God, and the almond tree blossomed."'

My mind wanders for a moment. I think of the kitchen, as it

once was, with uncle's bedroom directly off it, his curses audible through the half-open door. Martina is annoyed. 'You're not here again,' she says.

'One morning aunt Ourania departed on the early bus for Vathy,' I resume. 'She planned to be out for the day. "Come with me," uncle Andreas winked, soon after she was gone. He was in high spirits, released to do as he pleased. I was to be his unwitting partner in crime, the extension of his thin arms. He led me outside to the almond tree beside the house, and handed me a saw.

'"Cut it down," he told me.

'"Are you sure?" I asked.

'"The almond tree is a pest," he said, pointing to the young olives on either side. "It is interfering with their growth." Despite his assurances, I remained uneasy at sawing through such a young tree, ripe with sap.

'"It has not been producing well," Andreas added, as if reading my thoughts. Besides, it was too late, Martina. The tree was toppling to the ground. We cut off the branches and left them at the feet of a tethered goat. Her yellow eyes glinted in the sun as she chewed the leaves. Her teats swung in rhythm with her lunges and bites. I cut the larger branches into firewood, as directed, and stacked them in the *katoi*.

'Andreas harnessed the donkey and led it through the village. To every passer-by he called out, proudly: "Where are you going lazy bones? We are off to work!" We unwound from the hem of the village past a row of stone cottages to the family grove.

'"There are olive trees one thousand years old," Andreas said, tapping the trunks with his walking stick. "There are millions in Greece and no two are alike. Each one bears a character of its own."

He moved about the trees and inspected their lower branches, felt them with his hands, jabbed them with his stick, and finally settled on one. It jutted horizontally from the main trunk, one metre off the ground.

'"The branch is diseased," he pronounced, and told me to cut it in four parts. "*Siga, Siga*," Andreas advised. "Take it slowly." He sat down on a stone, leant on the stick and directed the work. Uncle talked. I cut. The diseased branch was reduced to four logs within an hour. Andreas tied them to the donkey with an expert hand and we made our way back. "Where are you going lazy bones?" he asked passers-by. "We have been to work."

'Nearing the house, he quickened his pace. "We should hurry," he said. "The bus from Vathy will soon be back. We will light a fire and have the kitchen warmed up by the time Ourania returns."

'He need not have bothered. She had arrived home early. And she was not pleased, Martina, not pleased at all. "Leave him alone for a moment and see what he gets up to," she sneered.

'I left the warring couple in the kitchen and retired to the bedroom from which I could hear Ourania, thundering. "You have cut down a neighbour's almond tree! That bit of land belonged to her! How could you? I leave you out of my sight and see what you get up to?"

'Ourania's accusations grew louder, more strident. Andreas erupted. "Shut up!" he roared, stamping his feet on the rotting boards of the kitchen. "Enough damn you! Leave me alone."

'They continued to argue back and forth until finally, the house subsided into silence. By the time I ventured back to the kitchen, Andreas had retreated to a neighbour's house to lick his wounds, Ourania had sunk into a dark depression, and the almond tree, far from talking of God, had disappeared into the bowels of a goat, and the dark recesses of the *katoi*.'

'I know all the places in the story,' says Martina when I end.

'Not the old kitchen,' I reply.

'I like the new one,' Martina retorts. 'The rest of the house is too old.'

That autumn, ten years ago, would be the last time I saw Andreas. He returned with me to Athens to spend the winter months with his daughter's family. Ourania had left to winter in Athens weeks earlier. Andreas' bags were packed and ready at five in the morning, well before the taxi arrived. He was unusually silent, brooding. Perhaps he sensed what was to come.

We left the house in darkness. Only shepherds were about on the road to Stavros, urging their flocks to pasture. In the *kafeneion*, taxi drivers and insomniacs sipped coffee. We glanced at the lights of the bakery as the taxi swerved from Stavros onto the cliff road, and I imagined the vista behind me as it appeared from the opposite direction, on the final approach to Stavros.

I had seen it many times, the shroud lifting to reveal Exogi, the highest village, and above it, the peak of the mountain, the folds sweeping down to the lower ridges. The undulations resembled green waves, lighter in times of drought, darker after the rains. On the slopes could be made out a scattering of hamlets, swathes of olive groves and cypress.

In my mind's eye I saw the northernmost hamlet, the Village of the Forty Saints, and beyond, to the last house overlooking Afales Bay: the cliff path ascending to the remains of the mill that Andreas had worked during the war. Its conical red-tin roof perched on the circular walls like a witch's hat. The inner steps spiralled to the grinding-stone. The mill's innards resembled the workings of a broken clock, stilled by neglect.

We had crossed the invisible portal and the northern heights were behind us. I too was now afflicted with the curse of Ithaca, the longing for the return, a desire that flared as soon as a parting was imminent. The black peaks of Kefallonia, towering over the three-kilometre strait between the two islands, accompanied us until, abruptly, they too were gone: locked from view as we negotiated a series of hairpin bends to the east coast.

The taxi sped towards the port of Vathy and, still, Andreas was silent. His silence persisted as we boarded the ferry. He stood on the upper deck, one hand on the rails, the other resting on his walking stick, and gazed at the procession of vehicles being directed into the hold. The lamps lining the esplanade were giving way to the dawn, as the ferry unwound from the inner harbour and set course for the open sea.

Andreas remained by the rails as the mountains grew smaller, less defined, until the island was reduced to two peaks, one in the north, the other south. Ithaca appeared like a coiled spiral, turned in on itself, on its intimacies and enmities, its ghosts and abandoned dwellings. *Stenos kiklos*, a closed circle, from which we were now shut out.

Other islands appeared, the chain known as the Echinades. The islets had been way-stops for smugglers and partisans, stepping-stones to the mainland, where corsairs once withdrew before stealing back to sea under cover of darkness. And where Andreas, the resistance aide, had hidden by day to avoid patrols of enemy boats.

Andreas remained on deck even as the port of Patras drew near. He sat by the rails with his chin pressed on the crook of the walking stick. Kilometres out to sea, the port appeared huddled at the base of a towering hill. The sun had lifted into the mid heavens, a golden disc over the Ionian: a sea of many returns, and one last parting.

———

Uncle Andreas died two years later. I was long back in Melbourne. In those final months he sat on the balcony of his daughter's apartment in Athens. His mind was wandering, his body falling apart, but he knew what he wanted. He leant on the balustrade and cast his words to the winds, to passers-by on the pavements, to anyone who would listen.

'Take me to Ithaca,' he shouted.

'You are not strong enough to return,' Ourania insisted.

'The wind is up. The boat is waiting' said Andreas.

'You need rest, hospital treatment,' the doctors advised.

'The boat is leaving. Take me to the port,' Andreas demanded.

'You heard what the doctors said,' interjected Ourania.

When no one was home, he would descend to the street and approach strangers. 'Take me to Ithaca and I will pay you,' he pleaded, and held out his wallet.

Days before he died, he rose from his hospital bed, grasped the walking stick, glanced about to make sure no one was watching, and stole out to the corridor. He steadied himself on the wall, and hobbled from the foyer.

'I am in prison, held captive by fascists,' he shouted at passers-by.

'The wind is up. The boat is waiting. I beg you, help me escape.'

Now, in keeping with the curse, I have returned yet again, and all that remains of my uncle's presence are the tales he recounted on the balcony, by the kitchen fire, on the decks of ferries, in coffee houses. And the tales I have heard of Stratis, my paternal grandfather, and Mentor, my mother's father.

This is my final accounting. I have assembled the journals in which I recorded Andreas' rambling discourses, Mentor's manuscript, penned in Greek, and the first chapter of my manuscript: a tale of a boat called *Brotherly Love*. At night, when Martina sleeps, I set them out on the living room table. The first task, I have determined, is to translate Mentor's memoir.

I prefer it here, in the living room, on the unsteady boards, beneath the ceiling ribbed with cypress beams. It is the room closest to the sea. The winter is approaching, and the chill has descended. The church bells have struck eleven. The village is wrapped in silence.

———

Ithaca. I cannot recall the first time I heard the word. I was raised on the opposite side of the globe, yet it had always been there like an ancient longing welling up from the sea. I grew up surrounded by water. An embankment sloped from the house to the mouth of the Patterson River. Port Phillip Bay was visible from my bedroom window, and one kilometre upstream the river fed the swamps. Perhaps Ithaca was where the migratory birds headed when they left for their flight north.

Manoli built boats in the yard of the house. It was his enduring passion. His rage subsided only when he was out on the bay. There were times when he stormed out and did not return for days. He rarely spoke of Andreas, his brother, or his mother, Melita, and he cursed Stratis, his father. He poured venom on his wife Sophia, and forbade her to visit Mentor.

When, at last, we broke the prohibition, Mentor claimed he could turn my mouse into a rat. All he needed, he told me, was a three-month loan of the mouse. I was ten at the time. The cage in which he housed the mouse stood on his worktable, beside the human skull he used as a weight on his manuscript.

Sophia told me the story many times—as I have now told Martina, who was born a year after my mother died—tales of the skull, and of her father, Mentor the hypnotist, the magician and kite flier, fiddler and fiddle maker, chef and self-appointed healer, the village boy who descended the mountain and set out for new worlds.

'After the death of my mother, Fotini, it was the kites that kept him going,' Sophia claimed. 'And the backyard shed in which he made them.' Years earlier, when Sophia was a child, he held the skull in his right hand on the night he performed his magician's act 'The defeat of the devil'. The back-curtain was draped with a painting of a flight of stone steps rising from ancient ruins scattered over a mountainside.

'The devil was dressed in black from hood to leather boots,' said Sophia. 'He held a pistol, finger on the trigger, while I waited on a ladder behind the curtain. I wore a white gown with angel wings. My father tugged at the curtain and I slid down on a rope, wings flapping. I hated it. I heard members of the audience snigger, but Mentor did not care what anyone thought.

'At that time one of my chores was to go outside and polish the plaque on the front gate. "Mentor the Hypnotist", the engraved letters read. "Can cure neuralgia, insomnia, headaches, nervous disorders. Relief guaranteed. Enquire within."

'The usually compliant Fotini put her foot down, and refused to perform this chore. My mother wanted nothing to do with Mentor's experiments in the occult. It was left to me. I polished the plaque until it glowed. I did not dare look up lest I caught the eye of a passer-by. When the job was done, I ran inside.'

'You have forgotten about the angel,' I reminded my mother.

Sophia laughed at the memory.

'I slid towards him, wings outstretched,' she said. 'My job was to tap him on the shoulder as I was lowered to the stage. As soon as I touched him his posture straightened. His resolve tightened. The touch of an angel gave him courage to face the devil. The devil adjusted his pistol, took aim and fired. The shot sent a shudder through the audience. Mentor caught the bullet between his teeth. The audience gasped. Cynics reached for their worry beads before remembering they no longer carried them. The applause was louder than the sniggers.

'When the curtain was lowered, I packed away my wings,' Sophia concluded. 'I could not get them off quickly enough. What could I do? I had to play the part, polish the plaque, and do what I was told. That is how I was taught, to do as I was told.'

———————

I set out with Martina on the mule path to Exogi, early in the morning. The path breaks from the road into a forest of oak and cypress. Drops of dew hang from ripening olives. A dung beetle hauls droppings five times its size. The forest floor is littered with yellow toadstools.

Halfway up the mountain we pause at the ruins known as Homer's School. The diggings are boarded over; in summer, archaeologists will resume their excavations. The roots of olive trees split through rock formations that villagers claim are millennia old. A yellow-striped lizard basks in the sun. Like the tortoise of the Agora, it slips away before Martina can grasp it. A flight of stone steps ascends against a rock face. The ancient stairway leads nowhere, yet figures large in Mentor's manuscript.

We return to the path, which widens into a walkway between perimeter walls. Minutes later, we see the blue dome of St Marina, and the first homes of Exogi, built into the mountain. Stone steps provide short cuts between clusters of houses. We pause by the pile of rubble that was once the home Mentor was raised in, and break clear of the village on a path that runs towards the gate of a chapel beneath the summit.

On the lee side of the ridge the land plunges into a hidden valley, its sides indented with derelict terraces. From our vantage point, Exogi appears precariously perched on the edge of a cliff. With just one tremor, it seems, the entire village would be torn from the mountain and hurled into the sea by an enraged Cyclops.

We climb higher. A black goat lifts its head and gazes intently. The lower peaks and escarpments extend beneath us. We can imagine the entire island, the full expanse of it. It is small enough to be known, yet large enough to contain mysteries. Its mountains are high enough to conceal valleys, and its coastline long enough to obscure harbours.

A sea hawk circles above us. We are mesmerised by its cool mastery of space, but moments later it is caught by a gust of wind and hurled off-course. The battle between hawk and wind continues as we scale a dirt path to the telecommunications tower. Satellite dishes flash in the sun. The earth is littered with goat dung. The sea, in a three-hundred-degree sweep about us, is a sheet of mercury.

We are fully exposed to the wind. It alternatively erupts in violent gusts and dies back to silences. Within its invisible kernel I discern a hissing and bellowing, a tumbling and rising like the sinuous notes of a violin. For a moment I am afraid that Martina will be lifted and catapulted into the waters far below us. I clasp her hand as we battle our way against the wind, the final metres over a field of boulders, to the summit.

BOOK III

Mentor's manuscript

MELBOURNE 1967, ITHACA 1895–1916

I T IS my curse. I am in love with the summit: underfoot, the rocky earth, between boulders smooth as dinosaur eggs. Beyond the boulders, the limestone crust curving over cliffs into solitary coves, the sea stretching like a rumpled sheet, north to the island of Lefkada and west, to Kefallonia. So close, I can make out the settlements within its mountainous folds. And the sun, moving, spotlighting shepherd's tracks, the lower hamlets, the silver flecks of an olive grove.

Even now, over fifty years later, the scene comes upon me as I walk the streets of Melbourne, the city I have lived in more than half a lifetime. I stop, lean against a wall, catch my breath and smile the blessed smile of a man who is grateful that the island exists on this earth.

Perhaps it is true what they whispered in the Ithacan Club after my first-born, Demos, died. 'Mentor has gone mad,' they sighed, as they arranged their cards. '*Trellos ine*. The death of his son was too much to bear. He was a master chef, a fiddler, an Ithacan brother. Now he no longer plays at our weddings, no longer stuffs the intestines of lambs, nor joins us for a hand of cards. What a pity,' they muttered with the distracted air of those who are intent on the game. 'A man who spends too much time alone courts madness.'

Who could blame them? I had left my job and retreated to the domed reading room in the State Library. I was no comfort to my wife, Fotini. Neither of us could be consoled. I needed solace. I wanted to understand the cruel logic of fate. I wanted to know my purpose on this earth. I unnerved them. I have always unnerved people, though it has never been my intention. It is the lot of silent ones to make others feel unnerved.

I can only stay true to my nature, and it has its advantages. In my silence I am patient, and because I am patient I enjoy solitude, even on busy Russell Street, at a cafe table in the Greek quarter. I have always sought the silence that lies behind sounds. I isolate them as Mikhalis the fiddler taught me to do, break them down into components: the grunt of a truck, a snatch of song emanating from the music store, the lilt of conversations drifting through cafe doors.

Fragments of sound draw out fragments of memory. We all have our fragments to assemble and make sense of. We all harbour the secret wish, like blind Homer, to take the lyre in hand and recount our tales. For now, let an old man invoke the scenes of his childhood. I am indulging in nostalgia some would say, but I don't see it that way. The memory lives, and is as real as the world I see around me.

Nostalgia may be a curse, yet it is also one of life's pleasures, a pastime for the mind. In my ageing it is a salve to conjure the past. It enables me to play with time rather than be its slave. Have you noticed how many times a day we check our watches? It is a symptom of our disease. We cannot even abide the few seconds it takes for the traffic lights to turn from red to green. I have seen drivers reading newspapers as they wait. We cannot sit still.

Once I came across a line that encapsulated my thoughts. I had not been in Melbourne long. It was my habit at that time to take a break from work and stroll to the State Library. It was a ten-minute walk from the cafe in which I worked to the wrought-iron gates on Swanston Street. The gates are no longer there but the stone steps remain.

I paused in the forecourt, stepped into the foyer, and climbed the marble stairs to the domed reading room. I picked out books at random and flipped through the pages to test my understanding of the new language. I piled selected volumes on a desk, adjusted the swivel chair, and began reading. I found the line in a compendium of sayings, and copied it down. Over the years I have kept it in my wallet: 'Man's problem is not being able to stay alone in his room.'

When Demos died, the reading room became my haven. There was space beneath the dome to weep and not be seen. I took comfort in the stacks of books that were lined up like mute witnesses to my follies. I sat beside readers quietly immersed in their obsessions. I rested my head on the leather writing pads and lost myself in the scent of ageing pages.

The loss of a child, however, is a wound that can never heal. Not even the memory of the summit can obliterate the pain. Yet the scene can assail me at any time. I have no choice in the matter. It can rear up without my bidding; and I return to the beginning.

———

I was born on the mountain. Within hours of my birth, my father stepped out, lifted me above his head and shouted, so loud he could be heard at the furthest limits of the village, 'I have a boy. I have a boy.' His voice carried over the terraces, mule paths and barren ridges of the upper reaches. He proclaimed the news loud enough to penetrate the skulls of the men immersed in card games in the coffee house.

They grabbed their winnings, or made do with their losses, rushed out to the streets, and dashed up the flight of steps that led to our house. Dimitri lifted me one last time, handed me to my aunts, and accompanied the men back to the coffee house for celebratory drinks. As you can see, I glimpsed the summit before I tasted my mother's milk.

In time I acquired the sturdy walk of those who are born on mountains. My thighs grew thick, my calves hard, and my ankles supple enough to withstand the shock of rocks and boulders. The peak greeted me each day as I stepped out of the house. It drew me to the path beyond the village, and above terraces planted with flax, corn and vines. The path arced past the last church and graveyard. I inhaled the incense trailing through its open doors, and climbed above the receding homes towards the chapel beneath the summit.

I dashed through the forecourt, skirted the belltower, hoisted myself over the perimeter wall, and clambered over the final barrier of rocks. I scoured the sky for the sea hawk. I wanted to exchange my arms for wings and survey the island through its predator eyes.

I had no need of company. I enjoyed the subtle presence of goats. I had only to follow the bleating of the mother to see the placenta within minutes of birth. The kid struggled up to the teats, while the placenta lay on a crag, pulsating, for a moment, before being torn to shreds by sea hawks.

On the mountain there are no creatures better to emulate than goats. They are sure footed and find sustenance where other creatures would starve. They tear the bark off trees and, if out of reach, piggyback on sheep to grab hold of succulent leaves. They know when a storm is looming, and when it descends, their faces peer from, and disappear into, the clouds.

I roamed the mountain alone, or with Stratis. Four years older, Stratis lived in a lower hamlet, the Village of The Forty Saints. I followed him like a faithful kid bleating at his heels. At night we became fiends. We raided gardens and ran from enraged dogs. We fled up trees like terrified cats and did not come down until dawn. We stole watermelons, but they tasted so bitter we threw them away. In the morning we saw that we had bitten into pumpkins. The daylight revealed the insanity of our nights, but when darkness fell we succumbed to the temptation all over again.

We crept out and met by the ruins of Homer's School. It stood on the wooded slopes midway between our villages. We gathered fallen branches, lit a fire and laid out a supper of figs, feta and olives, and washed down our feast with wine Stratis had siphoned from a barrel in the *katoi*.

One glass was enough to inspire us to howl like wolves. The shadows cast by the fire played upon geckos clinging to rock-walls, millennia old. We picked our way through the ruins to a flight of steps cut into the rock, stood on the highest rung, and ran a knife over our right thumbs. We pressed the thumbs together and declared ourselves blood brothers.

On ensuing nights we climbed beyond Stratis' village to the

Marmakas. We followed the cliff path above Afales Bay, paused by the mill, and advanced to the leeside where we slept in shepherds' huts. On windless nights we returned to the mill and dozed on the platform beside the grinding stone. On warmer nights we slept outside. We looked up at the skies and hurled abuse. We had learnt the art of blaspheming, and skies do not answer back.

Not content with the shepherds' huts of the Marmakas, we embarked on a more ambitious trek. Stratis guided me over mule paths from Exogi to the wooded slopes overlooking Polis Bay. We skirted the village of Stavros, and clambered over mountain passes to the isthmus that divides north from south. The sun was sinking as we climbed the slopes of Mount Aetos to the citadel ruins.

We gulped down wine and tested each other to see who could walk in a straight line. We stumbled over slopes littered with ceramic tiles, and dodged the remains of retaining walls. We scattered a flock of sheep asleep on their feet, lifted our arms to the heavens, and proclaimed ourselves kings of Ithaca. Our first act as monarchs was to fall into a stupor.

We were not the only ones who played pranks. One night I was awoken by a commotion in the square. I jumped out of bed and raced through the streets. Old Niko the drunk lay prostrate on a bier outside St Marina's surrounded by a growing crowd. Four pallbearers hoisted the bier to their shoulders. We followed the procession to the cemetery grounds. Niko was barely conscious as we chanted the incantations for the dead. The natural order of things was being turned upside down. A new festival was being born and Niko was its patron.

The pallbearers carried him back through St Marina's doors and laid him out on the floor. They placed two candles by his head, two by his feet. We retreated to the dark recesses of the church and waited until he awoke. Niko sat up with a start, stared at the candles and pressed his hands to his face as if making sure he was there. He staggered to his feet and stumbled from the church into the first light of day. We followed and mimicked his gestures. The younger children threw stones. 'Hey Niko, are you alive or dead?' we chanted. From that day on we greeted him with these words.

———

Old Niko lived in a hovel on a hillock that protruded like a vertebra from a spur above the village. He wheezed his way through the winter months and on warmer days sat sunning himself by the hovel door. He slept on a mattress amid rotting sea-trunks and wicker chairs. His skin was lizard bronze, his eyes rheumy brown. He was a mystery I could not fathom, a drunkard who had known better days. His isolation struck fear. He was being eaten by syphilis, the villagers laughed. The children kept a wide berth. I too kept clear of him, but there would come a time when he would give voice to my absent father.

The periods of my father's journeys were unfathomable. They had something to do with the waters that glistened below us, and the double-masted brig that vanished over the horizon soon after he left. He would leave when the winter was over. He would still be away as the days grew warmer, and our crops were ready for the reaping.

And just as I thought he had become a ghost of his former presence, he would be back. He returned when the harvest was long over, and the snakes had curled into their winter burrows. On each return he bent down, lifted me up, and drew me level with his eyes. He smelt of salt and wind, and the odour of forgotten days. He looked at me intently, measuring the changes since we had last met; then set me down and opened his knapsack to retrieve his home-coming gifts.

One year he brought me a Turkish dagger. He gripped the silver handle between his forefinger and thumb, and hurled it at the almond tree beside the house. The dagger caught the sun as it whirled. It vibrated as it lodged in the bark and came to rest embedded in the trunk. I carried the dagger with me whenever I roamed the mountain. I threw it at cypress and oaks, and fought hand-to-hand battles with imaginary foes. I sharpened its blade against the rocks and polished it with oiled cloth until it flashed.

The following year my father brought me a telescope. He did not hand it over immediately. 'We must catch the light before it dies,' he said. We followed the path that rose above the village. I felt small beside him as we walked, a little afraid of this stranger whose mind always appeared to be somewhere else. The sun was well on its descent when we scrambled to the summit.

'Close your eyes,' he said, as he handed me the telescope. 'Lift it to your right eye. Now look!' I made out the chimneys of houses on the slopes of neighbouring isles. I saw caiques at anchor and boats returning to port. I saw the wild foliage of un-pruned vines and the dense undergrowth beneath olive groves. I followed the final fifty metres of an old woman's trek to the doors of a mountain chapel and watched her step inside.

I swung the telescope round to take in the white cliffs called Sappho's Leap glistening off the Lefkada coast. I saw the sclerotic limbs of an olive tree jutting from a cliff face. A hawk swooped so low I recoiled from its claws. When I lowered the telescope all sprang back into its rightful place.

In the year of his final return my father lowered his knapsack and extracted jars of black caviar, an Armenian bracelet, and reams of silks for Erasmia, my mother. He presented me with a pistol, and promised to show me how to stalk hare and quail. 'We have made a great profit,' he boasted. 'We sold our wheat in Zakynthos at three times the price we paid for it.'

The celebrations continued late into the night. I fell asleep to familiar voices, and awoke, hours later, to the sight of the mountain. I could see the upper slopes through the window. I lay in bed full of the mystery of my father's return. I was close to the constellations and the half moon gliding over the summit, closer to the skies than those who lived in the lower hamlets. And my father was home.

———————

In the months of his final return my father woke me late one night. We crept out of the house and descended the mule path to Frikes Bay. To quicken our journey we scrambled between zigzag bends, grabbing hold of shrubs to break our fall. My father clowned like a child and challenged me to a race over the final metres to the bay. The crewmen were squatting on the waterfront. They smoked and chatted as dawn broke. The day was still unfolding as we lifted anchor and sailed south.

By mid afternoon we had dropped anchor off the town of Zakynthos. In the evening we strolled through arcaded streets to the opera house. A sun that had risen over Ithaca was now sinking over Zakynthos Bay. My father walked like an aristocrat in his one and only suit. From his waistcoat there hung a fob watch on a gold chain. We milled in the foyer surrounded by perfumed ladies in evening gowns and men in tailcoats and top hats. 'For a night we join the Venetian aristocracy,' my father joked.

A touring Italian opera-company performed *The Barber of Seville*. Members of the audience hissed when they detected a false note, and shouted bravo when an aria moved them. Within hours of the final curtain we were back at sea, sailing north. We dropped anchor in Frikes Bay one full day after we left, and trudged the final flight of steps into the village as the first rays of the sun lit the dome of St Marina's. It was to become one of the few memories of my father.

———

Carpets of spring flowers began to appear on the upper slopes. My father stretched his arms, rubbed the winter from his eyes, and I knew the time had come. That final year I was old enough to help. For days I worked with the crew to repair and ready the boat. When the repairs were done, we dragged the brig into the water and loaded it with wine, oil and currants. We hauled slabs of limestone from Kioni on horse-drawn carts, and lowered them into the hold to serve as ballast.

'What choice do I have?' my father said on the day he left, but in my twelve-year-old eyes he seemed as excited to be leaving as he would have been, months later, to return. My rage increased as the brig inched out of sight. I wanted to leap from the quay and force the crew to take me. As soon as the boat disappeared my vigil began. I returned to the summit and came to know what sky and ocean share in common: transparent flight paths and sea lanes, one belonging to migratory birds, the other to sailors and traders.

When boats appeared on the horizon my heart tightened. Each vessel was a potential return. There was always a boat en route ferrying unknown crew and cargo. I charted the ship's slow progress until, just as it seemed that it would always remain within sight, it would be gone. I longed to penetrate the mystery. Where did journeys end? Did they ever end? What lay beyond the beyond? What was my father doing at this moment?

I returned to the house lost in wild imaginings. My mother sat in the kitchen with her friends. I stood in the doorway and listened as they talked. They did not speak of their absent husbands. They did not speculate on where they may be, or where they were headed. They discussed their crops and laid plans for the harvest. They exchanged remedies for the ailments of their children and livestock. Only once did I hear my father mentioned. 'When he is gone,' Erasmia said, 'I feel dead inside.' She shrugged her shoulders and returned to work.

———

That year my father did not return. A sudden heart attack claimed him. It was a common enough tale. He was dead by the time the brig reached the nearest port. The bells of St Marina marked his passing. The villagers were accustomed to such news. By nightfall the house was crowded. They came to ensure that Erasmia and I were not alone long enough to fall prey to our thoughts, and they came night after night for weeks on end.

The kitchen was thick with smoke and talk. The women brewed coffee, poured brandy, delivered food, shrugged their shoulders and intoned, 'Ti na kanoume. Ti na kanoume. What can we do?

What can we do?' The men clicked their worry beads and muttered, *'Ola ine tikhe, ola ine tikhe.* All is luck, all is fate.' The younger women fought to restrain their thoughts from turning to their men at sea. The children, accustomed to absent fathers, soon forgot the reason for the gathering and ran wild, while the older men and women turned to their grandchildren and murmured, *'zoie se sas,'* life to you.

I retreated to the summit. For weeks I scanned the horizon as if expecting my father's return. I knew it was a futile quest, but the windy heights swept away errant thoughts and lifted me above the lament. It was Old Niko who brought me back to earth. I was returning to the village when, without warning, he was beside me.

'I have something to show you,' he said. I did not resist. I no longer cared. For the first time his vagrant smell did not disturb me. I followed him to his hovel. We sat outside, I on a rock, and Niko on a wicker chair. He leaned back, closed his eyes and burped away the previous night's drinking.

'I sailed with Dimitri, your father, many times,' he remarked. 'He was a skilled seaman, a cunning trader.' Niko laid out two glasses and filled them with wine. *'Exo ta vasana!'* he exclaimed, lifting his glass. 'Out with our troubles! And to your father, an honourable man.'

Niko swept his free arm in an expansive arc over the houses scattered about us. 'Built in retreat from pirates,' he said. 'Exogi was founded centuries before you and I were dreamt of. The islands were a temptation for passing corsairs. We withdrew to the heights and kept an eye on the seas.

'Mind you, we were marauders when we had the chance. More than once our ancestors hid by the shores and allowed the pirates to advance inland to plunder. While the pirates were gone they stole their boats, and waited. And when they returned flushed with their loot, the pirates were ambushed and killed to the last man. Life on the Ionian was retreat and attack, raid or be raided.

'One day soon that time will return,' Niko declared. 'The blood will flow again in torrents. I can smell it. We are a village born of fear, but it brought us close to the skies.'

Old Niko spoke slowly at first, in a drawl that I can hear to this day. Or perhaps this is how I imagine it. It doesn't matter. There comes a time when memories and imaginings are inextricably entwined.

'When the threat receded we ventured back,' he continued. 'The lower villages were our new offspring, and the lower slopes, a chance to carve new terraces. We reclaimed our bays, restored our boats, and returned to sea. It was the surest way of making a living on this rock-infested isle. No matter how many terraces we clawed out of the mountain, there was never enough to sustain us.'

The evening chill was descending. Niko invited me inside. He lit a lantern and held it over a sea-trunk, his one sturdy piece of furniture. The trunk was filled with nautical charts, maps and atlases. 'It is the fate of Ithacans to be governed by maps,' he said, as he unfurled one over the table.

'And first among them is this map of Ithaca. From afar it is a mass of limestone that juts out from, and plummets back into, the sea. See how it is made up of two fat landmasses, one to the north, the other south. See how the masses narrow to an isthmus slim as a heron's neck. One day, an earthquake will cut the island in two,' Niko laughed.

He refilled his glass and toasted St Nicholas, patron of harbours and sailors, and his ancient predecessor, Poseidon, jealous god of the seas. He toasted Zeus, the cloud gatherer, and Aeolus, lord of the winds. He toasted seamen past and present, and wished them all well. Each toast of mine was restricted to one mouthful, in case he was accused of getting a twelve-year-old drunk. Finally he toasted the two of us, by which time we were both as unsteady on our legs as if making our way from the island over angry swells.

'Now that we are on our way,' said Niko, 'and before we lose sight of Ithaca, let us start as all good tales should. *Arkhe tou paramythiou. Kalispera sas.* The fairytale begins. Good evening to you.' In that moment, despite the smell of damp, the hovel filled with warmth. Niko's tale became mine and as I recount it, many years later, I no longer know which fragments I owe to Niko, and which to others I have met who undertook the same journey.

'Your father joined his father who had once joined his father on the annual voyage to the Black Sea, driven by a hunger for wheat,' Niko began. 'I was a member of his crew many times. We sailed south, and rounded the Peloponnisos to Kavos Maleas. Each sea had its hazards, and in the Aegean it is the *Meltemi* winds. They sneak up on you in clear weather, and we had to fight to prevent them hurling us off course.

'We moved east as far as Lesbos, turned north by the lighthouse of Sigrion, and sailed into seas where Greeks are still lorded over by Turks. We berthed in Lesbos and sensed the uneasy truce between the conquered and cursed. We followed the coast of Asia-Minor, and dropped anchor off the island of Tenedos, where we sheltered from gales blowing from Anatolia.'

Old Niko unfurled a second map. 'British admiralty maps,' he stressed. 'Whatever is said about the English we can trust their nautical charts. See how the sea contracts when we enter the Dardenelles.' I followed Niko's index finger as it traced the route from the Aegean to the Narrows. 'On the western shores rise the rocky slopes of Gallipoli,' he pointed out. 'See how it juts into the Aegean. Just inside the entrance, stands the fort of Kilitbahir, and on the opposite shore, the town of Canakkale.

'Kilitbahir means lock of the sea,' Niko explained. 'And that is how it is: once a boat leaves the Aegean and enters the Narrows, it is locked in. Whenever we approached the entrance I thought of the blood that has been spilt here. Xerxes, millennia ago, led his Persian army from Asia Minor to Europe to strike at the heart of Greece. He marched his troops over the water via a pontoon formed of boats. Odysseus and the armies of Agamemnon and Menelaus, battled for years to capture nearby Troy. Empires have fought, and will continue to fight, to control this wretched strait.

'Even the currents were against us. Beneath the surface current runs a dense counter-current, conveying the warmer waters of the Aegean, but above it, and against us, flowed the cold waters of the Black Sea.'

Niko paused. Outside the wind was rising, beating against the walls. Inside, within the hovel, we were becalmed. The minutes stretched at their leisure as Niko poured himself another glass. He stood up and paced the room. His pace quickened, and with it, the tempo of his tale.

'At night the Strait swarmed with boats that did not possess lights. The sea has its share of wankers who create havoc. Our spirits lifted when we moved beyond the Narrows into the Sea of Marmara. We sailed towards the Bosporus lured by the sight of minarets sharp as fishmongers' tongues. I held my breath each time we veered from the Bosporus into the Golden Horn. Even *giaours*, infidel dogs like us, admire the city's beauty. We may hate the Ottomans, but we are smitten by Constantinople and remain captive to the *megali ithea*, our wretched longing for the return of the city to its Byzantine days.

'We dropped anchor among skiffs and barges, coal-powered steamships, and lighters. We moored between every type of boat known to man: caiques and gondolas, yachts piloted by aristocrats, Russian mail-boats, high-masted schooners, armour-plated frigates, corvettes, ocean liners, and our own Ionian trehadiri and brigs.' Niko cupped his hands over his ears. 'I can still hear it: the sighing of oars, the crack of the sails, the chant of the Muezzin from minaret galleries, the cry of navigators nervously steering their vessels in the teeming port.'

Niko's love of knowledge seemed to groan within him like the sigh of the hovel's rotting beams. It was Niko who induced in me a love of languages. He proposed toasts to individual words, but Niko would use any pretext for a drink.

'Dissect a word and you will extract its essence,' he said. 'Take the word port, from the Latin *portus*, meaning door. We see it in our Italo-Ionian *porta*. A port is a doorway to other worlds and the two-pronged Golden Horn is a perfect port, an amphitheatre as beautiful as our Vathy. The entire sublime-stinking drama called life unfolded before our eyes when we stepped through this door. The stench of a thousand farts mingled with bittersweet spices and perfumes. And everyone, even those of us who could only spare a day or two in port, swarmed through the arched entrance to the Great Bazaar.

'I would go there with your father. We stepped into a labyrinth of squares and fountains, crossways and alleys. We strolled beneath leaded cupolas and arcades of chequered stone. We jostled along-side plodding camels, ladies in sedans, merchants on horseback, and inspected entire streets devoted to one object: camel saddles, discarded weaponry, Turkish slippers, mountains of prayer mats and gilded Korans.'

Niko was on his feet, dancing about the hovel. The walls emitted the accumulated stench of spirits and cigarettes, the latest of which Niko clenched between his lips. 'Listen,' he said, again cupping his hands to his ears. 'Listen to the voices of merchants climbing over each other like ants scrambling for air. Cosmos is the most beautiful of words. Cosmos is a straining for perfection out of chaos. Cosmos means harmony, but first we must enter the chaos and withstand the howling of wild dogs.

'I strolled the streets beside Dimitri and saw the mongrel in us all, the traces of every race on earth, and the lie to our vanities about pure blood and superior ways. Arabs, Persians, Circassians, Negroes and desert Bedouins, eunuchs from Abyssinia, merchants and travellers from every corner of God's earth, or the devil's earth if you prefer, collided in the alleys of the bazaar. Constantinople was host to every breed of human that has crawled on this wretched globe.

'In front of their stalls stood the merchants, Turk and Armenian, Greek and Jew, entreating in competing tongues: "Please. Please. Signore. Caballero. Kyrie. Good sir. Please maestro, artista, connoisseur, dearest friend, come and look. I beg you, excellenza, my brother and treasured guest, may the Lord, praised be his name, be with you and your families, and with your ancestors and gods. Come! It cannot hurt. I am a humble merchant and my prices are better than my neighbours' who are all thieves, may they burn in hell. Trust only me. Come, feel the material on your cheeks. Lift it to your nose. Inhale its fragrance. Taste it if you wish.

"'All roads, sea routes and mule paths lead here, to this shop. All caravans and camels with flies gathered on their arses find their way to my emporium. See what they bring me—cashmeres from India, linens from Hindustan, carpets from Caramania, muslins from Bengal, shawls from Madras, tinted tissues from Cairo, porcelain crockery from England, black mastic from Chios. Chew it and forget where you are. Sit down. Take the load off your feet. Have a coffee spiced with cardamom, sweets from Smyrna, mint tea from Anatolia, a second cup. Take your time.

"'Yes. Yes. I am speaking fast, but I cannot help but be proud of my wares: Oriental spices, pickles, powders and pomades. Tablets for every ailment, and potions that allow your penis to swell donkey-size and remain hard and erect until you have satisfied an entire harem, let alone your mistress or, if need be, your wife.'"

The hovel was whirling, the dirt floor shaking and Niko was dancing his hop-like dance. 'And the women,' he said with a lecherous wink, 'the glimpse of a face beneath a veil, or the thigh of a streetwalker gleaming white beside a gas-lamp late at night, would drive us mad. We knew where to find them, just as we knew where to find them in every port. Syphilis is the seaman's most reliable export.

'On the way, in our excitement, we tripped over litters of pariah pups cowering at the teats of their mangy mothers, and side-stepped dogs dozing and sniffing, rutting and howling in the orifices of arcades and alleys. We scattered pigeons perched on mosques, congregating in courtyards, clinging to rafters, and messenger pigeons bearing missives from far-flung strangers scrawled in unknown tongues.'

Niko pirouetted towards his climax. 'Your father loved Constantinople!' he exclaimed, pointing at me. 'He was a man of style, dressed in his best as he strolled the bazaar, a carnation in his lapel, his moustache waxed, oiled hair slicked back. He moved about the Greek quarter, sought out friends, sat with them in coffee houses, and smoked the narghile. Dimitri was a *levendi*, a *palikari*, an honourable man.

'Enough. I am tired,' said Niko, abruptly. 'The night is old. The journey is long, but before we continue we need a good night's sleep. I am going to bed. And tomorrow night the same.'

———◆———

I walked home my head pounding with possibilities I had never dreamt of. Above me the summit brooded, a black outline against the night. In the waters beyond the Marmakas fishermen were spreading their nets. Beyond them stretched sea-lanes on which I saw myself sailing with my father and generations of Thiaks.

There are nights we remember for the rest of our lives, nights that tremble with mysteries. I thought of my father squeezing through the Narrows, vanishing over yet another swell. Lost at sea. Lost in the crowd. Lost in the skies. Lost in the cosmos.

Niko bellows the word: Cosmos, cosmos, cosmos, and I am falling through space, from the cosmos to the summit, from summit to shore, moving out to sea, sailing in ravines cut like deep wounds between mountains. Armies march over the bloodied channel, and I am locked in. The mountains lean closer. I try to prise them apart, but they are made of rock, and I am nothing but sinew and tendon, vein and artery, windpipe, pulsating lungs. I gasp for breath and wake up choking, relieved to see the summit through the window, free-standing. Breathing. Breathing. Breathing me back from my dreams.

———

I do not recall whether it was the next night or the next week when I returned to Niko's hovel, but I do recall that I could not wait to hear him resume his tale. And I remember the glasses of wine, our toasts to Poseidon, St Nicholas and St Basil, and gods ancient and new; and to blind Homer and one-eyed beasts, white-breasted Sappho and bards whose words still ring true. And to the Aegean, the Sea of Marmara, the Bosporus and Golden Horn, and to ports I had never heard of encompassing the seven oceans.

The list grew with each visit in keeping with Niko's unquenchable thirst and ended with a toast to Dimitri, the *levendi*, the most honourable of men, and Old Niko's refrain: '*Arkhe tou paramythiou, kalispera sas*. The fairytale begins, good evening to you.' And again we were voyaging in the rose tinted dawn, well stocked with provisions from Constantinople, with Niko, and my father, and men of the village, some of whom I knew, and others who had died, or gone mad, or vanished long before I was born.

'Alas, a day or two in Constantinople was all we could afford,' sighed Niko, 'before we continued our voyage. We tacked against the river's currents past homes rising from underwater foundations. We moved past fat men astride wheezing donkeys, and walled mansions shaded by citrus groves. We sailed by the walled fortress of the Genoese Castle, and Joshua's tomb on the Giant's Mountain.

We sailed until the great inland sea was upon us, a silver glow that disturbed our eyes under the midday sun.

'The Black Sea intimidated us,' said Niko, tracing his index finger over yet another map. 'Unlike the Ionian and Aegean, there are no islands within easy reach. In spring, melting snows swell the rivers of Southern Russia—the Dniester, the Bug, the Don and Donetz—and flush black earth through their deltas, trailing a dark stain out to sea. Currents battle the rising winds, and malevolent forces are let loose, inducing blizzards driven by abrupt wind shifts that can spin a boat like a top, and dash it to pieces.

'We coasted between anchorages and dared not move far off shore. We clung to the western rim and sailed past ships sagging under sacks bloated with grain. Travellers huddled beneath mosquito nets or squatted on deck dealing cards. Entire families lay prostrate on makeshift sheets or bare boards, worn out by weeks of flight from God knows which embattled kingdom or arid steppe.'

Niko was back on his feet, goaded by his countless toasts into his hop-like dance. He spat out his story as he whirled, and the spittle landed on fabled ports of the Black Sea: Varna, Constanta. 'The ports swarmed with thieves and dogs. Beggars stretched out their needy hands. Labourers stumbled under the weight of heavy cargoes. In the back streets tailors, shoemakers and jewellers cut and shaped, cloth, leather and diamonds.

'*Mavri Thalassa*. The Black Sea,' Niko recited. 'In the ports of the Black Sea we realised we were merely ants in search of hard-earned booty to haul back to our impoverished lairs. As we approached the Danube delta, birds and locusts descended on marshlands and swamps. Men in fishing boats cruised the estuaries and coastal waters in search of sturgeon bloated with caviar.

Shepherds in sheepskin caps and jackets, cow-skin moccasins and sun-beaten hides drove flocks over muddy passes.

'Beside them walked women with handkerchiefs woven into their hair, petticoats peeping beneath knee-high dresses. We gazed at these women and imagined what lay beneath their layers of clothing, but we had no time for daydreams. We were impatient to reach our destination, the Danube River ports.

'If ports are doorways to new worlds,' exclaimed Niko, 'then ports on the mouths of deltas are a succession of doors, linked by rivers to landlocked cities, inland civilisations. There are three mouths on the Danube: St George in the south, Kilia in the north, and between them, Sulina, our next port of call.'

Niko retrieved a map of the delta, and guided my finger to the river mouth. 'Twenty miles east of Sulina,' he said, 'we tacked between the shore and the Isle of Serpents, so small it cannot be seen on this map. On the southern shore, within its low-lying cliffs, basking on rocks, lay a mass of black serpents coiled in one tremulous mass.

'The isle was the home of Achilles, and a temple in his honour once stood there. A Greek historian has written that when he visited the temple, its surrounds were full of goats that sailors had left as votive offerings. Flocks of white seabirds took to the sea every morning, skimmed their wings on the waves, and returned to sprinkle the shrine. But I believe only what I see with my own eyes,' said Niko, 'and what I saw was a bare island pointing the way to the river mouth.

'Autopsy means "that which one sees with ones eyes". Autopsy is the seaman's curse. He sees so many gods he becomes godless. He sees so many mysteries he becomes weary. He sees so much he no longer knows what to believe. And I have no more to say. The night is old. The journey is long, but before we go on we need a good night's sleep. I am going to bed. And tomorrow night the same.'

———

I stroll home with my feet on the rocky soil of Ithaca, and my mind on other worlds. Niko's tales bleed into my dreams and I plummet from the skies to a pit of serpents spitting venom. There is nothing to hold onto but black night, black water, black winds and the black silhouette of my father, always beyond reach. He turns and is beside me, lifting me to his height. He places a telescope to my eyes, and the world springs closer, but my father is moving away, receding, dissolving in the dark.

———

The wine has been poured, the glasses are full, a map of the Danube delta lies on the table—a British admiralty map of course—and the toasts have been drunk, one to each god assembled on Mount Olympus, and to the gods of many nations. And to agnostics and atheists, pagans and idol worshippers, and those who are confused, and to those who believe that all that lives eventually returns to a void.

'No one should be left out,' says Niko, placing an arm around my shoulders. 'Even beggars have a right to be honoured. After all, didn't Odysseus return to Ithaca in the guise of a beggar, and didn't the gods disguise themselves as strangers, and when the wind changes and flings us off course, don't we become strangers?

Old Niko takes one last sip and swipes his jacket sleeve over his lips. '*Arkhe tou paramythiou, kalispera sas,*' he exclaims and we are entering the mouth of the Danube, sailing against wilful currents to the port of Sulina. Below us submerged banks of silt spread a yellowish tinge out to sea.

'Not so long ago,' says Niko, 'the silted mouth was littered with the hulls and masts of boats that had run aground. Sulina was a hamlet of mud huts built on stilts skirted by reeds, safe only for low draft lighters. One night, in the winter of 1855, twenty-four sailing ships and sixty lighters ran aground in a tempest. Since then dredges have cut a channel twenty-four feet deep, three hundred feet wide.

'Sulina grew as the channel cut deeper and larger ships sidled against its lengthening quays. Some of the buildings are said to be of Ithacan stone, the ballast of Kioni rocks we carried in the wombs of our boats. Can you imagine it, the foundations of a port spawned by rocks quarried from our own wretched Ithacan soil?'

I nod my head like an automaton, fully captive to Niko's hypnotic rant. 'Now that we are in Romania,' he declares, 'we must toast each other in the local tongue: sănătate. Good health to the Danube delta, its swampy waters and black sands, and to pelicans, ibis and sea eagles, otters, wolves and wild boar. Good health to marshlands and islets of beech, and to flocks of geese that obliterate the skies with their wings. And good health to deltas that shit silt into the sea; each year over one hundred million tons,' says Niko, twirling the fact on his tongue as he refills his glass.

'Good health to waterways lined with willows, and to a fisherman's paradise brimming with mackerel, bream and carp. Good health to flamingoes that have flown here from the Nile, and to marsh dwellers who set fire to reeds to pave the way for new growth. And, lest we forget, sănătate to the entire one thousand square miles of delta, even though it broods with intimations of death: In summer, clouds of mosquitoes feasted on our hides. We have lost Ithacan brothers to malaria, tuberculosis, and mysterious plagues. I have known Thiaks to waste away from nostalgia once the fever has taken hold.'

Niko pauses. The romance fades. The colour drains from his face, and I see that Niko is old and rotting, and drinking himself to death. Yet he is still moving, sailing upstream against currents, past oak forests and swampland to inland river-ports, and I am sailing with him, and my father, and fellow Thiaks. We drop anchor in Tulcea, where the three arms of the delta converge. We pause in Galatz, a river port encircled by forested hills. We fling our ropes onto the wharves of Vraila, and inspect warehouses stacked with freight.

In each port there are Ithacan merchants, shipping agents, river-pilots and entire families who dwell on houseboats. In each port we see them strutting to their offices, Ionian magnates, drawing up contracts, hiring crewmen for their ocean-going fleets. Every port is a homecoming, an Ithacan home to stay in, godfathers to bless us and godchildren to bless, and someone to place food beside us, a kitchen or coffee house to sit down in, to find out who had died, who had been born, who had married and divorced. Who had run off with a mistress, or gambled away his fortune, and who had contracted syphilis, or become wealthy since we last met.

We offload our cargo and put our brig to the river trade. We sail alongside steel barges and steam-powered tugs, built and piloted by Ithacan cartels. We move upriver with Ionian flotillas and return with cargoes of timber and dry goods. There is no shortage of work, no poor soils to restrain us, no backbreaking slopes. For a

few blessed months we are masters of the river, at liberty to deter-
mine our fate. And when the chance arises we stray from our
purpose long enough to sail within striking distance of the great
inland city, Bucharest. We drop anchor, draw lots, and leave the
loser with the barge groaning under its load of grain.

'Bucharest was Mikhalis the fiddler's great love,' says Niko. 'He
sat day and night in cafes that never closed, ears cocked to Tzigany
bands. We left him sitting like a man possessed and set out for the
gambling dens. The Romanians are even greater gamblers than the
Greeks. Perhaps it is the Greek blood that flows somewhere in their
veins.

'We hailed coaches for the fun of it, drawn by Russian horses,
ebony black, with black manes, whipped on by Russian exiles
dressed in black velvet tunics embroidered with gold braid. They
conveyed wealthy travellers to and from theatres, opera houses,
brothels and casinos, back to their hotels where French waiters
served French wines and cuisine prepared by French chefs.

'Sănătate,' says Niko, and swills another glass. 'After three days
in Bucharest, our heads were spinning and our wallets empty. We
tore ourselves away from the gambling houses, dragged Mikhalis
from his Tzigany bands, staggered to the station and returned to the
river trade. After all, this is what had lured us to the Danube, against
swells and gales, and silted waters that threatened to run us
aground.

'The pursuit of grain transformed us into salmon leaping over
the tides to the wheatfields of the Danube basin, tended by armies
of peasants for aristocrats who lorded it over their feudal estates.
They spent their leisure hours in Bucharest palaces, while their
peasants tilled the soil and battalions of priests kept them in

check. At times the currents ran so strong, oxen dragged our boats upstream, pulling on ropes from the riverbanks.

'We traded our oil, currants and olives for grain, and left before the cold took hold. We filled every space with sacks of grain: stacked it on the decks, stuffed it in the Captain's cabin, the sleeping quarters and in the holds. We would have swallowed it and shit it out, or shoved it in our underpants if we'd had enough room!' Niko exclaims.

'The return journey was faster despite the load. We emerged from the Black Sea into the Bosporus and bypassed Constantinople. The Great Bazaar could no longer entice us, nor the most alluring of brothels tempt us now that we were on our way.

'Despite the favourable currents, the journey seemed longer as we drew closer, because we finally allowed ourselves to think of our homes. We relived the same illusion each time,' Niko tells me. 'The island glowed in our mind's eye. If the winds dropped we shook our fists at the heavens. If storms impeded our progress, we railed against our fate; and if the grain prices in Zakynthos were high, we detoured to make a quick profit. Each successive sea brought us closer, yet the agony increased.

'Your father was talking of you,' says Niko, tapping my shoulder. 'Dimitri allowed you to return to his thoughts. He could endure months holed up in ports, whittle away days in taverns, or spend weeks loading boats and haggling over the price of grain, but the final hours as he neared home were unbearable. He searched the horizon for the familiar outline of the two islands, Kefallonia and Ithaca.

'At first, they seemed as one. Only when the mountains of Kefallonia receded, and Ithaca assumed its shape, did he allow his breath to ease. Only when he could make out the shepherds' huts on the Marmakas, and glimpse Exogi struggling through the clouds, did he allow his spirits to rise.

'As we drew up to the waterfront, Dimitri had to restrain himself from leaping off before the boat was secured. He set his eyes on the summit like a navigator setting his sights by the North Star. He ascended the familiar path, rucksack stuffed with presents. His heart was filled with expectation, his body light with anticipation. He was about to look upon your face.'

Niko swayed on his feet, as if giddy from the voyage. He leaned on a wall for support. The hovel was his still point, an axis within a chaotic world. 'We returned home and succumbed to the pleasure of feeling the earth beneath our feet,' he says, wearily.

'And, for a while, we were content. Until the weeks became months, and the homecoming was long over, the winter at an end, the vipers back on the prowl, and our coffers running low. We crawled out of our beds, returned to the quay, loaded our boats and prepared to set sail. What choice did we have?

'Enough! I am tired. My journeys are over and I am not content. New journeys are to be made, and I am too old. I am going to bed. And tomorrow night the same.'

———

I walked home, confused. I looked down at the hamlets, sprinkles of lamplights on the lower slopes. A sudden clutter of hooves and a goat skittered into the dark. I made out the moonlit trails on the mountain opposite, disappearing into the groves. Above me stood the summit, powerless at yet another departure, another descent to the bay. For the first time I sensed what the women called *erimia*, desolation. Each year more men set out. We were becoming a village of absent fathers.

I spent my time in the company of women. When I awoke, my mother was long up in the pre-dawn dark. Erasmia had prepared the bread and wine, and loaded the mules. The time of the olive harvest had arrived. When we stepped out we were not alone. Families were making their way to the Marmakas' groves. They had no time for regret. The mountain took care of that. The energy required to carve and work it, absorbed the sting and bent their backs.

I trudged beside my mother, aunts, and uncles who no longer had the will to tend their boats. They had no need of lamps to light the way. The paths were as familiar as the veins hardening in their arms. We paused at the edge of the groves, built a fire, brewed coffee, and chewed bread before setting to work.

There is nothing more pleasurable than fatigue after a day's labour. The smells released by the mountain were more pungent when we trudged back. The heat of day was gone, the mountain attuned to the sound of voices. I ran ahead, climbed through gaps in the perimeter wall, and dashed home to the barking of familiar dogs.

'The best food is when you're hungry,' so the saying goes, and after a day on the mountain I was ravenous. As soon as I finished eating, I made for the door. 'Why do you spend so much time with that syphilitic?' my mother said, but I was gone. Nothing could hold me back. I climbed beyond St Marina's to the spur on which Niko's hovel stood. He was seated outside, smoking, and pointed towards Afales Bay.

'Who else would call it Afales, Bellybutton Bay,' he wheezed. 'We Thiaks think our island is the navel of the universe. From the summit, Exogi lies at our feet, planted by God knows whom. It was wise to build the village on the heights. We can lose our heads in the clouds and forget the shit below.'

Niko retrieved a leather-bound volume from the trunk. The pages were thick parchment. Inside the cover lay a foldout map of Ithaca, dated 1806. Lines marked the routes across the narrow channel to Kefallonia.

'Written not by Greeks, but an Englishman,' said Niko. 'The Germans and English come here in search of Odysseus. They love Ithaca more than their own soil. They stumble about in the midday sun with copies of *The Odyssey*, and comb through the rubble in search of buried cities, lost worlds. They pore over the script as if deciphering a code. They pick over each word and interpret it like a biblical text.

'And they explore the usual suspects, south to Rock Korax, the Raven's Crag, and the Spring of Arethusa where, surely, Odysseus' faithful swineherd, Eumaeus, watched over his pigs. They travel further south, to Marathia, where they are convinced Odysseus met the loyal swineherd soon after his return. They poke around in the vain hope they may find signs of the swineherd's hut, and the courtyard in which he welcomed and fed the disguised king.

'They move back north to the cave of Dexia, and are certain they have stepped into the grotto where the nymphs wove purple fabrics on looms of stone. And they inspect the nearby shores of Phorcys Bay where the sleeping Odysseus, on his return, was surely deposited by the noble Phaeacians.

'They hire mules and inch their way further north, and pause just below us, by the ruins of Homer's School. They dip their hands in the Melanydros Springs, where they believe Homer cured his blindness when he washed his eyes in its mineral waters.

'They explore each bay as potential sites for Odysseus' landings, and scour each hill for the remains of his palace. Each bends the text to suit their case. "Surely the palace stood on Mount Aetos," says one, and he points to the ruins of the citadel and the excavations of Schliemann, the archaeological dreamer. They spend hours pacing between stones marking out Penelope's chamber, the servant's quarters, the Banquet Hall and pillars, and are convinced that it is the exact place where Penelope's suitors met their bloody deaths.

'"Bah, that is impossible," argues another. "The palace stood on the slopes overlooking Polis Bay. The sheltered port corresponds to Homer's Reithron anchorage. And the little island of Dhascalio, off the Kefallonian coast, barely visible two miles away, is certainly Asteris, where the suitors lay beside their beached ship in wait for Telemachus, determined to kill him before he reached Ithaca."

'"No, you have missed the point," argues yet another. "The site of the palace is Pilikata Hill where, as it is written, there are distinct views of three bays," and Niko swivels his arms to take in Afales, Polis and Frikes to underline their case. 'I must give them their due,' he says. 'They know their ancient Greek. They quote chapter and verse, and recite whole passages by heart. They slog manfully on steep terrain in the heat to fulfil their quest.

'Perhaps we envy them. They are wealthy and have time to potter around. We bend our backs to work our fields when we would rather look to the skies. They bend their backs willingly and crawl on all fours to sift the earth. We envy them the luxurious boats that await them. They seek their meaning under the ground, and that is where I will be soon enough.'

———•———

Years later, in Melbourne, in the State Library, I came upon a copy of the same volume *The Geography and Antiquities of Ithaca*, written by William Gell, esquire, member of the Society of Dilettantes—shelved among its rare books.

On the dedication page the author had composed a hymn to his 'King's Most Excellent Majesty'. He lays his humble manuscript at 'Your Majesty's feet', and is 'encouraged by the hope' that his description of Ithaca 'may not be entirely uninteresting to a Monarch who, by the success of His arms, and the wisdom of His counsels, has extended the influence of Britain to every quarter of the globe'. He remains his 'Majesty's most dutiful servant, and faithful subject'.

I arranged for the prints in Gell's book to be photographed, and have glued them to one of the walls of my shed. I look up from my manuscript through the window and catch sight of my bantams foraging. In an open cage above my work desk sits a cockatiel. He flies down to perch on my shoulder, screeches in my ear, and remains quiet for hours. I would not know he is there except for the occasional brush of feathers against my cheek.

The walls are lined with books on aerodynamics, the art of hypnosis, travellers' accounts of Ithacan journeys, and field guides to birds. On the rafters hang kites and violins. My worktable is littered with materials and tools: tins of lacquer, saws and planes, dowelling, sheets of paper, reels of string, files and pliers, hammers, chisels; and a cage housing my grand daughter's mouse.

What more is there to do now that Fotini is gone, succumbed to illness, and my daughter Sophia married to crazed Manoli? I look down at the magician's skull I now use as a weight on the manuscript. For whom am I writing this tale? Who knows? My grand daughter, Xanthe? She too is cursed with the thirst for knowledge. I see it in her eyes. The ancient Greeks believed it takes three generations for a family curse to wear off.

Xanthe is wary of this shed, but also drawn. She brought me her mouse when she last visited. I promised her I would transform it into a rat. I feed it a mixture of cereals and grains and it is well on the way. In return I showed her the copies I have made of lithographs in Gell's book, etched almost a century before I was born.

Most of the prints are without people. Where Ithacans do appear they are dwarfed by the landscape. The artist's eye is focused on ruins and sites that resemble Homer's descriptions. The sketches are impressive in their detail, neat and polite. There are no sharp edges, nor the stench of shit or the odour of panic rising from a lamb about to be killed. There are no junipers and prickly oak wedged between the stones. There is no sign of the placenta shredded by a ravenous hawk, nor the pulp of overripe figs bulging through blackened skins.

There is no sign of a violent sun setting fire to a violet sea, nor scenes of the parched soil cracked open, crops wilting, heralding another winter of distress. There is no hint of voices rising from the fields on harvest days, and no sight of celebration, our fingers tearing strips of roasted flesh, nor of the dancing stoked by wine and the strains of Mikhalis' violin. No sense of the raw labour, the bloodied fingers liberating patches of barren earth.

And not even the faintest echo of my mother's savage cry when she received the news of her husband's death, and the cry of the women who mourned with her, as they had mourned their own. I still hear it. A frantic keening, alternating with quiet sobbing. Ending hours, or days or weeks later, in a shrug. I see them, now, as if spying through the window: my mother, and a chorus of black widows huddled together, their youth contracted into a premature lament.

It was their fate to wait: for the boats, for the letters, for the flow of money from foreign lands, for the return of men who had become strangers demanding their conjugal rights. This is the virtue thrust upon us: the capacity to wait, to endure the storm, to perch on the summit, bodies alert, ever vigilant for an enemy attack.

None of this is in the lithographs. They are not my Ithaca, but a fantasy. Now that I have not been back for fifty years, perhaps Ithaca has become my fantasy. Perhaps what I write is a confusion of dreams and nostalgia, yet I return to the shed, light my desk lamp, and take up my manuscript. Let the fairytale begin. Good evening to you.

'Perhaps we are the Ithaca of old. Perhaps not,' Niko had said. 'It does not matter. It is enough to believe it. Whatever the truth about the past, we remain seafarers to this day. To survive we are condemned to leave this rocky island and travel to the ends of the earth.'

———————

We are gathered in the village square, in the spring of 1912, seated at tables beneath the plane tree. Couples are dancing tangos, dressed in their European best. The musicians are playing: Makis on accordion, Vassili on clarino, Mikhalis on violin. Basted lambs are turning on the spit. Children are running between tables, darting from shadow to light.

I leave the wedding party with Stratis and climb above Exogi. The music evaporates; the square is a diminishing circle of light. We leap over the chapel wall, crest the summit and scan the sea. Stratis picks up a handful of stones and flings them into the unknown. 'I am leaving,' he says. 'Joining my godfather Thomas, in Australia.'

We balance on rocks that have retained their warmth after a day in the sun. I shrug my shoulders. It is a familiar shrug that says: 'Well, you are leaving. So what? That is how it is. *Sto kalo.* Go on your good way.' I am seventeen years old and I have inherited the fatalist gesture. And Stratis is twenty-two. He is married to Melita, a girl from the mainland town of Zaverda. He is a father with a son, eighteen months old, and a second, soon to be born. He has crossed the boundary into adulthood, but the bond between us remains strong.

'There is nothing here,' he says. 'Thomas has been away ten years. He manages an oyster bar in Kalgoorlie, a city built on gold. He says it's still possible to find nuggets scattered on the desert sands. In five years I'll return with enough money to buy a caique and double the size of my groves. What can I do with just a few hectares of land?'

We remain locked in our thoughts. Far below us a ship crawls by en route to the Adriatic or some foreign port. From this distance it is a ship of phantoms, and its lights are fireflies that have come aboard for the ride. I detect the contradictions within Stratis, his yearning for adventure. I know it well.

I pick up a rock and hurl it as far as I can. In this moment I hate my father. I hate Stratis. I hate the sea and distant lands. I want to expunge myself, to erase all hope. The rock hurtles into the darkness clear of the slopes. I turn my back on the summit and begin my descent.

Mikhalis calls me over when I return. The celebration is at its height. Couples are dancing closer, moving in the shadows. 'I learnt this tango in Bucharest when I went there with your father,' he says. He rests the violin on his knees. "Play the wind. Play the wind," the Tzigany would say. To know an instrument is a great gift. Better to be a musician than one of the guests. We are present but also apart, a step away from trouble,' he winks.

Mikhalis lifts the violin in preparation: 'A good musician is an unobtrusive presence,' he says. 'We see the budding romances, the flirtations, the winks and caresses. We know couples that can no longer bear to touch each other and sleep well apart. We observe the widows and wives with absent husbands, and know those who are resigned to their fate, from those who steal away to regain a man's touch.'

The musicians resume. A circle is forming. Mikhalis hands over his fiddle and breaks in. The men squat and clap to Mikhalis' solo dance. He weaves and feints, and lowers his body to sweep the dirt with his palms. His steps are emboldened by the circling men urging him on with their quickening beat.

Days later, when he teaches me the melody on the violin, Mikhalis will tell me that dancing the *zebekiko* in a circle is the Turkish way, while those who perform solo are dancing Greek style. He will tell me this is our eternal tension, the conflict between individual and group. He will tell me that within our men there is an urge to break away, to travel alone. Even so, the lone dancer is encircled, supported by the group.

He will tell me that the *zebekiko* is played in 9/8 time and he will teach me the complex rhythm, how to capture it in the sliding pressure of the fingers, the movements of the bow. It is a rhythm that turns against itself, a rhythm that wants to defy rhythm and impel the dancer to hurl himself beyond all bounds. The nine in the equation is our defiance and anarchic spirit, the eight, our need for each other. Keep them in harness and all will be well.

Old Niko spent too much time alone, Mikhalis will say. He jumped ship once too often and disappeared for years on end; and when he returned he could no longer look us in the eye. He harboured secrets, and his hands trembled. He could talk only when fuelled by wine.

Mikhalis is dancing the *zebekiko*. His upper body remains poised, the steps are improvised yet contained. Around him, each man is dancing alone, but held within the orb. Above them, the mountain performs its own silent dance dictated by millennia of hail, wind and storm. Within two years every man in the circle will be gone: to war or sea, or alien lands.

Mikhalis accompanies me as I walk home and places an arm around my shoulders. 'A true Ionian musician returns to the first sounds: wind, sea and earth. He understands that the winds rise from and return to stillness. He knows that the earth shifts, however subtly, with the tread of his feet. He discerns the faint pulse of undertows in the sea-depths. And he detects the silence at the core of all sound. He cleans his mind of thoughts and does not forget what he hears and the moment he first heard it.

'Some day, while standing watch late at night aboard ship, or stranded on some alien shore, the memory of what you hear now will keep you company. How many sounds can you discern? Put them together and allow them to harmonise, and you have a *cantatha*, a serenade. Take them apart, but keep yourself together, and you have the *zebekiko*. And take away the musicians and you will return to the heart of all music: natural sound.'

Mikhalis puts a finger to his lips. 'Listen,' he says. We are standing on the path beside the uppermost house. I hear a rustling of undergrowth, the sound of laughter cascading, fading and, even at this height, a mere decibel above the silence, the breath of the sea. We are enveloped in it, above it, yet a part of it.

I open my eyes and Mikhalis is laughing. His mouth is open. I see a flash of gold filling. His face is a paradox of lines without care. He places his arms around my shoulders. 'That sound is in me, as in you, as it once was in your mother's womb.'

That night I dream I am surrounded by water, floating on a sliver of firm earth. *Terra firma*, yet nothing remains still. Islands collide and drift apart. I try to pin them down, but they are gone. My father is gone. Stratis is gone. Mother is dressed in widow's black, and Old Niko's hovel door is locked, the windows barred. The women are scaling the paths back to their groves, walking their slow, damned walk.

And I am running past them, enraged, scaling the heights. I am above the island and Old Niko is below, hopping and spitting and speaking in tongues, and Mikhalis is laughing. It is the laugh of the devil. I am dazzled by the gold in his mouth. I peer inside and see oceans churning, armies clashing, seamen drowning, predatory birds circling on wild winds. His enlarged tongue expels baying mobs like pieces of dirt, draws back everything it has expelled and, moments later, spits it all back out.

Stratis left for Australia in the summer of 1912. As he voyaged south, others were sailing back. The call had gone out. It resounded in the coffee houses and workplaces. It was heard in waterfront taverns and shipping offices. It sought out the crews of far-flung freighters and ocean liners. It ascended flights of wooden stairs into the smoke-filled rooms of Ithacan brotherhoods dispersed over many lands.

'Come back,' the voices whispered. 'Return and fight for your country, your God. We will regain our stolen lands from the enemy Turk and grab some more while we can. After all, to the victors belong the spoils.'

The young men downed tools, packed their bags, drew the curtains, locked their doors and made their way to the wharves. They journeyed back from sojourns in Australia, the Americas, Africa and Asia. When they arrived, they set out with their countrymen for the battlefields of the Balkans. Each village possessed at least one or two men who left for the front.

I yearned to go with them. The impulse to respond to the call to battle flows deep in the blood. My mother argued I was too young, and that father was no longer alive. I pleaded, but I had no choice. My father's death was a scar that kept me tethered to the house like a captive goat. I was needed for the sowing and harvest, to burn the pruned olive branches clogging the groves.

I stood on the slopes and heaped the branches on the fire. Through the flames, the waters of the Ionian looked like tattered sheets of green. I herded the blaze from wind shifts by pouring water on its flanks. I cursed as I dodged the embers and revelled in the heat.

Soon the photographs began to appear. Boys I had grown up

with had sprouted beards. They stood with their comrades on the battlefields of Ipeiros, Macedonia, Western Thrace, the new theatres of war. Or they stood alone, rifles by their sides, cartridge belts strapped from shoulder to waist. Even in the photos we saw that their boots were cracked, their uniforms baggy, coats stiff with dirt. They held their bodies at attention and did their best to look proud. Their mothers and wives framed the photos, hung them on walls, placed them on chests of drawers beside icons of favoured saints, and lit candles in homage to their warring boys.

And there were photos that were not allowed into children's hands, images of men brandishing the severed heads of the enemy, of burnt out villages and charred homes, and of the enemy put to flight. Photos of triumphs and cruelties and fields splattered with the entrails of the dead.

By year's end the men began reappearing. They returned to the island as victors. They acknowledged our cheers and garlands, listened obediently to patriotic speeches, but something had changed. Some were limping, or nursing more subtle wounds: a nervous tick, a haunted look that suddenly overcame them mid conversation, mid step.

Half a century later I cannot name the individuals. Perhaps I did not want to dwell on them, even though they were feted by those who had stayed at home. Perhaps we did not allow ourselves to listen when we heard the screams with which they awoke, or the flaring of their rage.

When they did speak of their deeds they did not boast, but muttered, 'We did what we had to do.' They had caught the fatalist's curse. They had left for battle with an *elelef*, the ancient cry of joy uttered by Greek soldiers at the start of battle, and had returned subdued. Their tales seeped out in fragments, little confidences, remarks dropped in coffee houses as they dealt the cards. I hung about, still young enough to be regarded as a neutral listener, yet old enough not to be shooed away.

They spoke of the odour of iodine in the corridors of military hospitals, and of sitting by the beds of comrades who lay with the glazed eyes of gutted fish. They spoke of wounded soldiers in crowded wards extracting maggots from their gangrenous wounds, and of men flopping about like deranged beasts as they drew their last breath. They whispered tales of battles that left bodies decaying, and of marching for so far and so long that day and night became one.

They lit up with talk of nights on leave spent in the brothels and cabarets of Salonika, and their bravado returned. They spoke of the busloads of women one sympathetic lieutenant had sent to ease their hunger. Their eyes glowed at the memory. Their lust stirred at the thought, and flickered back to life. They licked their lips and returned to work with renewed relish.

We could not foresee that the first victories were the prelude to a prolonged and bloody battle. Except for Old Niko. 'Ah, the fairy-tale truly begins,' he said, after we had drunk our usual toasts in his hovel one night. 'It is an old tale. One that never ends, but merely lies dormant while soldiers limp home to lick their wounds.'

I see him now, his mottled skin, and bloodshot eyes, a small man, wasted by drink and self-neglect. His restless gaze darted with the rapidity of a man on edge. 'It has all been written,' he said. '*The Iliad* is a book of prophesies. Read the opening stanzas and you will be overcome by Achilles' rage, his lust for vengeance. War is a chain of rage begetting rage. Every era has its Trojan wars. Every generation finds ways of devouring its young.

'In my years on the world's oceans I learnt of the deeds that men must commit to retake their piece of dirt. One act of terror unleashes a chain of vendettas and, in time, no one even knows when the first took place.' The Balkan Wars, he insisted, marked the beginning of a long and treacherous night. He could see it as clearly as the sun declining on an inglorious day, a period of unabated turmoil and pillage, and hillsides littered with unmarked graves.

'For us it is a war fuelled by dreams of a greater Byzantium. Of avenging bygone humiliations, the loss of Constantinople, and throwing off the imperial yoke. And for our enemy, the Ottoman Turk, it is a threat to a disintegrating empire. They have ruled the roost for so long they are not about to give up. A tyrant does not willingly give up his slaves. And for young men it is an age-old call to savagery and death.'

Niko's hand trembled as he poured the wine. He paced about the hovel. His thin body seemed to shrink further within his shabby clothes. 'Beware of those who speak of cultural purity and build citadels, walled borders and cast out those who belong to other tribes. They sing the same song and chorus as they loot and kill: "We are pure, and God is on our side, while our foes are in the service of the devil. May they rot in hell."'

I wanted to run. His words mocked everything I had been taught. I smelt the drink on his breath, the rot in his blackened teeth. 'We must tear words apart to liberate their meaning,' he shouted. 'Every nation thinks they are civilised, and the others are barbarians. Look hard at the word. Dissect it. Put each syllable under a magnifying glass. Ba. Ba. Ba.' Niko barked the words. 'Ba. Ba. Ba. It is the babble of foreign tongues. Ba. Ba. Ba. The babble of those who speak a language other than one's own.

'Every empire has taken its turn to hoard land and gold. Yesterday's allies become tomorrow's enemies and we turn on each other to fight over the spoils. Revenge circles the battlefield like a hawk scanning prey. Neighbours who have lived in peace set fire to each other's homes. The looted become the looters, and former slaves become masters who become slaves, and so it goes.

'And each nation thinks they possess what the ancient Greeks called *mesotes*, measuredness, while the others are cast as savage mobs. We forget that when given a chance, we have been just as cruel as any other race. Read *The Iliad* and you will see it. We were not angels in Troy. Listen to returned warriors in the quiet of the night, or when they have drunk too much, as they unburden themselves of the horrors they inflicted in the name of their cause. Enter their dreams and see the deeds they have had to commit, and which they have wiped clean from their waking hours.

'Travel deeper still, and discover that their comrades ran to their deaths with tears flowing down their faces, and the names of their mothers on their lips. And know this is what is truly meant when we speak of the Underworld.'

His words were treasonous. He would have been driven from the coffee houses and the company of men. He would have been cast out of gathering places and banished from the tribe. 'You are spitting on the brave deeds of our soldiers,' I shouted.

Niko shook his head. 'A seaman comes to know the madness,' he said. 'He sees it with his own eyes. I have seen what men do to each other. I have sat on hillsides and looked at the smoking ruins of razed villages. I have watched fleeing peasants leading donkeys piled with quilts and mattresses, ox-drawn wagons crammed with pots and heirlooms, and panicking children clinging to the roofs of overcrowded trains. I have heard that howl of infinite grief that accompanies the news of a loved one's death. I have travelled far. I have seen too much. It is a disease far worse than the syphilis the villagers are so sure I have.'

I returned to the fray. I rested my case on the tale of the women of Zalongo. Every schoolchild could recite it by heart. On 18 December 1803, in Zalongo, a cliff in Ipeiros, fifty-seven women chose to die rather than be captured by the Turks. They moved together, hands held in a circle dance. One by one, they approached the cliffs, threw their children over, and jumped to their deaths.

I spoke of the battle of Lepenti, fought off the mainland, not far from our shores, an epic struggle that had secured the Ionian Islands for the Venetians from the Ottoman Turk. I spoke of the siege of Messolongi and of our people's brave deaths. Niko clutched his bottle and laughed. 'Yes, they were brave, but you are a monkey performing his master's tricks. One day you will learn we are all captive to our tribal myths.'

I ran from the hovel as if fleeing the devil. I heard Niko's mocking laughter as I ran, and in the time I remained on the island I never spoke to him again. I slipped away whenever he approached, but his words would return to haunt me. He had planted the seeds of doubt and robbed me of the certainty that would have given my life a simple purpose.

Years later, I came to understand Niko's agony. He was filled with too much knowledge. He had gone beyond the myths that keep nations together. His years at sea had eaten away at his certainty. He had absorbed truths that are all but impossible to bear. He had strayed too far from the circle and was left to dance alone.

With the return of the men from the Balkan Wars a new wind began to blow, a whirlwind of courtships and romances. The returned soldiers desired the comfort of women. It was a time of weddings and pregnancies, the tribe making up for their dead. Mikhalis' band was in demand. Rarely a week went by without a bride being paraded through the village to the groom's house.

Then, like the Ionian squalls that erupt without warning, the winds changed. Men who had just married, or become fathers, talked of leaving the island again. They laid plans to set out for the countries they had returned from. They had forgotten the harsh struggles of previous sojourns. *Afstralia* was a country beyond the reach of war, they claimed, and riches were there for the picking. When their wounds healed they set off, farewelling their pregnant wives and infants with the promise of wealth and swift returns.

After each departure I felt more stranded. I received letters from Stratis. Kalgoorlie was an Eldorado, he wrote. The main street was lined with businesses run by Ithacans. In five years he would see Melita and his boys, Andreas and Manoli. He would return to the island a wealthy man. Meanwhile he would seize his chance. 'Come and join us,' he said. 'Work awaits you. You will not be alone.'

My centre of gravity shifted from the summit to the bay. The world appeared different at sea level. The water was close. Enticing, yet forbidding. There were breezeless days when the seas were dead. When squalls erupted, the waters were hurled against boats moored by the quays. Fishermen hastened to fasten the ropes or hauled their vessels ashore. They leapt from deck to jetty and worked furiously to protect their boats. And when their work was done they retired to the coffee houses to sit out the storm.

I preferred days of fair winds, and the steady procession of fishermen making their way to sea and returning with their daily catch. Crews lowered their sails and guided their vessels to the waterfront. Dusk was a time of returns and departures, a changing of the guard. Day fishermen gave way to those who took their chances at night.

I inquired at the shipping offices in Vathy. I had made up my mind, but it was no longer easy to leave. Warships patrolled the seas. News reached us of blockades in the Bosporus. Trading routes were cut off. Our arid soils mocked us and our crops were stillborn. Children ran about bare-footed, in threadbare clothing. Destitution stalked the island. It was time to leave. Not even the danger of war could deter me.

It was Mikhalis who helped me on my way. The journeys to the Black Sea had long ceased. Mikhalis had adapted my father's boat, and ferried cargo to and from mainland ports. I left in the northern spring of 1916.

When the time finally arrives, the parting is always abrupt. I left at the first cry of a newborn lamb. I left as the first rays of sun flooded the blue dome of St Marina. I left while the villagers were stirring, moving about their kitchens like sleepwalkers in search of light. I left with my face set, like a sail, waiting for wind. And I left alone, to avoid tearful farewells. On my back I carried a rucksack and violin.

I glanced back at the flights of stone steps that divided the village homes. For the final time I scanned the valley, the mountain terraces, the windmills on the heights. The eight sails lay dormant against the rising light. The sails are nets that trap the wind was the odd thought that reared in my mind.

I descended the path littered with mule droppings and bound by perimeter walls. I paused beside the ruins they call Homer's School and recalled the night Stratis and I sealed our pact. I moved between olive groves and vineyards, and chapels shadowed by cypress and oak. The summit vanished in the mist and for a moment my heart tightened. I quickened my steps on the steep descent to Frikes Bay.

I boarded Mikhalis' boat and gazed at the wake as it moved out to sea. It churned with infinite possibilities. It hummed with the melody of movement and change. A journey that had begun with a descent was now progressing on an even keel. I walked to the foredeck and watched the bow part the water before me. I returned to the wake that streamed from the stern like the aftermath of a difficult birth.

I sailed in the wake of Stratis and my great uncles and their kin. Old Andreas Lekatsas had been the first man of Exogi to spend time in the Great Southern Land. He sailed the pre-Suez-Canal route by way of the Cape of Good Hope, a voyage of many months. He jumped ship in Melbourne in 1851, and joined the rush for gold. So the story goes, from mouth to mouth, from cafe to cafe, from story to myth.

Andreas' nephew, Antonios, left in 1877; he was twenty-four years old. He began his ascent in the city of Melbourne sweeping kitchens, washing dishes, putting out rubbish, and waxing cafe floors. He polished the boards so hard and so long the floors began to glisten. Mountains of dust were transformed into bank notes. Within two decades he had amassed a small fortune, which he invested in coffee palaces and restaurants. So the story goes, from mouth to mouth, from story to myth.

Antonios' younger brother, Marinos, voyaged in his sibling's wake. A cabinet-maker and fiddler, he played the music and carved the instrument that conveyed it. Marinos joined his brother in Melbourne but he had visions of his own. He struck out for Tasmania. As he drew close he had the sensation he was coming home. He hired the most inventive architects of the day, and sat with them as they drafted plans based on his designs. He beheld the image of the grand Opera House of Zakynthos, and when the work was done, he sent home news cuttings of the gala opening.

The Princess Theatre in Launceston opened its doors on 1 September 1911, the first night of the southern spring. Giant flame arcs illuminated the outside walls. Every one of its 1800 seats was occupied. A symphony orchestra entertained the guests. Marinos was hailed as an entrepreneur of great energy and skill.

These were the legends that accompanied me as I set out. I did not want to look back. I was wary of what I might see, but like the biblical Lot I could not resist. Ithaca was fading from sight. The summit was the last to sink. Then the island was gone. I fought an impulse to jump overboard and swim back. No one had warned me of this.

With each kilometre my panic increased. I could not rid myself of the thought of my mother's resignation, her silent reproach. The crew jostled with the sails and resorted to the engine when the winds died. Even though I knew them, they remained detached, doing their job. There was no going back.

The waterfront hotel, where I spent my first night in Patras, smelt of neglect. I slept in a room of strangers, on cots with sagging springs. The cries of seamen loading boats, and the revelry of sailors on shore leave, threaded in and out of my sleep. And I dreamt of the summit. I held the telescope to my eyes. A sea hawk flew into the circle and veered towards me, talons outstretched.

I wrenched myself clear, tumbled over the cliff, and flapped my hands to stem the fall. I searched for currents that would keep me aloft, and eased myself into flight. My eyes took in the northern peaks, the hamlets and harbours, escarpments and coves. I surveyed the entire island. It whirled about its axis until reduced to a single peak. Ithaca was sinking, the last peak fading, and I could not control my flight. I awoke to the blare of ships' horns, and the late night commerce of the street. Never had I felt so alone.

———◆———

Nights flowed into days and back into nights at sea, from Patras through the Corinth Canal, and from Piraeus to the Aegean, engines throbbing in the dark. I lay in the hold and listened to passengers stirring, speaking urgent gibberish in their sleep. Oil lamps caught the grimaces on their faces. The air was hot with unwashed bodies.

We sailed to the southern extremes of the Mediterranean. Egyptian sailing boats slipped unannounced between troopships and freighters. The gaping delta of the Nile yawned invitations to the unknown. I rested my eyes on its eroded banks and learnt that water is stronger than stone.

We disembarked in Port Said and searched for onward passage. Notices plastered against dusty windows proclaimed cheap fares to any destination, but passage was hard to obtain. I prowled the corridors of shipping offices, rode creaking lifts, waited in queues and pursued false leads. Boats to Australia in a time of war were rare.

I was overjoyed when, in the street, I saw Laertes, a seaman from Kioni. He confirmed the saying that in every port you will find a Thiak. We wandered the streets of the wealthy quarters and admired the porches of spacious homes. We gossiped in waterfront cafes to the smell of hashish drifting from back rooms. Port Said remained a city of small-time smugglers and traffickers, traders and perfumed whores; and the harbour, a hive of merchant fleets and converted liners weighed down with troops.

I moved into Laertes' lodgings. He was looking for work on the cargo boats, while I continued my search for a ship to the south. I finally found passage on a Norwegian freighter. We sailed the Suez by night; the boat was blacked out for fear of attack. Out in the darkness I imagined troops moving, maps being re-drawn, millions dying as empires warred. By day I saw army camps, sand-hills of flaming white, and strings of camels and Bedouins clustered at Red Sea wharves. I conjured visions of monks and emaciated hermits meditating in Sinai Desert caves.

We drifted through the invisible portal that divides north from south, and there were days that I saw nothing beyond the imprint of the past. The view from the summit crystallised and assumed permanent shape: the limestone ridges curving over cliffs into solitary coves, and the sun, forever moving, spotlighting shepherd's tracks, the lower hamlets, the silver flecks of an olive grove. And, as if awakening from a trance, I saw a dark cloud moving towards me.

Only when the cloud was directly above did I realise it was a flock of birds. Suddenly the birds descended on the boat in the hundreds. They perched in every crevice, on the masts and rigging, the portholes and decks. For one full day the birds remained, preening and chattering like excited children, and when they left, I followed the flying cloud and saw that we were approaching the west coast of the new land.

Deserted beaches stretched uninterrupted as far as the eye could see. The weight of the ocean surged into swells that broke on vast swathes of sand: the Ionian is free of such tides. I observed the breakers through the telescope my father had given me. I was adrift without past or future, and the faintest trace of war.

BOOK IV

Mentor's manuscript

KALGOORLIE 1916

WATER is stronger than stone. Dreams are more potent than reason. The ocean batters in vain against desolate coasts. These were my thoughts as we approached the final port. An albatross glided across the bow. Fremantle Harbour was a delta where sea and river collide. The scent of burning eucalyptus mingled with the smell of bilge and brine.

Cries of farewell reverberated from a troop ship passing by. I ran my telescope over soldiers crowding the deck rails and riggings. They gazed at the retreating shore, as had I months earlier from the stern of Mikhalis' boat.

I turned to those gathered on the quay where the departing ship had been moored. The uncertainty in the eyes of those on the troop ship making its way out to sea reflected the uncertainty in the eyes of those they were leaving behind. I swung between the crowds on the quay and the ship, as one by one they turned their backs and returned to their separate lives.

I focused the telescope on a second quay and saw a hospital ship edging towards its berth to the strains of a military band. Our passage was temporarily stalled as its gangplank was lowered. I saw the returning troops carried off on stretchers, descending in wheel-chairs, leaning on crutches, stumbling on unsteady feet.

Stratis was waiting as I left the customs office. He was not the Stratis I had slavishly followed as a child. His face was drawn; he walked with the stoop of a burdened man. When we embraced I felt the tightness in his body. He ushered me over wooden planks smudged with seagull droppings. I was seeking my way on firm land, shedding my past like a weathered skin.

We made our way past the crowd assembled by the hospital ship. The wounded were to be ferried to the barracks in South Terrace, Stratis pointed out. There were so many, some would be taken to a makeshift hospital on the Fremantle football oval.

I had witnessed a rare moment, a changing of the guard. The troop ship, ferrying the able-bodied to the European front, was out of sight, while the returning wounded were being ferried ashore. The entire world was at war. I saw it in the anxious faces of those straining to catch sight of a father, a husband, an injured brother. Their heroes had returned broken men.

For a moment I panicked. I wanted to run from the clamour of new arrivals, the sound of the foreign tongue. I envied the seamen who would soon be gone. I craved their anonymity. I longed to join them, and see the shore receding, the port disappearing, to remain within the coming and going, the never arriving. Out of that dark labyrinth we call memory, one voice arose: Old Niko chanting the name of an ancient port. Kalitbahir. Kalitbahir. I was locked in. There was no going back.

The windows of the London Cafe in Perth were boarded. Stratis glanced about warily as he unlocked the door. Broken chairs lay upturned against the walls. Fragments of glass that had eluded the broom glinted in the dull light. The shelves had been stripped bare, and the shop fixtures ripped out. A gutted cash register lay on the floor.

We made our way to the back room where a group of men were playing cards. I recognised Ithacans who had left the island over the years. We embraced and kissed each other on the cheeks. The men swamped me with questions about their families, festering feuds, disputes over village land.

Anastasias, the manager of the cafe, emerged from the kitchen with bowls of oysters and crayfish. 'He is from Castellorizo, but we don't hold it against him,' Stratis joked. 'We are all fools on the same sinking ship.'

We lowered our heads to the table and ate to the sound of shells cracking, earnest chewing and the slurping of wine. Only when our bellies were full were they prepared to tell me the tale. It moved around the table from teller to teller. Voices tumbled over each other, disputing details, adding interpretations, embroidering the drama.

It had begun the previous Friday evening. On the following day the country was to vote in a referendum on conscription. The streets were crowded. The air was charged with impassioned pronouncements, extravagant claims. Orators proclaimed their opinions on soapboxes. Speakers thundered that those who would not fight were impostors and cowards. Others countered that the lives of the country's young men were being sacrificed to foreign interests, Imperial powers.

As darkness fell, a group of soldiers and civilian youths assembled at the Beaufort Street Bridge to drink and hatch plans. They egged each other on with talk of 'enemy aliens' and 'the foreign traitors among us'; then set out, on the run, for the fish markets where they were sure to find them.

Anastasias spread a street map on the table and traced the route: from the bridge to the markets, where the enraged men came across two fishmongers, Lakidis and Mavrokefalos, manning barrows with the afternoon catch from the Sicilian boats. The markets had closed. Their quarry had eluded them. The mob would have to make do with the fishmongers. They upended the barrows, scattered the prawns, and marched from the markets brandishing looted crayfish, singing patriotic songs: 'Australia will be there', 'It's a long way to Tipperary'.

A drunken soldier tore a Union Jack from a building and waved it in front the cheering men. They paraded the streets behind the flag, until, responding to the directions of a ringleader, stampeded to Murray Street. They came to a halt outside Kyriakos Manolas' restaurant, uncertain of what to do next. One of the men at the back of the crowd, growing impatient, hurled a crayfish at the glass. One begets many as is written in the book of Genesis, and a hail of crayfish battered the windows.

When they were done, the men regrouped and marched through city streets led by a soldier blowing a bugle. Their appetites had been whetted. They craved more action. They recalled newspaper articles and cartoons that had lampooned their pro-conscription patriotism, and dashed to the offices of *The Truth* on Hay Street.

The last crayfish rebounded from the plate glass with a dull thud. The men scurried to a pile of road metal, grabbed fistfuls and returned like a swarm of soldier ants to continue their assault. When the windows gave way they rushed to the offices of the *Daily News* on St George's Terrace, gathering an assortment of missiles as they ran.

Anastasias paused with his finger on the map, to work out the route the mob had taken from the offices to his cafe. 'What does it matter?' he finally said, shrugging his shoulders. The men had surged into the cafe and cleaned out his entire stock.

The mobs continued their rampage, laying waste to Panos Koronaios' Royal Dining Room. They raided the English and Continental Cafes owned by Russian émigrés; and attacked Sam Epstein's Moana Cafe. 'I am a naturalised Briton,' Epstein pleaded, and was jeered at as the rocks took flight. One hundred patrons fled through a shower of glass. Looters sprinted inside and hurled boxes of chocolate out to the pavement. Children grabbed fistfuls of sweets and leapt for joy at their unexpected fortune.

The undermanned police called in the Light Horse picket from the Claremont Camp. The crowd scattered and broke into smaller packs as the horses charged. Fistfights continued late into the night, and in the morning, when my compatriots surveyed the damage, they realised years of toil had been reduced to waste.

'No matter how hard we try to remain quiet we have not escaped notice,' said Anastasias. 'We mind our own business, but every day there are newspaper reports about the Great War as they call it. They know that King Constantine's wife is the sister of Kaiser Wilhelm and they believe that the palace is riddled with pro-German spies.

'They know that mobs on the streets of Athens are attacking the republican followers of their ally, Prime Minister Venizelos, but they do not care to know that most of us support him. They have no time for subtleties. Their boys went off to do battle as if setting out for a picnic, and now that their loved ones are dying they need to wreak vengeance.'

'It did not start yesterday,' said Stratis. 'They have despised us for a long time. It irks them that some of us have done well. They hate the sound of our foreign tongue. They hate the way we keep together. No matter how hard we try to be more British than the British we remain black traitors. So let's split open a few more oysters and talk our gibberish, and they can go to hell.'

Stratis pushed back his chair and circled the room singing. For the first time since I stepped ashore I saw the old Stratis, slipping over the stones of Aetos, barely able to hold a straight line, Stratis and I sealing our pact on the steps of Homer's School with blood and a swig of wine.

I rose to my feet and joined him. We lifted the stripped crayfish from the plates and brandished them in imitation of the mob. We marched around the room singing mock renditions of patriotic songs, and fell about laughing. When we came to our senses, we heard a voice rising: first as a humming, then as a wave building, voices sought each other out, easing into harmonies. Conversations gave way to *cantathas*, the most loved of Ionian musical forms.

'*Mavri xenitia*,' one of the men muttered as our voices trailed away. 'Our black exile. We are marooned in a foreign land, and despite our constipated smiles and declarations of loyalty, our hopes of redemption are turning to dust.'

Stratis and I left Perth by train the following morning. Our compartment was crowded with soldiers on leave. One leant against his wife, the only woman among us. Another sat with an arm in a sling, brooding. We were men without women headed for the Golden Mile. For the first time in my life the coast was out of sight. I had lost my familiar companions, sea and mountain. As we advanced inland, the trees grew smaller, shrinking to stunted shrubs upon stony dirt.

'The first volunteers,' said Stratis, 'signed up in August 1914, when Britain declared war on Germany.' He spoke softly, lest his Greek attract wary glances. In recent months men of foreign appearance had been attacked and beaten for speaking their native tongue. 'The recruits came running: stockmen and drovers, railwaymen, labourers, carpenters, miners, gold prospectors, bushmen, timber contractors, office workers and shearers, from every corner of the state, young men, teenage boys.'

'Like the Ithacans who volunteered for the Balkan Wars,' I offered.

Stratis ignored my remarks.

'Hundreds gathered at the Kalgoorlie station to farewell the recruits who had been drinking all night. The town's people pushed beer and baskets of food through the carriage windows. They waved Union Jacks and cheered when the train pulled out. The same scenes, I was told, were repeated at every station. The next day, the recruits were marched to the training camp at Blackboy Hill on the outskirts of Perth. Ten weeks later they were on their way to Fremantle where they boarded two troop ships.'

Stratis paused, and noting the blank expressions on the passengers in the compartment, lowered his voice further. 'I was in

Fremantle, packing oysters in ice for the journey to Kalgoorlie. The wharves were crowded, brass bands played, streamers were thrown on board as the ships cast off. The recruits did not know where they were going. Many believed they were bound for Britain or the European fronts. Days later, on the Indian Ocean, the two ships joined a convoy of thirty-eight.

'Imagine it my friend!' Stratis exclaimed, 'a flotilla of ships had sailed from New Zealand and Australian ports, and assembled in the port of Albany. Now they were on their way to the continent we had sailed from so recently.' He shook his head in wonder. 'Odysseus entered Troy with troops hidden in the bowels of a wooden horse. Three thousand years later, troops and live horses are sailing to do battle on the opposite ends of the earth.'

Stratis leaned closer. 'By the end of November the plans had changed,' he said, his voice almost a whisper. 'Under orders from the Imperial command in London the troops and horses disembarked in Alexandria; and five months later they were dying at the hands of the Turks, not far from the battlefields of Troy, their bodies strewn on the shores of our Aegean.'

We continued our journey in silence. The land was scattered with oases of woodlands, copses of salmon gum, wild flowers, all the more brilliant because of the emptiness that surrounded them. We stopped at isolated stations: single timber waiting rooms beside a signal box and water tank. Passengers disembarked and vanished into nothingness. And just as it seemed the world itself had disappeared, Kalgoorlie was upon us, a dusty mirage rising from an ocean of red dirt.

We sit around *trapezia*. This is how we find each other, at backroom tables scattered throughout the globe. We unfold our arms, lean forward, enter conversations, lean back and fall silent, then re-enter the fray, even as we curse, *malacca*, you wanker, even as we shake our fists and lament our black exile. And this is how it was, at the very first table, on my very first night in Kalgoorlie, in the back room behind the Parisian Cafe.

My Ithacan compatriots were there to welcome me as they had in Perth: cafe proprietors, oyster mongers, tobacconists, fruiterers and confectioners. And the backroom boys: waiters, dishwashers, cooks and cleaners, apprenticed to uncles, older brothers and fathers, biding their time until they too would have enough capital to set up shop. Their tales fell from their lips in tandem with the cards they slapped on the table. And holding court among them was the Gambler, the know-all of know-alls, the patron saint of new arrivals, the loudest mouth in the room.

Dressed in a jacket, waistcoat, white shirt and bow tie, his upper back was curved in the premature stoop of a man who had spent too many nights hunched over tables. His crooked nose accentuated the sharp features of his elongated face, and a mop of hair straggled from beneath a felt hat to his jacket collar. A cynical smile played upon his lips.

'See what has become of the children of Odysseus!' he laughed. 'We have abandoned the seas to become city-mongers. Our clothes smell of rancid fruit and gutted fish. We are so tired we doze off on our feet.' The Gambler shuffled the cards with a deft hand as he talked. A cigarette wiggled in his mouth, but barely interfered with the flow of his tales. His companions tried, with little success, to get a say in edgeways, while I listened in silence, a naïve newcomer hanging on every word.

'I did not want to remain a slave for the rest of my life,' he said. 'After all I come from Kioni, the most beautiful village on Ithaca. I can see it now,' he declared with mock nostalgia. 'The three windmills standing like sentinels on the rim of the peninsula, our homes on steep slopes with perfect views of the harbour. Alas its beauty could not support us. Without wealth the most beautiful scenes appear ugly. When I have accumulated enough money I will return. This is what I live for.'

'Ah, here it comes, the old chorus,' interjected Stratis, winking at me. 'We have heard it all before. Now you will tell us about your days at sea.'

'Why not young man?' the Gambler retorted. 'After all, I spent a decade on cargo boats. The best voyage is always the maiden voyage. By the third voyage, sea-life becomes a weary succession of familiar ports. By the twentieth, I had endured enough of being tossed from wharf to wharf. On an impulse I jumped ship in Fremantle.'

'Ithacan compatriots can be found in every port. I soon found work. The proprietor, from Vathy, worked me eighteen hours a day, and paid me a pittance. I doused myself with cold water to stay awake. He expected me to be grateful he had given me a job.

'At first I thought I had little choice. I worked as a dishwasher and cleaner, and hauled the stinking rubbish bins into the lane. I held my breath to avoid the stench, brushed away the flies, returned to the cafe, and saw it in a new light. It was obvious that the action was centred on cards. There was money to be made at the backroom tables. Life is a gamble so why not make a living as a gambler, I reasoned. I threw off my apron, and told my boss to get fucked. I had discovered my mission in life. A game of cards, a group of men assembled around a table, this is what I live for.'

'As long as you have control of the bank,' laughed Stratis.

'Why not, young man? I provide a service. I follow my compatriots and fellow riff-raff wherever they go. I seek you out wherever you are scattered on these godforsaken wastes. I have found you crawling in mine shafts, and scavenging oyster beds. I have seen you bent over stoves, waiting on tables like timid servants, smiling to prevent yourselves from throwing up. I have tracked you down herding cattle on stations as large as our entire island.

'I sit with people wherever I find them and unite them with a pack of cards. I organise the bank, keep all in order, prevent needless fights and arguments, and in return I receive the gossip. A good story, Mentor, this is what I live for,' he said, turning to me, his one willing listener. 'I know every tale of every Greek who has had the misfortune to stumble into these parts.'

'Now he will tell you about the Jacomas brothers,' Stratis warned.

'Why not, young man? The Jacomas brothers are the cunning heroes of journeys that would make Homer rejoice. Their native island, Castellorizo, is more destitute than ours, and doubly cursed since it lies off the Turkish coast. I have docked in its harbour many times en route to eastern ports.

'Castellorizians were marine traders. They roamed the Mediterranean like wily Ithacans. The Ottomans, may they burn in hell, controlled the harbours and crushed them with taxes. They denied them access to the Anatolian forests where they obtained the timber for constructing their boats, and to rub salt into the wounds, the new European steamers outgunned the speed of their home-built craft.'

'We do not need a history lesson,' grumbled one of the men, impatient for his next hand of cards.

'How can we understand a man's fate if we do not know of such things?' snapped the Gambler. 'The Jacomas brothers did not suddenly appear from the desert! They came here because they were running away from the plague that has afflicted us all. A little bit of history won't go astray. The brothers arrived here in the footsteps of Paddy Hannan, the prospector who first came upon this madness we now call Kalgoorlie.'

The Gambler leant forward and rubbed his knees as Spiro Karpouzis, the cafe owner, delivered a tray of coffees. 'The smell of coffee, the sight of the *kaimaki* frothing on the top, the anticipation of the first sip, this is what I live for!' he exclaimed. 'Who could have imagined that so much pleasure resides in such a tiny cup?

'Paddy Hannan is the reason we are stuck here, in this black hole,' he continued, addressing me, cigarette in mouth, cup in hand, unsure of which to indulge in next. 'Hannan journeyed with his face glued to the ground, driven by the memory of the famine he had known as a youth. He had fled a country where his compatriots' lips had turned green from their diet of grass. For thirty years he followed every gold rush, south to north, west to east, and across the Tasman Sea to the New Zealand coast. He scanned the earth for so long, he forgot there were skies.

'He was fifty by the time he plodded here beside two pack-horses and his companions, Shea and Flanagan. The three men staked their claim on the tenth day of June 1893. Every one in Kalgoorlie knows the date; it is inscribed on the pepper tree in the street that bears Hannan's name. They set up camp when there was nothing but ugly stretches of scrub. They clawed at quartz embedded with fragments of gold. They found nuggets of alluvial gold scattered over the ground. The rumours travelled fast. Within days there were hundreds of prospectors pawing the Kalgoorlie dirt.

'Now you will boast that you knew Hannan,' said Stratis, 'even though you were not here at that time.'

'I didn't meet him,' the Gambler confesses, 'but of course the Jacomas brothers knew him. Like me, they made it their business to know people. Hannan was forever heading somewhere else, the brothers told me. He would disappear for weeks and return with the same secretive expression. He would have made a great poker player.

'"What have you found?" the brothers asked in towns that had known better days. Hannan looked around as if making sure there was no one who could overhear him, then whispered, "I have found nothing. Nothing at all."

'The brothers were not so foolish. They had our islander cunning in their veins. They quickly saw what was what. Why waste one's life grovelling in dust? They acquired wagons, loaded them with crowbars, picks, tomahawks and saws, pegs, nails, five-gallon drums filled with water, bags of sugar, tinned pudding, sacks of flour and potatoes, and set out like the gypsies who pass through our Ithaca.

'They journeyed on routes inscribed by wagon grooves and bullock hooves, and raised their hats to graves marked by wood crosses and cairns. They paused by lone prospectors wheeling their belongings in barrows made of branches and bark. They greeted bearded men trudging with all they possessed on their backs, and stopped to serve weary prospectors foraging over parched creek beds. They collected water from condensing machines on the shores of salt-water lakes, and sold it to disoriented wanderers wilting from thirst.'

The Gambler paused to dab his forehead with a handkerchief. 'Like Ionian seamen, the early prospectors reaped the winds,' he continued. 'They hurled top sand into the air, and the dust was blown away, leaving behind specks of gold. They knelt like pious worshippers beside wooden cradles and rocked them to sift the dirt.

'The Jacomas brothers could barely see them through the dust as they approached. They built a fortune selling cloths that wiped away the mess. They bartered and traded and took gold nuggets in lieu of cash. They knew every teamster, miner and merchant in every town and settlement on every field from Kalgoorlie to the west coast.

'And they knew the Mahomet brothers, Faiz and Tagh,' the Gambler powered on, encouraged by my attention. 'In 1892, they had trekked overland from South Australia with 250 camels. Within two years there were thousands of beasts and their turbaned handlers. They took possession of them in Fremantle, when they were led off ships from India and Afghanistan.

'The cameleers taught us what a good camel is worth. Their slow movements are deceptive. They cover long distances faster than horses and bullocks. They trek for up to six days without water. They forge paths where no rails can be laid. A single camel can transport a pair of fat men one hundred kilometres in a single day. One camel is known to have carried a grand piano on its back.

'You don't believe me? Then you don't know camels. The skill lies in the tying. If the ropes are in order the camel can cope with the rest. I have seen them hauling water tanks, railway sleepers and sheets of corrugated iron. I have seen them in teams of twenty, harnessed nose-to-tail, close enough to lick each other's bums. They eat plants that not even a goat can stomach. Their padded feet cushion them against stones and the scalding earth.

'We should import camels to Ithaca,' laughed Stratis.

'They stink,' said Spiro, 'and sink to the ground when you whisper *hooster*. I have seen it during a camel race. The race-goers shouted *hooster* and the camels collapsed to their knees. The cameleers were angry. They had put good money on their prized beasts. One of them ran onto the track and tried to whip his camel back to his feet in front of the laughing crowd. As it struggled up, the crowd bellowed *hooster* and down it went again.'

'We are all gamblers,' said Stratis. 'It is a way of aborting years of sweat. A roll of the dice, a shuffle of the deck, and our worries are over. We prefer cards. Australians prefer horses, and flies crawling up walls. The Afghans put their hard-earned cash on camels and wrestlers.

'The Afghans had a rival for our Gambler,' said Spiro. 'Aesop, he was called. His enterprises were more varied. He gambled on foot races, wrestling, billiards and boxing.

'Yes. Yes. The Jacomas brothers knew Aesop,' butted in the Gambler, intent on regaining the spotlight. 'They met him many times in the streets of Coolgardie. When he was young, Aesop would take on all comers in wrestling contests.

'His challengers quaked in their boots when they faced him. He was a giant of a man. He drew himself up to his full height, arms folded, moustache bristling, biceps flexed, and stared his rival down. He would simply wait while his opponent fidgeted and finessed and tried in vain to get a hold. Then with one swift move he would pin him to the ground.

'Yes. Yes. The Jacomas boys knew him, just as they knew every miserable soul who has been lured to these parts. They knew those who made it, and those who toiled in vain. They knew those who struck it rich and those who went mad.'

'Now he will tell us about Stellios Psichitas,' predicted Stratis.

'Why not young man? Stellios' fate is a warning to us all. He should have remained in his native Syros and never set foot in this ill-fated land. Alas, his brother Ioannis owned a fruit shop in Lawler, on the Murchison fields, and Stellios could not resist the call.

'In 1902 Ioannis brought him over and set him to work in his shop. Stellios envied his older brother. He coveted everything he possessed. He complained of the long hours he was made to work. The men despised each other with a hatred known only to brothers. One day, Ioannis left for Leonara to stock up on supplies. Stellios remained in the shop with his brother's wife, Sophia. She held her newborn baby in her arms. Some say that she mocked him, or that he tried to embrace her and was rebuffed. Others argue Stellios demanded a share of his brother's riches.

'Whatever the reason, it drove him into a murderous rage. He felled Sophia with an axe and slit her throat, and her baby's throat, with a razor. He staggered out into the desert babbling. A search party found him cowering in a creek bed with the bloodstained razor in his hand.

'He was tried here in Kalgoorlie. It took the jury fifteen minutes to convict him, and the judge one minute to sentence him to death. He was transferred to Fremantle jail. He begged his brother for forgiveness. He begged forgiveness from father Antonios Lambradis, the wandering priest. He begged forgiveness from anyone who came near him until the day he was hanged.'

'We are all beggars here despite our growing wealth,' Stratis cut in. 'Our compatriots feared reprisals because of Stellios' crime: it reflected badly on all foreigners, as those of us who are not British are called.

'My letters were misleading, Mentor,' he said, turning to me. 'It took me time to see how it is. One of us quarrels with his brother and we are all fratricides. One of us exploits his workers and we are all parasites. One of us is preferred for a job and we are all fucking scabs. One of us murders and we are all potential murderers. Our compatriots may have pitied Stellios, but they were not sorry to see him hang.'

———·———

I left the cafe with Stratis and strolled the streets of Kalgoorlie, overwhelmed by the Gambler's barrage. Stratis guided me past Ithacan businesses: rooms leased by our compatriots and fitted out as oyster bars and cafes, grillrooms, tobacco and fruit shops. We saw crowds of drinkers through the swinging doors of public bars, leaning on balustrades, and bent over tables in billiard rooms, drinking to steady their aim. 'Beer and whisky are the holy waters of Kalgoorlie,' Stratis laughed.

We leapt on a cable tram, and leapt off in Boulder twenty minutes later, and continued our stroll on streets alight with drinking saloons. At that late hour they appeared to be replicas of the streets we had just left. Stratis again pointed out businesses run by Thiaks. The doors were bolted, the shutters down. Except for the locks, we could have been walking past homes in Ithaca, slumbering in the dark.

The streets petered out at ridges carved with mines. Treatment plants were still at work. Head-frames, smoke stacks, boilers and storage vats stood against the sky. Tailings dumps formed a range of hillocks that swelled like milk-filled breasts. We were walking the Golden Mile, the richest gold field in the world, Stratis declared.

The days of surface mining were long over, he explained. The alluvial gold had been quickly exhausted, and prospectors tamed into waged workers who plumbed ever-deepening seams. They laboured in dimly lit underworlds of galleries, tunnels and shafts. They drilled into lodes clogging their lungs with toxic dust. They jammed explosives into rock crevices and ran for their lives. Metallurgists, engineers, managers and foremen were the masterminds of the new order. Capital flowed to and from London offices. The miners were worker bees ferrying nectar to distant hives.

We struggled up a tailings-hillock on our mountain-goat legs. All that had loomed large, moments earlier, shrank in the star-filled night. Stratis swung his arm in an arc. 'We are standing on a seabed, seven hundred million years old,' he said, shaking his head in wonder. It was the oldest land surface in the world, here long before any creature walked the earth, and hatching inside its rocks was the gold that would reunite two Ithacan fools on a hill of waste millennia later.

'The land is not as empty as it seems,' Stratis explained. 'Inside there is movement. Seeds lie dormant, waiting for rain. And when it finally falls, fields of flowers sprout overnight. It is said that while Europe lay buried beneath glaciers, natives were extracting edible roots from what we see as barren earth.'

I looked at the outline of Stratis' face as he talked. I understood, as never before, the meaning of friendship. Our pact had taken on new meaning in the three days since I stepped ashore. We shared a passion for knowledge. We were blood brothers reunited on a mutual quest.

A day that had begun by the sea was ending in a city that had risen on desert sands. Beyond the revelry and the huddle of saloons, beyond the tunnels where men toiled to extract wealth, beyond the wood frames and iron girders, stretched unknown space. I was marooned. I bent over, ran my fingers through the tailings dirt, and shivered.

My life assumed a new rhythm. I alternated between the Parisian Cafe and Spiro Black's oyster saloon. With my primitive grasp of the new language I was not yet fit to wait upon tables. I was relegated to kitchens, and unloaded oysters from the Perth train. And on my days off I strolled the streets of Kalgoorlie with Stratis.

Perhaps only inspired madmen could erect a city so quickly. Within a decade the founding fathers had piped in water and built baths to wash off the dust. They fashioned wide streets out of red dirt to accommodate camel trains and bullocks. They graduated from canvas tents and bark-sheds to homes of stone and mortar. They erected courthouses to try thieves, and banks to protect their expanding riches. They built town halls and offices and engineered mines a kilometre deep in the ore-bearing ground.

Progress and order were their guiding values. They were men of enterprise. Empire builders. 'Men of soaring energies,' Stratis called them. Well-groomed bearded men, with a purpose in their stride hurried through the streets oblivious to the midday sun. They made their way to the Mechanics Institute, its fanned smoking rooms, billiards hall and lounges. They prided themselves on their public library in Hannan Street, where I spent hours bent over English texts.

I stepped out of the library with Stratis one Saturday, and strolled to the racecourse where we lay on shaded lawns. Lawn was the highest aesthetic of the city fathers. Lawn defied nature. Lawns stood in opposition to ancient contours. Lawn neutralised stone and boulders, and smothered the grime. Lawn was a sedate boast that the wilderness could be contained.

We strolled back to the town centre with the post-race crowd and strayed into the back streets. We paused in front of a double-fronted house where a man and two teenage children sat in wicker chairs by a table on a veranda. The table was covered in a white lace cloth, baskets of ferns and pot plants hung from the galvanised roof. A woman emerged from the house with a tray of white cups and a pot of tea. It was a scene of contentment gilded by a late-afternoon sun.

We made our way to the Palace Hotel, climbed the carpeted stairs and sat back in easy chairs on the balcony. We were dressed in double-breasted suits, white shirts and cravats. Our hair was pomaded, our moustaches waxed and curled. We lit cigars and sipped liqueurs, gentlemen's drinks. I stood up and leaned on the balustrade overlooking Hannan Street.

Townsfolk were stepping off cable-trams, hailing horse-drawn cabs, navigating bicycles and automobiles through the evening crowd. A white Oldsmobile bedecked in ribbons ferried a bridal party, followed by a convoy of men wearing cream silk suits, and perfumed women in evening dresses.

We continued our stroll as evening fell and strayed beyond the fringe of the city. Beyond the final street stood a huddle of dwellings, a confusion of clay and canvas, galvanised tin and eucalypt branches. A group of blacks sat on kerosene tins around a fire. The women were dressed in cotton skirts, the men in shabby suits and open necked shirts; the children ran about barefoot.

The camp clung to Kalgoorlie's edges like the serrated hem of a neat skirt. Nearby, Afghan cameleers were pitching tents beneath a cluster of salmon gums. Their beasts stretched out in the sand, at rest after a day's labour.

I am drawn to thresholds. I long to follow things back to their source, to the drone of Byzantine chants flowing through the doors of St Marina. I move away and out of range, but the impressions linger. Beyond all sounds, said Mikhalis the fiddler, can be discerned the eternal hum we call silence; and from this silence there rise melodies that give shape to our longings.

The fragile space between town and desert hummed a different music. The cameleers were singing. Their voices evoked the call of the muezzin urging the faithful to prayer. We wanted to approach them but we held back. They were a cosmos unto themselves, and we were interlopers. We stood and watched from a distance, then turned and walked back to the well-lit streets of the city.

———

It began early morning, a howling of wind and dust. It swirled from the desert, from disused shafts, open-cut mines and tailings dumps. Horses snorted, dogs whimpered, camels sank to the dirt and refused to walk. It invaded the balconies, peppered the roofs and settled on verandas. It funnelled through junkyards and timber yards, and assaulted the racecourse lawns. It infested our jackets, and crept into our boots and pockets. It lashed our eyes, clogged our nostrils, soured our tongues, and swept us off the streets into the back rooms of our cafes. We drew the curtains, brewed coffees and surrendered to the Gambler's cards.

The afternoon sun illumined the dust when we finally stepped back out. Dogs scavenged, tails up, noses to the ground, sniffing at novel smells. Cart wheels whipped up dust as they rolled by. Horses oozed sticky sweat from their rumps. Children itched. Tempers flared. Women cursed. Men coughed and flicked dust off their jackets as they hurried back to work.

Then I saw him. He emerged from the dust in a soldier's uniform. His hair was matted, and perspiration flowed in dirt-stained rivulets from forehead to neck. He clasped his hands to his ears as he limped. And he howled. People averted their eyes and edged out of his way as he approached. He fell beside the cable tracks and beat the gravel with his fists. He beat the sides of his head and still he howled. It was an animal keening, the high-pitched wail of a wounded dog.

I stood on the pavement, transfixed. I followed the soldier as if willed by an unseen force. He stumbled through the back streets, to the double-fronted house I had seen, weeks earlier, bathed in tranquillity. The older man, who had been seated on the veranda, and the woman who had served the tea, were waiting as he limped though the gate. The older man pinned the soldier's arms to his side and wrestled him to the ground. The soldier bucked and clawed until the older man prevailed. The couple led him into the house, subdued and trembling.

I remained rooted to the spot after the front door closed. The blinds were drawn, the house silent. The potted plants were wilting from neglect. Weeds had begun to sprout beneath the rim of the veranda. The soldier had enlisted two years earlier as a teenager, and had returned from the battlefields to his parents' home, weeks ago, insane.

From that day on, whenever I strolled in the back streets I knew, instinctively, the houses of families who had lost a son, a brother, husband or father. The houses were stained by an absence. Those who entered and stepped out were marked by grief. It was evident in their drawn faces, their distracted air.

I was plagued by the thought of the simultaneity of events. Somewhere in the city a father, a mother, a wife, was being informed of the death of a loved one. At the same time, a crowd was waiting on a quay in Fremantle for the first sight of a shell-shocked husband, a maimed son. And on a battlefield, far from home, a soldier was being blown apart.

I hurried from the house to the bordellos on Brookman Street, and exchanged a week's wages for a woman's warmth. I observed my sun-darkened hands moving over fair skin. I chose a second partner and paid her to remove the thick powder on her cheeks before we embraced. I inhaled the perfume on her smooth skin. I wanted to wipe the slate clean.

———•———

The dust storm was over but a greater storm brewed in men's hearts. We arranged our goods in the display windows as we assumed polite citizens should. We waited on our customers neatly dressed, and greeted them with good cheer. We controlled our gestures and spoke sparingly to obscure our foreign tongues. We cooked to their tastes, and hastened to serve them, but no matter how we tried, we were looked at with growing distrust.

The Gambler kept us informed of news from the battlefront. He sat at the backroom table and translated daily reports from the *Kalgoorlie Miner*. He leaned back, broadsheet in hand, and read out the honour rolls of soldiers killed, and lists of the wounded and missing-in-action. He translated reports of battles in Serbia, Romania and Macedonia, and as if reaching the climax of a performance, he paused at news from Greece. He pondered over the text like a scholar, consulted dictionaries, and weighed up each word before translating.

King Constantine, he finally informed us, had stalled on Allied demands to hand over his reservists' guns. In the first week of December, English, French and Italian troops landed in Piraeus. Fifty were killed in skirmishes with the reservists. French and Greek soldiers exchanged shots on the slopes of the Acropolis. Allied shells had fallen in the centre of the city. Athenians were fleeing to the plains of Attica.

As reports of the 'Grecian Crisis' grew more strident, customers we had believed were friends began to avoid us. I saw the transformation of familiar faces, from habitual friendliness, clouded by a hint of mistrust, to hatred, glinting in eyes riddled with suspicion. Stratis was spat upon in Hannan Street. Rumours were circulating.

The Gambler's translations became more considered. He savoured the attention of his audience and took time conveying the meaning of terms such as 'gross treachery'. He stroked his chin, nodded his head like a sage, and announced that editorials had accused the Greeks of unprovoked attacks upon the Allies. Athens had become a slaughterhouse. Armed royalists, loyal to King Constantine, were attacking republican supporters of Prime

Minister Venizelos. King Constantine was accused of colluding with the Germans in torpedoing hospital ships in the Aegean.

The Gambler pondered over the editorial: 'It was high time that shilly-shallying was abandoned in dealing with Greece,' he read. We waited for his translation. The Gambler revelled in our attention.

'It's "high time" you stopped "shilly-shallying" with us,' Stratis finally snapped in a concoction of English and Greek. We laughed until our bellies ached.

On the day the madness broke, the newspapers reported renewed atrocities. Venizelists had been 'done to death like rats,' wrote one correspondent. Diplomatic relations with the Greek government were to be suspended. The Allied governments threatened to impose a blockade on Greece until they received reparations for the loss of troops. 'King Constantine must be held accountable for complicity in the crimes committed,' thundered Allied leaders.

Again I was plagued by the simultaneity of events, the currents that bound us to actions taking place in distant continents. We were being viewed through distorted lenses. Our protestations of loyalty to Australia were sneered at. Our claims that we were supporters of Venizelos, who sided with the Allies, went unheeded. We were enemy aliens. Sinister presences. Dark-skinned barbarians.

'We must tear apart words to liberate their meaning,' Old Niko had shouted. 'Every nation thinks they are civilised while the others are barbarians. Look hard at the word. Dissect it. Put each syllable under a magnifying glass. Ba. Ba. Ba. It is the babble of foreign tongues. Ba. Ba. Ba. It is the babble of those who speak a language other than one's own. Each nation thinks that they possess what the ancient Greeks called *mesotes*, measuredness, while the others are cast as savage mobs.'

I glance down at the page I am writing. The Greek script is whirling. Alpha is waltzing with omega. The beginning is dancing with the end, and the end has become the beginning, and all that has happened will happen again. I watch the ink flow from my pen. I observe the moment in which it dries. Perhaps this is the moment when words die. The descent from the living thought to its death is swift. Perhaps this is the precise instant when a manuscript begins to gather dust. It cannot be seen yet, but the process has set in.

The bantams have stopped their cackling. The mouse that is now surely a rat has stopped gnawing. The cockatiel is asleep on my shoulder. I am tired. The night is old. The story is long, and before I go on I need a good night's sleep. I am going to bed, and tomorrow night the same.

———

Arkhe tou paramythiou, kalispera sas. The fairytale truly begins, good evening to you. It begins on Saturday, 9 December 1916. Shoppers are foraging for Christmas bargains. The House of Brennan boasts poplin trousers, elastic braces, cashmere socks, and Galatea knickers. McKay's display-windows blaze with women's millinery. Pellews of Boulder is doing a brisk trade in Formosa hats, silk Assam suits and dress materials: muslin and organdie, satin laces, camisole embroidery, tweeds and linens. Montgomery Brothers' Monster Christmas Fair offers green bamboo veranda blinds, beribboned corsets, trimmed underskirts. The stores of Kalgoorlie rival the fabled bazaars of Constantinople.

When darkness falls, the blinds are drawn, stores locked and bolted and the fulcrum shifts to the pubs and hotel balconies. The Lyric Pictures is showing *The Miracle of Life*. Powell's Palace Pictures is screening a Keystone comedy; at interval models will parade the latest creations of Paris. The Kalgoorlie band is playing at an open-air concert on Hannan Street. For a fee of two shillings, gents gain entrance to the weekly dance at the Theatre Royal, while ladies are allowed in free. At the Goldfield's Athletics' club Albert 'Kid' Lloyd of Victoria is stepping into the ring with local boy, 'Kid' George. The house is full. The audience is baying. The blood sports are about to begin.

A group of soldiers and civilians gather in Commonwealth Park and make their plans. They reassemble two hours later by the Town Hall. A shrill whistle signals the charge. The Olympia Cafe, Mangos' fruit shop and Spiro Black's oyster saloon on Cassady Street are the first to be attacked. Among the rioters there are those who had gulped down our oysters, sipped our sodas, slapped our backs and called us 'mates'. Now they chant, 'Go back to where you fuck'n' came from you sons of whores and traitors. While our sons die in your filthy lands, you lift our hard-won cash from our hands.'

The beer and whisky are flowing. It is a carnival, a substitute for men whose wives no longer make love, a means of vengeance for soldiers who have lost a comrade, a cleansing for those who have lost a loved one. Shops are torn apart, furniture smashed, fittings ripped out. Stock is scattered over the street. When a rioter is arrested the police are kicked and jostled by the mob.

Drinkers on pub balconies egg the rioters on. Rocks and bottles are hurled through windows. The stock is there for the taking.

Looters scurry off with cigars and spirits, cartons of cigarettes, crates of fruit and oysters. Children stuff sweets into their mouths, in their pockets and underpants.

The Gambler runs from the Parisian cafe chanting 'I am a loyal citizen.' His stout legs are working overtime. A group of men mimic his words with exaggerated accents. One of them grasps him by the lapels and heaves him to the ground. The Gambler, no stranger to brawls, covers his head with his arms as he is kicked. Stratis and I run from the cafe. We lift him by the arms and drag him back through the dust. Blood trickles from gashes in his forehead. 'I am a loyal citizen,' he bellows.

The many have become one, and the one are many, and in the many there is a clear purpose. I envisage tribes over millennia emboldened by flags and anthems, united beneath coats of arms and banners. I observe those who hang back, and those who succumb and move forward to become part of the one. I observe the potent brew of elation and hatred, the contagious bravado of the mob. Children ape their fathers. Women find common purpose with their estranged husbands.

We flee by the back door as the windows of the cafe shatter, and run to Panos Pitsikas' house where our compatriots are gathering. Children are crying, adults consoling, young men enraged by their impotence. Throughout the night the door is opened to those seeking refuge.

When the Greek businesses of Kalgoorlie have been taken care of the rioters cram into cable trams, and pour out in Boulder. The crowd has swelled to two thousand. They tear apart shop interiors and hurl crockery against the walls. They clear the shelves with one swipe of their hands and hurl the spoils through smashed windows onto the pavements. Scavengers scuffle over jars of pickles, puddings and cutlery, pipes and tobacco. Papadopoulos' fruit market is set alight.

Time is expanding, the sky impassive. We pace the rooms and endure the passing hours. We creep back into the streets as the sun begins its ascent. Women and children are darting into gutted shops to sift through the rubble. A child runs to his mother with a jar of preserves. She sends him back to continue his search. Municipal workers are sweeping the debris and nailing boards over shattered windows.

After the crowd disperses, we pick our way through the wreckage. A gust of red dust swirls in the rising heat. The stench of beer and vomit still lingers. We gaze at the remains of years of toil and know our days in Kalgoorlie are over.

For nine days, Mikhalis Raftopoulos and his son Yianni, cower in a shed for fear that the riots have not ended. We delay our departure until we find them, then tear up our leases, write off our debts and pack our possessions. We make our way to the station and leave as we had arrived, with a suitcase in hand and the clothes we are wearing. And in the years since I have often wondered, who moved in after we left to claim our gutted shops and aborted leases? Who sweated in the kitchens and warded off the flies as they dragged out the rubbish bins? Who sifted the rubble to claim the spoils of our losses?

Stratis and I formed other plans. We drove east from Kalgoorlie with the Gambler in his white Studebaker following the rail-tracks of the wood-lines. They extended, like octopus tentacles, hundreds of kilometres from the goldmines. The trees closer to the city had been axed in the early years of settlement. Entire woodlands were felled and the stumps prised out by gelignite, so fierce was the hunger for fuel. The tracks snaked beyond the new wastelands in all directions as the loggers moved ever further in search of timber.

We reached the first of the camps late afternoon. The men were trudging back from work beside logs loaded on horse-drawn wagons. Their clothes were heavy with sap, their hair infested with slivers of bark. They looked like scrawny scarecrows that had known too many suns. We helped them transfer the logs to wagons moored by railway sidings from which they would be ferried to Kalgoorlie.

The Gambler approached the workers' quarters after the evening meal. They quickly agreed on the fee he charged for controlling the bank, and the game was on. The timber-men were Italians. In the previous year, their Slav workmates, former citizens of Austro-Hungary, had been interned as enemy aliens on Rottnest Island. The Italian workers outnumbered Anglo-Australians four to one. The ratio increased in the summer when the Italians stayed on despite the heat.

The Gambler was the great tempter. He wore the guise of a genial uncle but his jovial demeanour masked his cunning. 'We are brothers,' he proclaimed, drawing on his pidgin Italian, 'in search of a way back to our true homes.' He was a messenger bearing news from distant mines and camps, a slow moving Hermes, ample bellied and plump.

The mood changed as soon as the first hand was dealt. The players were riveted, their nerves finely tuned. They crossed themselves and gripped the cards more tightly as their losses grew. They lost track of the passing hours, and forgot their years of hard labour.

One player kept a bottle by his side to urinate in, lest he miss the round when his luck would surely change.

The Gambler stole into their lives at nightfall and was gone before dawn. I wondered about the men back in the camp as we travelled further east. They would be splashing cold water from the washing trough on their faces, and leading their horses from the stables. The Gambler would have appeared as an apparition, a thief in the night. The men would have cursed him for their empty wallets or rejoiced in their unexpected wealth. They would have envied his easy means of accumulating cash while they were condemned to trudge to the woodlands for another day of back-breaking work.

We drove beyond the furthest reach of the camps and set our course by the Kalgoorlie–Port Augusta line. The railway, fifteen hundred miles long, was being constructed from both ends. We passed camel teams carting massive pipes and bore casings. The thick-wheeled wagons were harnessed to pairs of camels. We came upon mail coaches and rail inspectors in horse-drawn buggies.

Water bores rose on spindly legs. Condensing plants, wells and storage tanks quenched our thirst. The way was littered with earth-works, ballast pits, concrete culverts and sandbanks. Locomotives conveyed tip-wagons loaded with sand to the head of the rail-line. Steam shovels excavated the ongoing route. Horses dragged earth up steep inclines and shaped them into smooth banks. Automated tracklayers set out rails and sleepers, and battalions of workers straightened them out. Gangs of spikers and bolters secured them in place. Man and beast battled the earth to clear the way for new tracks. I thought of the Ithacan terraces clawed out of the mountain dirt.

As soon as work on one section was done the entire gang moved on. The rail-workers were nomads, adept at shifting camp. They dismantled their tents and machinery, and reassembled them before the day was out. In their wake, on the new tracks, came hospital cars with dispensaries and lavatories that removed the waste.

Stratis and I occasionally obtained a day's work unloading sleepers. A new map was being inscribed before our eyes. Heat and toil were levellers, uniting men who had been born far apart. We were all dark skinned under the desert sun: Irish and Scots, Welsh and English, Italian, Indian, Afghan and Greek, in harness to a common cause. At night we fell into the deep sleep of those who are too spent to think. We were a temporary cosmos unto ourselves, far removed from a warring world.

And into that cosmos stepped the Gambler, ever vigilant for the main chance. He set up games during overnight stops at railway camps and boarding houses. He organised rounds during midday breaks in the shade of solitary gums. There was no time for idle talk. The men were mesmerised by the cards. They fastened their eyes upon their fate. Those who lost became more obsessed, and those who won were tempted to ride their luck. As soon as their foremen ordered them back to work, we hurried to the Studebaker and were gone in a haze of dust.

The road was an ill-defined track traced by convoys of lorries and camels tending the rail-line. Our bums were sore from relentless jolts, our faces caked with dirt. We stopped beneath the overland telegraph line by the peg marking the West- and South-Australian border, and cocked our ears in a mock attempt to detect voices coursing through the wires. Whenever we stepped out to relieve ourselves, our piss evaporated in the hot earth.

The Gambler gripped the steering wheel with his right hand, freeing the other to grasp the cigarette that accompanied his insatiable talk. 'To see settlements and camps appear and vanish, this is what I live for,' he declared. The dust whirled and settled, and in the temporary clarity we saw three blacks: an older man, a teenager and young boy. They stood naked on an escarpment and stared at the Studebaker as we drew closer. We stopped to greet them but they were gone by the time we stepped out.

The three natives unnerved me. The absence of sea and mountain disoriented me. The landscape seethed with the matter of millennia. It required fierce persistence to subdue it, and the litheness of nomads to endure it.

'We are strangers here,' I muttered. *Xeni*. Outsiders.'

'You think too much,' replied the Gambler. 'Do not speculate. Curb your wandering mind. Approach life as a game of cards. Accept the hand you are dealt. What choice do we have? We may as well believe that all has been pre-ordained.' I glanced at his comfortable body cushioned by the seat, and envied his potbelly ways.

Our journey to Port Augusta was nearing its end. On our final night we parked by a waterhole. We scavenged for wood, heated tinned food, and salivated at the memory of sheep crackling on spits. The Gambler opened a bottle of whisky, gulped the first mouthful and passed it on. 'Let the wankers who destroyed our businesses burn in hell,' he said. We drank until the bottle was empty. The Gambler hurled it into the dark. 'Fuck them all,' he bellowed. 'Fuck them all.'

For the first time since leaving Ithaca I reached for my violin.

I blew off the dust, opened the case, lifted out the instrument, adjusted the strings, and applied rosin to the bow. My fingers were stiff, the bow movements uncertain. I had not played for many months. I found my way to a hesitant czardas, and settled on a *zebekiko* Mikhalis had taught me. The Gambler heaved himself to his feet. He had not shaved in the weeks since we left Kalgoorlie.

'Fuck them all,' he said, as he lunged into a dance. His belly bounced as he swivelled. He lurched from side to side, yet managed, by instinct, to stay upright. Despite his weight and drunkenness he exhibited a measure of grace, but he tried one ambitious move too many and landed on his back. 'Fuck them all,' he chanted, as Stratis helped him to his feet. They placed their arms on each other's shoulders and resumed the dance. 'I do not know these constellations,' the Gambler said, casting a deck of cards to the breeze. 'I do not know these constellations,' he repeated as the cards fluttered to the ground.

'Perhaps there are palaces buried beneath us,' said Stratis. We paced out the imagined grounds, marked the spot where Odysseus slew Penelope's suitors, and gazed down longingly where we envisioned the legendary marriage bed. We aped the gestures of travellers scrambling over archaeological sites clutching copies of *The Odyssey*, reciting chapter and verse. We crawled on our knees and sifted the sand in a mock search for artefacts. We staggered to our feet, chased each other over the dry waterhole and collapsed by the fire.

I lay on my back, and rested my head on my arms. When I looked down at my outstretched body, I saw nothing but the sky curving away from my feet. The galaxies were dervishes, rotating towards the culmination of a dance. I fell into a stupor and when I came to, I stood on the summit straining my eyes for a view of the neighbouring islands. The Ionian flowed far below me, yet tantalisingly within reach. It vanished and in its place stood Old Niko's hovel.

He led me to the trunk, drew out map after map and unfurled them over the table. Each map was a confusion of hamlets connected by barely perceptible tracks. I bent down to inspect them, but did not know whether they led to Exogi or to desert camps. The tracks faded, and I laboured up a flight of stone steps to the family house. On the roadway children were stuffing their mouths with sweets. I peered through the window and saw a gang of men hurling crockery at the walls.

'Go back to where you fuck'n' come from,' they chanted. A dishevelled soldier emerged from the back room. He shoved his forearm towards my eyes and I saw puss oozing from a gaping wound. He thumped his temples with his fists, stumbled up flights of steps to the upper village and howled. As I scrambled after him towards the summit, the entire village broke from the mountain and plummeted into the sea. I dared not look back.

The summit dissolved and in its place appeared the bordellos of Brookman Street. Prostitutes sat on the doorstep and beckoned me inside. I followed them to the back rooms, and did with them what I wished. I closed my eyes and when I reopened them, I was standing at the base of the mountain. I could see it in its entirety.

'I do not know these constellations,' the Gambler bellowed as a storm broke out. 'I do not know these constellations,' he repeated beneath a hail of fluttering cards. Then the mountain was gone, flattened. I ran over shallow dunes of red dirt, but stayed rooted to the spot. No matter how hard I tried I could move neither forward nor back, and in desperation, willed myself awake.

BOOK IV

The fire had died down. Stratis was curled up like a foetus and the Gambler lay sprawled on his back. A crow cawed from a stunted eucalypt, a wombat sniffed at the tyres. The night sky obliterated the horizon. I was lost in space: and did not know the constellations.

BOOK V

The weatherboard house by the bay

THE storm is brewing, the winds rising; Zeus the cloud gatherer is at work. Martina is stirring in the next room. I leave Mentor's manuscript on the walnut table, and sit by the bed until she settles. I move from room to room, fasten the shutters, stop in the kitchen and bring the briki to the boil. I pour the coffee and return to the living room. I am about to resume my translation, but on an impulse I put Mentor's manuscript aside. It is time to move closer to the present and the chain of events that has brought me here. I approach the task with a sense of dread.

Ti na kanoume. Ti na kanoume. What can we do? What can we do? *Ola ine tikhe. Ola ine tikhe.* All is luck. All is fate. It is an ancient lament, a dirge that villagers chant with a fatalist's shrug, the words islanders mouth when one of theirs succumbs. Rarely a year goes by without a young man being taken by the sea.

Last year it was a youth on Lefkada. He awoke to a day of spring perfection and left for the bay with his heart singing. He boarded a caique with his diving partner, and cast off in anticipation. He cut the engines in the strait and drifted at anchor. On the lower slopes he would have made out the village he called home.

On the waterfront he would have seen the night fishermen unloading their haul.

It was midday when he made the fatal dive. On shore the shopkeepers were closing the doors and shutters, preparing for the siesta. He adjusted his mask and snorkel and leapt from the boat clutching a spear gun. He held no fear for these waters. When he did not surface at the expected time his diving partner raised the alarm.

When the news reached the village the screams of the young man's parents shredded the skies. His mother stumbled through the streets tearing at her hair, beating her fists against her thighs. 'He was so beautiful this last summer,' his grandmother cried.

'I am nothing but a dead man walking,' his father intoned. 'The sea has finished for me,' he vowed. The young man's body was retrieved by divers and laid out on the waterfront. His mask-like face retained the hint of a smile. Death, it seemed, had come as no surprise.

One year later, the villagers gathered to commemorate the event. They set the table for the wedding guests and for the groom who would never be. They wept for the woman he would not impregnate and the children he would never sire. They ate and drank, and spoke of his lust for the sea, the fatal disease.

Thalassomania, the affliction is called. *Thalassa. Thalassa,* the Sirens hum. If you have ventured too far down, do not be alarmed. Your body is transparent, weightless. Allow the water to take you. You are safe in its cool embrace. What better way is there of passing?

'There have been times, under water,' cousin Andonis has confided, 'that I imagine I possess special powers. I dive deeper with great ease, and think I can hold my breath for hours. I am overcome by a wish to dissolve in the depths. Perhaps it is the memory of the womb that lures me, a lethal desire to return to my true home, a primal yearning.'

Perhaps this is how Manoli should have died, deep within the waters of the Ionian, with a spear gun in his hand and the shores of Ithaca within reach. A smile on his face, and his body at repose, divested of the rage that would accompany him to the grave.

———————

I was ten in the summer of 1967, when we moved to Carrum, to the weatherboard house by the bay. Unpacked boxes and possessions littered the rooms and passage. Sun streamed in through the windows. Young boys, stripped to their shorts, dived from the highway bridge into the Patterson River. They clambered over the rails and leapt with their knees clutched to their chests, egged on by friends. They hit the water, swam ashore, scrambled up the embankment and returned to jump again. I watched them from the living-room window in awe of their daring.

Never had I seen Manoli, my father, so animated. He paced the rooms, pausing to gaze through windows at vistas of sea, river and estuary. From the kitchen window could be seen the full reach of the peninsula, sweeping to the head of Port Phillip Bay. He had plans, he announced, surveying the rooms, talking aloud.

He would gut the house, knock down walls, rip out the linoleum, and restore the floorboards. He would get rid of the ancient fittings and replace them with the brand new. He would abandon the building sites, where he worked as a carpenter for other men, and invest in his own concerns. Instead of confining himself to refitting shops, as he had in his few previous ventures, he would build blocks of flats, entire shopping centres. His ambition knew no bounds.

And, in his spare time, he would build boats: cabin cruisers and dinghies, clinkers, single-sail sloops. He would design sleek hulls, ribbed with beech, teak or pine, and when he was done, he would moor them by the embankment that sloped down from the house. He would sail them on the bay equipped with the very best navigation aids, the latest engines, converted car motors with greater horsepower. He was, he declared, a man of the contemporary world.

His mind was so fixed on his plans he did not see me in the shadows. I had learnt to keep quiet, to observe and stay out of his way. I kept my eyes on the boys leaping from the bridge with triumphant howls; and for a moment I allowed myself to think, perhaps we would be happy here.

———

Soon after moving in, Manoli built a small jetty on the river below the house. Diagonally opposite, beyond the highway and railway bridges, stood a fire station. Despite its proximity it did not help old Mr Burton, three houses away. Burton set his bedroom alight when he fell asleep while smoking a pipe. I was awoken by the bells, quickly dressed, and ran outside to join the crowd. We watched, transfixed, as the firemen carried Mr Burton out. He did not return and the singed house remained boarded up.

The fire station was hired out for functions. On party nights beetles hurtled around the dusty lamps over the entrance. I crept to the windows, drawn by cascades of laughter and the strains of the band. The guests danced waltzes and tangos, the pride of Erin and foxtrots. The light cast by the hall windows gave way to the dark. I imagined the goings on in the swamp where nocturnal creatures cruised the muddy waters in search of prey. I looked back at the sea: somewhere out there Manoli was spreading his nets.

It would remain my most enduring image of him, Manoli motoring out to sea. He scurried down to the jetty at twilight carrying a change of clothes stuffed in a duffle bag. He dragged the nets down the embankment and hauled them aboard. He untied the ropes, allowed the boat to drift, started the engines, and advanced through the river mouth.

Congregations of terns scattered from the rocks by the estuary. Seagulls screeched and swooped over a bucket of bait. I watched the boat's steady progress from the veranda until it dissolved between sea and sky. Hours later I would wake, move to the bedroom window and know it was not a dream. Manoli was out there. I did not think of him as my father. For as long as I can remember he was a separate entity, someone apart.

I remained by the window until the first train trundled over the railway bridge. Starlings roosting under the bridge were shrieking the discordant chorus of a newly awoken flock. I stole out to the veranda to watch Manoli's return. It was the one time I could be certain his anger had been tamed; yet I kept my distance from the jetty, in case his mood suddenly changed.

I followed his steady progress to the estuary. The boat battled the swell where the river's flow met the surging tide. There was majesty in the boat's passage through the turbulence, and a lumbering grace in Manoli's movements as he stood by the stern, tiller in hand.

Once through the entrance the prow cut through more placid waters, sending wavelets towards the banks. Nearing the jetty, he cut the engine and steered his craft towards its berth. The deck was flecked with blood. Manoli tied the boat to its moorings, heaved the nets ashore, and squatted beside them to disentangle the remnants of the catch.

When he was done he dragged the nets up the banks, and carried buckets of fish to the house. His wellingtons left thick imprints in the mud. He walked with a swagger: he was a fisherman returning with his catch, and before the day ended Sophia would have gutted and fried them, and Manoli would have distributed the rest to friends.

I had eyes only for the crabs. I stole down to the bank to free those trapped in the nets. 'You are an idiot,' Manoli said in disgust, when he passed by. 'What do you think? In this world it's eat or be eaten.'

Manoli built boats in the backyard. There was always one moored by the banks, a boat-in-progress on wooden blocks, a third on the drawing boards, and yet another daring design taking shape in his mind. He studied boating journals and drove to the Mordialloc boat yards in search of new ideas.

While the latest boat was being built Manoli tended the one in use. He serviced the engine and washed down the decks. He secured the tyres that cushioned the boat against the jetty and replaced the frayed ropes. He was not given to sentimentality. He allowed no overt sign of it, yet he named the boats *Levantes. Maistros. Sirocco.* Ionian winds.

He built shelves in the garage that became scattered with lines and hooks, reels of twine, containers of nails and screws, tins of varnish, paintbrushes, barometers, compasses, manuals, and paperback copies of the works of Karl Marx, seasoned with a fine patina of salt. 'Read these works,' he proclaimed. 'That is all one needs to understand the ways of the world.'

The trestle table-cum-desk was a jumble of pencils, rulers, erasers, sharpeners, set squares, lists of addresses, and scraps of paper covered with sketches of boats to come. The concrete floor was stacked with planks of timber, coils of rope, propellers and shafts, tins of fuel, dismantled motors, forty-four-gallon drums, tyres and winches, and stiff nets in misshapen piles. The grease-stained workbench was littered with wood-dust, engine parts, chisels and hammers, saws, sanders and planes, propped against each other, in disarray. The walls were bare except for a crayfish trap, inadvertently netted in the bay. It dangled like a hunting trophy from a nail hammered into a timber support.

'I am not sewing doilies, moron,' he exclaimed when Sophia complained about the mess. 'Look what I have created. When I die I will leave much behind. What will you have to show for yourself?'

Once, when I was certain Manoli was out, I stole into the garage and leafed through his designs. There were sketches of boats with stylish cabins, outboard motors, and plans for boats, I would one day learn, were modernised versions of Ionian caiques. There were notebooks scrawled with the addresses of suppliers, and fruit-crates stuffed with marine charts.

I sat back on the sofa positioned beside a tiny window with a view of the sea. I had often seen Manoli through the garage door, sitting here reading, or lost in thought. I dozed off to the smell of varnish and sawdust, and the rhythm of waves breaking. When I awoke he was standing over the sofa. In the past it was the dark scowl that frightened me, and the odour of his rage. It could come at any time, a blackness skittering over his face, yet in this moment, there was something else.

I had opened my eyes and caught him unawares. I saw the anguish of a man who wanted to reach out, but had long forgotten how. I can see Manoli's look of despair to this day. In that moment he was a shy stranger, bewildered and inept. The divide could not be breached. We dared not speak for fear of what we would say. Or betray. We were locked from each other like monks vowed to silence. We averted our eyes to the tiny window, drawn by the welcome diversion of the tide.

———

It rains and the river swells. Water spouts from open drains. Water infuses water. Rain beats upon the swamp. Rain floods the estuary and flows over the banks. Salt water collides with fresh water and swirls into the bay. Rain unites sea and sky, and Manoli is motoring out to sea. Rain cruises down his face. On the water he is lord and master of his home-built craft. He does as he pleases, and roams the bay all night. The water lifts and licks him, and washes the world clean.

When the rain eases I unleash the dog, clamber down the embankment, and walk the path one kilometre upstream to the swamps. I have ventured into forbidden territory, but Manoli is out. The pointer sniffs the ground, picking up scents newly released by the rains. Ducks and egrets glide the channels between reeds and matted grass. Dragonflies hover motionless above the surface, then zigzag off in pursuit of prey. The swamps are speckled with birds foraging waters that have sprung to life. They probe the wetlands with their elongated beaks in rapid sewing-machine strikes.

The pointer rushes in circles and barks furiously. She disappears and returns with a frog in her mouth. She releases it at my feet, and it instantly leaps out of sight. A network of logs forms makeshift bridges leading deeper into the swamps. I stand at the rim of more hazardous territory and dare not go on.

The rain returns as a gentle patter, and when it thickens I hurry home. Sophia watches from the veranda as I scale the banks. I burst into the kitchen with the pointer at my heels. The dog shakes herself vigorously, splattering mud over the linoleum floor. Her wetness permeates the room.

Manoli is out on the bay. He had studied the weather forecasts and noted the times of the tides before setting off. The winds are mild despite the rain. Sophia and I are anxious for his safety, but we cannot help being relieved that he will be away for the night.

———— · ————

I wake at dawn to the urgent cackling of hens, and stuff the pillows against my ears. No matter how hard I try I cannot stifle the sounds. I venture out to the backyard. Manoli, dressed in paint-splattered overalls, is in the pen, running the hens down, strangling them one by one.

I run back to the bedroom and bury myself under the blankets. When I wake, the house is full of cooking smells. The voice of a soprano can be heard from the radio over Sophia's movements. She is preparing food for the busy week ahead. Four hens are soaking in water, and Sophia is plucking the fifth. In the backyard, the carcass of a sheep is impaled on a spit, discharging fat in anticipation of the summer guests.

Uncle Cherry Ripe is the first to arrive. I wait for him on the highway bridge. The sun bounces of the duco of his restored Bentley in a blinding flash, heralding his coming long before he skids to a halt. Cherry Ripe brings with him the promise of better days and a glove box stuffed with white knights, violet crumbles and cherry ripe bars. 'My holy trinity,' he calls them. He is not my uncle by kin, but he was raised in Manoli's village. Like so many Ithacans, he is known by his *paratsoukli*, his nickname.

'Hop in my little bird,' he says. The interior exudes the solidity of wood and leather, the chrome-plated hubcaps wink at passers-by. And Uncle Cherry Ripe, dressed in white linen trousers and summer shirt, oiled hair slicked back, is crooning *Come with me to Blue Hawaii*. He pulls up at a highway shop for flake and chips.

When they are ready we continue our drive. Cherry Ripe swerves across the bridge, and brings the car to a halt by the foreshore. When we have eaten our fill we feed the scraps to seagulls. As soon as the first chips are thrown out, they swoop down in screeching droves. We observe them through the windscreen fighting over the spoils. When the gulls depart, Cherry Ripe steps out with a cloth and wipes the duco until it regains its shine. Everything about him shines: the windscreen, the leather upholstery, the chrome bumpers, and the foil wrappers of the cherry ripe bars that we devour for dessert. He sings *roll out those lazy, hazy, crazy, days of summer*, as we drive back to the house.

Next to arrive is the Gambler, in an ancient Chevrolet, a dilapidated beast that reeks of incense and dusty journeys on outback tracks. The battered body is covered in grime, and dangling from the rear vision mirror is a framed image of St Nicholas. The Gambler is slouched back on the seat, belly protruding. One hand grips the wheel, the other fiddles with a necklace of amber beads. St Nicholas swings as the Gambler hums Byzantine chants.

He is ninety years old, so it is said. The car veers gently from gutter to white line, yet somehow remains under control. 'I take my time,' the Gambler declares. 'Wherever I go, whatever I do, I move as if riding a swell. We come from the sea, and one day we will return to the sea. My friends, this is what I live for.'

Aunt Penelope arrives by train and walks over the highway bridge in scarlet stilettos, silk stockings, a tight black skirt and white blouse. She clatters up the veranda steps trailing the scent of the Myer cosmetics department in which she works. After a quick greeting she disappears into the bedroom and re-emerges, freshly powdered and rouged, and wraps me in a perfumed embrace.

Alexis the wrestler follows soon after. They say he had been a Greek national champion and represented his country in the Olympic Games. He is a massive man with a reddish face. His muscular build is sagging towards fat now that his fighting days are done. Alexis walks with stealthy steps, arms slightly akimbo, as if instinctively poised for a sudden attack. He sinks down on the couch, drops his guard and falls asleep with a grim smile.

Mentor arrives mid-afternoon, alone. He nods a silent greeting, retires to the couch beside the dozing Alexis, lights a pipe and observes the company with a detached gaze. 'Your mouse is fattening,' he tells me. The pointer moves to his side and settles at his feet. Mentor bends over to stroke her, and within minutes the dog lies fully extended, asleep.

All day they arrive, an assortment of distant cousins and aunts, uncles and godfathers, Ithacan crewmen on leave from boats in port, and relatives I have never seen. It does not matter; they come from the same island, *sympatriotes* nurtured in Ionian villages. They will return to their jobs in city restaurants, fish markets, cafes and fruit stalls, on factory floors and in infant businesses, after one week by the sea.

At nightfall the company strolls over the bridge to the carnival on the opposite bank. I tag along from stall to stall, ride the carousels, aim ping-pong balls at gaping clowns' mouths, and fire pellets at moving targets, while Uncle Cherry Ripe urges me on.

The company returns and converges on the veranda to eat and talk. I have never seen Manoli so broad-hearted in his gestures, and so generous in the slabs of roast sheep, stuffed intestines, and chicken that flow from the kitchen in his massive hands. But his awkward manner, and the manic shrillness at the edge of his voice, keeps me tense and alert.

Conversations flare and recede, and just as the silence is about to claim us, the Gambler lifts himself to his feet, expands his chest, and detaches his cigarette from his lips. He extends his arms in a dramatic gesture, and begins. His hooked nose and wisps of white hair are silhouetted in the veranda light. The jacket, waistcoat and bow tie he wears, no matter the time of day, or state of weather, are illumined by a faint glow. I am mesmerised by his fat hairy fingers.

He had made a fortune, he tells us, and had travelled the land to practise his calling. He had followed his compatriots wherever they laboured and set up card games. Now he lives his final years as a wealthy man with rents flowing from his properties. He stands on the veranda, a man whose life has straddled two centuries, the seven oceans, one thousand and one ports, smoke-filled back rooms, and flings his stories at the night sky.

'Enough of your tales,' exclaims one of the guests, interrupting the Gambler mid-flight, 'we've heard them all before.' And the company bursts out laughing. Laughter gives way to conversations that subside to whispers and, finally, silence. And from the silence, a solitary humming, then one voice, giving way to two, and soon many, finding their way, hesitantly at first, like the blind stumbling in the dark.

The voices search until they are in full harness: to each other, to the lapping of the river, the drift of laughter, the breaking swells on the incoming tide. The singers look like a flock of birds that have returned to their breeding grounds, and I am glad to be of them, and a part of them. They possess something as vast as the heavens, and as mysterious as the horizon that yokes the stars to the bay. The melody belongs here on this veranda by the mouth of the river, yet it belongs, more surely, somewhere else.

Ithaca. I cannot recall the first time I heard the word. It has always been there like an ancient longing welling up from the sea. Perhaps this is where the birds go when they leave the swamps for their flight north. Perhaps Ithaca is the goal of their migrations, an island beyond the limits of vision, somewhere out there in the dark. Ithaca is in the harmonies of *cantathas*, a mystery that fills me with awe and warmth.

The *cantathas* give way to quiet talk that returns to the croaking of frogs, the trill of crickets, the muted thud of boats against their berths. One by one the guests fall silent, leaving behind the last sentences that had slipped from their mouths; and when I wake I am back in bed and the sun is out, the curtains drawn. From the kitchen comes the sound of laughter, the clutter of dishes, and I come upon the guests seated at the kitchen table, bent over their coffees, eating and talking, as if this is the company they keep every morning.

After breakfast they set out, the men in jackets, white shirts and ties, stove-piped trousers and pointed shoes, the women in flared cotton dresses and high heels, carrying fold-up stools, picnic baskets, buckets and blankets which they deposit in the verge of bush that extends between the foreshore and road.

When the tide is out we clamber over the reefs, a tribe of scavengers, buckets in hand, to prise mussels from the rocks. I swim with my distant cousins, and run about in the midday sun. *Ela tho.* Come here! Our mothers shout and finally draw us to the blankets they have spread beneath gums and tea-trees. The blankets are covered with food: stuffed tomatoes, fried marrows and eggplant, feta in oil, fish roe dips, and slabs of meat left over from the slaughter of the previous day. When the eating is done and washed down with wine, the older guests lie back on the blankets and doze, while we run back to the water for relief from the sweltering sun.

Late afternoon the company trudges home, bellies full, bodies tired. They disappear into the cool recesses of the house to resume their siestas, and re-emerge hours later on the veranda. Conversations ebb and flow, and the nights beget days that beget afternoon sojourns crowded in Manoli's boat, from which the company returns in the evenings, to veranda nights by the bay.

And by the seventh night they are gone, leaving behind the dying echoes of their songs, the ripple of their laughter, and my father's brooding presence, and night sorties out to sea. They disappear as surely as the boat over the horizon. The summer is over, the veranda empty, and Manoli is somewhere out there, the night prowler, alone.

'I will not go to that house,' Manoli shouts.

He paces the rooms.

'I want nothing to do with Mentor and your accursed family.'

Sophia and I remain silent.

'Look at you, eh! The hen and her chicken,' he says, with contempt.

Sophia holds her ground.

'Stuff you,' he hisses. And turns, slams the back door and retreats to the car. Minutes later, he is gone.

I walk with Sophia to the station. A neighbour is cutting his lawn with a hand mower as he does every Sunday morning. A horse grazes in a paddock, swishing its tail at flies on his rump. The starlings beneath the railway bridge are taking flight. I wonder where they will spend the day. A boat emerges from under the bridge, backwash rippling from its stern. We pause to watch its progress to the bay.

The train can be heard approaching. We hurry to the station and arrive in time to dash in through the carriage doors. The railway runs beside the highway, lined by houses and shacks. I glimpse the sea at the ends of streets running from the tracks to the beach. I watch for the familiar landmark, a dental surgery with window displays of life-size dolls that appear to be suffocating against the panes.

As the train moves inland, I look down from the carriage windows at a succession of backyards. Tricycles and toys lie where last discarded. Clothes droop from lines and hoists. A woman in a black scarf cleans a tombstone in the Cheltenham cemetery. Approaching the inner city, the rails multiply into a lace-work of tracks. We disembark at Flinders Street Station, and continue our journey north by tram.

Mentor awaits our arrival in Brunswick, seated on the veranda in a wicker chair. He walks to the gate and escorts us into the house. My grandfather possesses gravitas in all he does. Fotini had died three years ago, and though tidy, the house is neglected and dark. Sophia draws back the heavy curtains and allows the light in. Mentor insists on making the tea, and sets out the cups and saucers on the kitchen table. Sophia stays behind to air the house, while Mentor ushers me into the backyard. 'The rat is waiting for you,' he says with a conspiratorial wink.

A gaggle of bantams peck at a crop of tomatoes interspersed with basil and marigolds. A well-tended grapevine trails against the walls of the washhouse. Mentor unlocks the door to the shed. Bookshelves line two walls. Years later Sophia will remind me that they included volumes on hypnotism and architecture, travellers' accounts of journeys to Ithaca, magician's manuals, and books on the occult. Violins and kites hang from the rafters. Against a third wall stands a gramophone and beside it, a box containing vinyl platters of violin concertos and arias recorded by singers of pre-war times.

On the gramophone stand framed photos of Enrico Caruso and Yasha Heifitz: one the greatest singer, and the other the greatest violinist, of all time, Mentor claims; and beside them a photo of Mentor playing the violin at a community function as a young man. He wears a tuxedo and bow tie, and is recognisable by his upright bearing and the dignified expression on his face.

On the desk sits a manuscript beneath a human skull, and on the wall above, hangs a cage housing a yellow cockatiel. A map of Ithaca is glued beside a small window, and, in the margin there's a hand drawing of a sea hawk in flight. Mentor allows the cockatiel out, after making sure that the door is closed. He reaches over, lifts a cage from the floor and places it on the desk. 'I have kept my promise,' he says, pointing to the fat rodent scurrying inside. 'Your mouse is now a rat.'

'Diet is the secret,' he adds. Mentor speaks sparingly. He opens a drawer and takes out a biscuit tin from which he extracts a gold brooch. The brooch is cast in the shape of Ithaca, the gold moulded to the contours of the mountains. The hamlets are marked by tiny pearls, the larger villages by minute rubies. The paths between them are silver, one millimetre wide. The port of Vathy is a stone of turquoise, and the summit, above Exogi, a diamond embedded in the gold.

After his death the brooch passed to Sophia, and since her death, nine years ago, it has become mine. I have brought it to the island and placed it on the table alongside Mentor's manuscript. The brooch has returned to its rightful place.

———•———

Mid-afternoon I walk with Mentor to a nearby park, carrying a kite shaped as a sea hawk. I handle it with care, as if entrusted with a mission. 'Do not think life is a mere plaything,' he says. Mentor speaks to me as an adult, though he places a hand on my shoulders as if guiding a child.

We move to the centre of the park, a field of parched late-summer grass, well clear of a verge of eucalypts and shrubs. Mentor places the kite on the ground and lifts it up on its end. I hold it in place by the apex as he backs away, unravelling the string. As soon as I loosen my grip the kite breaks for the sky.

Mentor works with an economy of movement. Just a few gentle tugs and the kite swirls in figures of eight. It gusts upwards, shifts sideways, and hangs stationary, mid-air. When the kite is stable he passes the baton into my hands. I am shocked by the strength in the wind: it almost tears the baton from my grip.

'Hold fast,' Mentor says. 'Fix your eyes on the kite.'

'Feel the currents through the string,' he adds. 'Follow the hawk.'

For a minute, the kite obeys my desperate tugs, then, plummets nose first into the ground. I run to the wreckage as if coming to the rescue of a wounded bird. Mentor walks calmly behind me. The shaft is broken, the cloth torn. I look up, expecting his stern gaze, but instead, I am greeted by a smile.

'Air currents are cruel,' he says. 'Just as you think you are in control, they tear you apart. They are as forceful as ocean currents. Not even a powerful eagle can withstand their force.'

———

It is dark when Sophia and I leave Mentor's house. The city is now a different beast. The passengers are focused inwards, lulled by the sway of the tram. The faces of the town hall clock look like silver moons. We hurry from the tram to Flinders Street Station, and down a flight of steps to the platform, in time to catch the next train on the Frankston line. It hurtles out of the city past shadowy backyards and well-lit rooms, inhabited, I am certain, by families far more harmonious than mine.

Nearing Mordialloc, the smell of the sea begins to drift through the windows. We are moving back into familiar territory, returning home after all. The streets of Carrum are deserted, the shopfronts dark. We glance from the bridge at the empty berth, and know Manoli is out.

He would return at dawn, but this Sunday would be the last time we saw Mentor until, months later, when I filed by his open coffin in church, and viewed him laid out in a tuxedo on a cushion of white silk. I gazed at his sunken eyes and thought of the skull on his work desk.

At the wake in his house, after the funeral service, I mingled with the guests: Ithacans farewelling one of their own. I slipped out to the backyard, and saw the garden run wild, the grapes shrivelled on the vine. I switched on the light in Mentor's shed, sat down at his desk and, with great trepidation, moved the skull and examined the manuscript.

I ran my eyes over the Greek text with little understanding of Mentor's neat script, and with no inkling it would one day reveal so much. And for weeks I dreamt of his face in repose, carved out of cold stone, dissolving into a skull, and awoke, in fright, and recalled my final glimpse of Mentor alive, standing by the tram stop, waving, then slowly turning for home, his bearing erect, walking through the streets of Brunswick, carrying the burden of his gravitas.

———

I walk the road from Stavros with Martina at night. There are things we see now that we do not notice by day. Exogi is a cluster of lights eyeing our progress from the heights. Cats scurry across our path, but their strength in numbers neutralises bad luck.

Martina is awed by the outline of animals corralled behind mesh wire fences that lean by the road. The last donkey of northern Ithaca grazes in a paddock of its own. Sheep huddle in an almond grove. 'Animals are clever in the dark,' Martina remarks.

When Martina is asleep I return to my manuscript. Where she

discerns wisdom, I see only fragments. By putting them down on paper perhaps they will fall into place. I am working my way through the seasons in some attempt at sequence, though the images I conjure span the four years I lived with Manoli in the weatherboard house.

I recall unexpected reveries at random: an autumn sun descending over the bay. The rays flow through the estuary, contained by the riverbanks. They are channelled upstream beyond the highway bridge, and cast a red sheen upon river, sea and swamp: a three-part harmony of water. One moment the sun is there, a burning red dome above the waterline, and then it is gone, and in its wake, the gift of serenity, despite it all.

***

'Do not go to the swamps,' Manoli has warned me. I wait until he is out, and take the pointer on the upstream walk. On the rim of the wetlands we come upon wader-birds in the shallows. Disturbed by our presence they rise like a rush of arrows.

Within minutes there are thousands, wheeling and regrouping. The few have become many, and the many one vast flock concealing the skies. They wheel and change direction as sinuously as wisps of smoke. In their collective movement there is strength, and in their whirring, a resonant hum. They move apart and descend to their feeding grounds.

When I return to the bay, a flock of gannets circles above shoaling fish, fifty metres off shore. There is frenzy in the water, and madness in the air. The sea churns and froths. There is no order, nor decorum, but a brutal whirl of feathers as each bird readies itself for the assault. When they attack, it is sharp and abrupt. They bombard the water with vertical dives and emerge with their prey in their beaks. They carry the struggling fish to a nearby outcrop of rocks, gulp them down, and return to the fray.

Manoli is right. It is kill or be killed. It can be seen in the cool menace of the predatory bird, circling, in command of space. It can be seen in the frenzied bombardment that continues above the shoaling fish. It can be felt in the sting of the jellyfish, the sharpness of the gannet's beak. It can be sensed in the bleached ribs of dead birds washed up on the beach. And it can be seen in the stealthy stroll of a curlew in the shallows, curved beak readied like an unsheathed sword.

Within weeks the curlew will be bound for its northern breeding grounds, and flocks of waders will sweep up from the swamps, on the first leg of their marathon flights. They will crowd the space above the water and quickly ascend to the heights. I will follow their trajectory from the foreshore until they are no longer within sight. Their departure takes place in a matter of days, heralding the coming winter and the descent of darkness upon sea and swamp.

I associate the departing birds with Ithaca, and with that nebulous place called the North. At some point I will begin to know something of the species and their routes. I remember sitting beside Mentor scanning a book of maps depicting migratory routes. There are birds, he claims, that sleep on the winds while they continue their flights. 'The sky is criss-crossed with invisible trails,' he says, pointing to flight paths extending to the extremities of the earth.

———

Like Stratis, years before me, I have returned to Ithaca well prepared. I had packed them between clothes so they would not be damaged: books on wetlands, field guides to migratory birds, and essays with contending theories about their flights. I consult them at the living-room table as I write. Their journeys to and from the bayside are far more astonishing than I'd imagined as a child.

The eastern curlew, sharp-tailed sandpiper, and greenshank make for the Siberian wastes. The bar-tailed godwit heads for Alaska and the Arctic, the Latham snipe for the north islands of Japan. The birds refuel on interim feeding grounds before resuming their flight. The round journey to Siberia is twenty-five thousand kilometres. There are birds that fly up to five thousand kilometres in one uninterrupted leg; and tiny sandpipers that clock enough distance to have flown to the moon in the course of their lives.

There are many theories as to how they navigate. Some say that the sense is embedded in their genes. Others claim they employ the earth's magnetic field, or navigate as the seamen of old, by the movement of sun, moon and stars. They cover vast distances, yet return with faithful regularity at the appointed time. They live their lives in perpetual motion between their breeding and feeding grounds. And they journey to survive.

My ancestors were also driven by a need to find fertile feeding grounds. I think of the frenetic tales of Old Niko. At first, Ithacans had voyaged to places from which there was a possibility of annual returns. As the routes to the Black Sea were cut off they journeyed further still. They breached the hemisphere with the promise that they would return wealthy men.

They could not foresee there would come a time when their

journeys would stall. Perhaps their instincts failed them. Perhaps, they were compelled to eke out a living on pastures new. Perhaps they were constrained by endless warring in the old world. Or perhaps, like Manoli, they delayed and prevaricated too long. He once booked an airline ticket to Ithaca, Sophia told me long after he died, and had intended to take me with him. But he had pulled out a week before the scheduled flight.

This much I now know, the true impact of his journeying can not be deduced from maps and nautical charts, but in the unguarded moments I recall, decades later, by the living-room table in the patriarchal house. I write them as they come. The only attempt at order, as I have said, is the succession of the seasons. Like the Black Sea traders of old, I follow the passage of the seasons in determining my route back home.

———

The small park on the foreshore by the river mouth is deserted. The carnival gypsies, who park their caravans in summer and set up tents and carousels, are long gone. In the centre of the park stands a monument to soldiers of the Great War. From the pediment there rises a granite statue of a soldier in a slouch hat. He stands fully upright, holding the barrel of an upturned rifle in his right hand.

We file from the primary school to the park bearing wreaths. Our teachers shepherd us through the streets towards the foreshore beside the highway bridge. We assemble by the statue and the Anzac Day ceremony begins. On the pediment are listed the names of Carrum residents who, the headmaster says, had made the supreme sacrifice in the Great War.

I am afraid of the word sacrifice. It speaks of death and the admonitions of old men. The soldier is young, yet he reminds me of Mentor as I last saw him, laid out in a casket. Mentor, in death, seemed carved out of cold stone. The statue, however, is hot under a mid-morning sun. The sun beats down on the parched grass, and the headmaster's voice is a distant drone. I can no longer look at the soldier. He is eternally trapped in an ideal of sacrifice, back turned to the bay, condemned to stare at rail-track and bitumen, highway and commerce, the demands of every day.

My eyes are drawn to the sea behind him. For the first time I see the bay as Manoli sees it, as a place of drama and boundless life, and a source of freedom, a means of escape.

———

Dusk has fallen. The winds are gusting. They batter the weatherboard like a horde of brigands. They attack the windows and tear corrugated sheets from the roof. They propel the tide over the full extent of the beach and whip the river over its banks.

Cormorants tuck their heads beneath their wings to shield themselves from the onslaught. Two terns struggle above the water's surface in search of fish. They dive when they locate prey, but are blown off-course. Water drips from the ceiling and we place buckets under the drops.

Sophia and Manoli stride out into the night to do battle. 'Do not dare leave the house,' father warns. The water rises to the veranda and licks the steps to the front door. The pointer leaps about in the kitchen. Lightning cracks the skies apart, and I catch them through the window in the momentary light. Manoli is scaling the ladder to the roof, while Sophia, on the ground, holds the lower rungs. Her upturned face is streaming with water. They return to the darkness as abruptly as their bodies had lit up.

Manoli remains outside long after Sophia returns. I see him by lightning strikes, battling to fasten a billowing tarpaulin over a boat propped on blocks in the backyard. He is doubled over, arms flailing as he attempts to secure the ropes. When he is done he bursts back into the house. The rain drips from his clothes and hands. A strike of lightning illuminates Sophia and Manoli's faces. In this rare instance, they are partners, united in a common task.

In the morning, when I walk the foreshore, I find dead gannets and terns. Their powerful bodies are intact, washed clean by the tide. They have succumbed to the gale, but not without a fight. The beach is littered with windswept branches and mounds of kelp. One of the terns is still gasping for breath. By the time I bend down, it has expired.

———

Manoli sits on the garage sofa, mid-winter, and threads a large needle. He bends over a pile of netting, and lifts part of it up by the hems. He passes it through his fingers like a man feeling his way in the dark. There is tenderness in his hands and stillness in his concentration. He looks up, but does not see me watching from the yard. He returns his focus to the net and continues to mend.

———

There are languid weekend afternoons warmed by winter sun. Manoli is at work on a new boat. He has laid the keel and is fitting the ribs. He works slowly. There is no other way. The demands of labour dictate the pace. The air smells of sea breeze and brine. He ferries the bent ribs to and from the garage and fits them inside the hull at right angles to the keel.

The afternoon is punctuated by bursts of hammering, the whirr of a saw, the buzz of an electric drill. As the work progresses, the exposed ribs curving up from the keel begin to resemble the skeletal bones of a fish. The sky expands with afternoon light. The yard breathes at a leisurely pace. It is the pace of the boat yard, of a craftsman at work, an antidote to Manoli's restlessness, his saving grace.

Yet always, the ominous lying in wait. I recall a row of slain foxes, tied by their feet on a paddock fence, their coats clotted with blood. They have been shot and left to rot. They are vermin, I have heard said. Yet I can see how beautiful they must have been while still alive. Perhaps among them are foxes I had seen in the back paddocks at dusk, pelts flashing in the long grass, setting out on nocturnal hunts. They would send the pointer into a barking frenzy. She pursued them, but they were too swift and cunning, intent on appeasing their hunger and thirst.

Manoli cannot stay still. The state of the house is a mark of his indecision. He knocks down a wall between two rooms, fits in a lintel, and abandons the project to embark on something new. He rips up the linoleum and exposes the floorboards, but leaves them as they are. He revives his plan to convert the weatherboard house into a brick veneer. 'The house must be brought up to date,' he says. 'Brick veneer is the way of the future.'

He tears down the veranda and scours building sites for discarded bricks. He brings them home in a trailer and unloads them where the veranda once stood. I help after school and on weekends, cleaning the bricks. I chip off the mortar, scrape off the dirt and scrub the surface until my wrists ache. Manoli pours a terrazzo; the concrete subdues the contours and enables him to lay the bricks against the timber boards. When the brick cladding is a metre high he loses interest. It becomes one of a mounting number of aborted renovations.

There is only one activity he sees through to the end: the creation of boats. When one boat is done, he sails it for a year, then sells it to make way for the new. He completes a bigger boat, a cabin cruiser with an outboard motor, and when it is finished he realises it is far too large to drive out.

Manoli orders in a crane. The neighbours gather to watch the operation. They are buoyed by the free entertainment. The crane is positioned in a dirt lane behind the back fence. Someone has alerted the newspapers and a photographer is on hand. The boat is winched up and sways above the fence. The crowd pulls back. The boat is steadied and lowered to the lane. The following day a photo of the operation appears in *The Sun*. For several days Manoli is a *cause célèbre* in the neighbourhood, as much for his folly as his enterprise.

————

Manoli comes and goes as he pleases. When he is at home he tends the blaze in the living room fireplace. He drags in logs and tree-trunks, and feeds them whole into the fire. The ends stick out beyond the grate. When one end has burnt, he kicks the remainder into the flames.

Sophia restores order. She cleans the grate, stacks the remaining logs by the fire; boxes the kindling she has scavenged from the riverbanks, and scrunches wads of newspaper to re-ignite the fire. She works in his absence, afraid of the sound of the door opening, Manoli returning inflamed with rage.

I see her now, Sophia when she was tall and slim. See her before she succumbed to a premature curving, a leaching of the bones. See that it is work that kept her from going insane. See her when mounting debts and Manoli's erratic behaviour force her to seek work further afield.

She leaves the house early morning. I hear the door close behind her, and register her departure fifteen minutes later when the first train rattles over the bridge. She works in the city for Sevasti, a distant cousin and recent arrival from Ithaca. A gifted seamstress, Sevasti had established a business making wedding dresses to order. Newly arrived girls from the island and other parts of Greece, spend their workdays at sewing machines to convert her designs into masterpieces.

Sophia, Australian-born, stands at the counter, receives orders and helps out with the accounts. She leaves for work in the winter dark, returns in the dark, and heats up the remains of last evening's meal. She comes and goes from the city, and when she is gone, she moves in her own mysterious world. For a time, she too is a lone navigator embarking on voyages of her own.

———

I am woken by a cry. I run to the backyard. Sophia is distraught. I see a scattering of feathers, two patches black, the other white, the remains of our three hens. The mesh wire cage is empty.

'They have been taken by foxes,' Sophia cries. 'They drag them by their mouths to their lairs, or bury them for future meals.' I have never seen her so distressed. 'I should have noticed the opening beneath the mesh.'

The backyard is tainted by slaughter. There are sinister forces lurking. Foxes are staking out the neighbourhood, waiting for nightfall, a gap in the fence. And somebody is watching us now. I turn and see Manoli standing by the back door. He surveys the yard and takes in the carnage. For a moment I think he is about to offer a word of consolation. He steps forward, hesitates, then hurries to the car.

'Bah! What do you expect?' he says, with contempt. While the car idles, he opens the gate. He reverses into the lane and drives off without a backward glance.

Sophia and I pick up the feathers. We do not stop until there is not a single one left. That afternoon Sophia repairs the cage. Days later she returns from work with a hen and two chicks. She releases them from the cardboard box, then stands back, and watches with satisfaction as they take to the yard.

The two chicks stay close to the mother. They fossick from dawn till the fading light. The sound of low-key babble has returned to the yard. Sophia has held fast. Order has been restored to the world. She turns to me, and smiles, triumphant.

There are many absences at the heart of this tale, yet even in their absence the men are present. Mentor, Manoli, Andreas, Stratis: voyagers and seamen, sojourners, gamblers. Providers. Builders. Community leaders. Self-appointed bards. Their voices ring loud, their deeds are apparent. Each has his version of epic journeys to new worlds, each can boast of forging new paths.

Yet where is Fotini? And other women whose names I had heard about the house: vague talk of Fotini's sister, Adriani, who had remained on Ithaca, of Melita, Manoli's mother, who died when he was a child. And of her sister, my grand aunt Irini, who was still alive somewhere over there, in that other world.

I fight to insert them into the manuscript. Perhaps this is how the helmsman feels at the tiller when trying to turn his boat in adverse winds. The weight of the sea courses through his hands. He strains against its power and battles to stay upright. Only with persistent effort does the boat come about.

I have few memories of Fotini, my grandmother. She once stayed for several days, before we shifted to the weatherboard house. She was in remission from the cancer that would soon claim her. I recall her white hair, puffed like cottonwool, and her smile. She possessed the quiet resolve of a woman who, I would one day learn, had journeyed, years earlier, from Ithaca as a proxy bride.

'*Ola ine gramena,*' Fotini would say, with a shrug. 'All has been written.' That is all. Two gestures: a smile and a shrug. Far removed from the world of men, passed down through the generations. My heirlooms.

———

I walk beside Sophia on a busy Melbourne street. The sky, contained between buildings, is a restricted blue. We enter one of the buildings, and step from the lift into the corridor on an upper floor. Fotini is lying in a far bed by the window of a public ward.

Sophia moves her seat close, bends over, and whispers. Fotini can barely talk. They fall silent, as if observing an unspoken pact. I turn my eyes to the window, where the light is streaming in. When I look back at Fotini I see that her white hair is lost in the white pillows. Her tiny face frames a stoic smile.

She reaches out a hand and I bend over to take it. She strokes my cheek. Her eyes glow and follow me as I retreat. They hold me from a distance. Glowing. Growing smaller. And years later, they still reach out, as the doors to the ward swing open and shut.

———•———

Manoli comes and goes as he pleases, to the pub, out on the bay, on hunting trips with Ithacan friends, and to the inner city, the mysterious rooms of the Ithacan Club. 'Come,' he says, gruffly, one evening, as if acting on a whim. He places a hand on my shoulders and ushers me to the car. It is the closest he can come to affection.

He drives the longer route, the beach road rather than the highway. Once past Mordialloc the road follows the shoreline. At times the sea is directly beside us, at others, at the foot of sandstone cliffs. We see the city lights and further still, round the bay, concentrations of lights between stretches of dark.

We park in the city, climb wooden stairs above a shop on the corner of Elizabeth and Lonsdale Streets, and enter the rooms on the second floor. As soon as he steps in, Manoli's demeanour changes. He is among compatriots and friends. I recognise summer guests: Alexis the wrestler, Uncle Cherry Ripe, the Gambler.

They look different in this company, harder. Intent. They hold the cards to their chests like well-guarded secrets. They greet me, turn back to the game and vanquish me from their minds. It is an abrupt shift in focus I have come to expect. I have seen it at picnics and family gatherings. They are engaged in men's business and are not to be disturbed.

When we leave the clubrooms Manoli is anxious to return to the bay. He drives directly to the beach road, veers right mid-journey, and descends the gravel path to Half Moon Bay. He parks the car by the bluestone seawall. One hundred metres offshore we make out the hull of a warship, scuttled years ago to create a break-water. A man lounges on a stool at the end of the pier, on guard behind three fishing lines. From this position the bay appears vast. We sit and watch for a while.

It is not the first time I sense that Manoli is trying to reach out. I imagine his lips on the verge of moving, about to confide. Then, like a crab pulling back within itself, he starts the motor and adjusts the clutch. '*I zoie ine mia trippa mes to nero,*' he says. Life is a hole in the water. He backs the car from the wall and returns to the highway. We do not speak on the drive home.

———

Manoli comes and goes as he pleases. He brings home new friends from the pub, Swedes and Italians, long-time Australians. He makes no distinctions. 'I am a citizen of the world,' he says, with his arms around his new brothers. He offers them work on sites where he works on his latest ventures: shops he is fitting and renovating. He tells them of his long-held plans to build blocks of flats and shop-ping centres. His ambition revives as he talks. He will take them out in the boat on fishing expeditions, he tells them. His generosity knows no bounds.

Sophia delivers plates of food, and cups of tea. Manoli draws on his stocks of refrigerated beer. The men talk politics, thump the table and speak idly of revolutions yet to come. They talk of the snapper, the 'big buggers' they had caught the previous day, and of the thousands currently swimming the bay. They talk of the starfish they had found in the snappers' gutted bellies: 'Will eat anything when they're hungry.' Fish talk.

Manoli is light-hearted with drink and camaraderie. He never drinks to ugly excess. I prefer this Manoli, content with drink, seated at the head of the table in earnest discussion with his new circle of friends. It is his soberness I fear.

———

Manoli's comings and goings are more frequent, his outbursts more strident. It has something to do with letters arriving from Ithaca. I glean bits of information from conversations. Stratis, his father, is very ill. He lives on the island, in the *patriko*. He is a subtle presence beyond my understanding, made more mysterious by distance. There is not one photo of him in our house.

I am woken late at night by the sounds of voices. 'Leave me be,' Manoli shouts. I hear him walking to the living room, and, soon after, sobbing. I creep from my bed. The door is ajar. Manoli sits on a sofa, his back turned to me. He clasps his forehead in his hands. He sits up and beats the armrests with clenched fists. It is the first and only time I see him weep.

In the morning he is gone, and Sophia has left for work. At dinner that night, she tells me that a telegram had arrived the previous day with the news of Stratis' death. Manoli has taken out the boat. He is gone for days and when he returns, he is haggard and drawn. He stalks the house like a wary beast.

———

Manoli is crumbling. His business ventures are failing. His body is succumbing to years of toil. What is there to show for all his efforts? For the forced smiles in the offices of bank-managers? He is wilting, becoming reckless. He attends races, spends hours pouring over form guides. His bets are increasingly daring. He drives to mid-week meetings at country courses. He is a familiar figure, known for his big bets, and his couldn't-care-less demeanour.

'*Den peirazi,*' he says when he loses. '*Den peirazi,*' he says when he wins. 'It doesn't matter. Nothing matters. Life is a hole in the water,' he laughs. I lie in bed at night and try to fathom it. How does one make a hole in the water?

He drives the beach road and detours to join fishermen on jetties. He baits his line, hurls it into the water and settles back on a canvas stool. He keeps two buckets, one with bait, the other for the few fish he is able to hook. He does not care whether he reels in fish or kelp. He does not care if his line is robbed of its lure and bait. He does not care when the chill descends. He remains seated for hours in the dark. *Den peirazi.* Nothing matters.

———

Manoli's comings and goings are more erratic. I am alert to the sound of his return, the brutal sound of his departures, the door slamming. One evening, he motors out to sea and vanishes. There are reported sightings by friends who claim to have seen him moored by wharves in various parts of the bay. We do not report him missing to the police. We are well accustomed to his ways.

He returns after a month like an apparition risen from the sea; steers the boat to the berth, mid-morning, and climbs the embankment. His lips are chafed and cracked, his skin singed and flaking.

He is a dishevelled stranger cloaked in the last vestiges of pride.

The fight has left him. He sits in the garage, idly sketching. The nets are unravelling. The engines he regularly oiled and greased are rusting. He spends his days among stacks of rotting timber, moth-gnawed sails and unrealised visions. He has grown ill and dispirited. He will never sail again.

———

Manoli died in 1971, in the first weeks of spring. I was fourteen. He died suddenly, felled by a stroke. He died within months of his final return from the sea, and within a year of the death of his father. He died when wild freesias were appearing, the wattle and jasmine blooming. And he died with the return of the birds. They descended in the tens of thousands. The skies were eclipsed by their density; the wetlands disturbed by their collective breasting.

'Do not go to the swamps,' Manoli had warned me, but I was now free to come and go as I pleased. I nestled against the dog, and watched the newly arrived birds feeding on the muddy banks. Pelicans landed on billabongs, generating a confusion of eddies. Reeds and wild grasses swirled, then eased back into uneasy silences.

Manoli's final boat strained like a dog on a leash at its berth on the river. He had transported it down to the water days before his death, and readied it for the warm months ahead. It was, in retrospect, one last flurry of activity. The boat bobbed with the tides and currents, emptied of promise. What can I say? Manoli was gone. We did not know whether to rejoice or cry. That is how it is. Life is a hole in the water.

———

When the news of Manoli's death reached him, Andreas placed the telegram under his pillow and took to bed for a week. Finally he rose, ate breakfast and scaled the path to the cemetery. He picked his way between cypresses and tombstones, and mounds of earth that marked the graves of the recent dead. He lifted his hat in acknowledgment of those he had known, and stopped by the family tombstone where Stratis' name had been recently inscribed beside the name of his first wife, Melita.

Andreas was an avowed atheist, but found himself, this once, drawn to the ritual. He cleaned the stone, removed the weeds and lit two oil lamps, one for Manoli, and the other for his father. He placed the lamps behind the glass in a bronze urn at the head of the grave, closed the lid and stood back to contemplate the flames.

He moved to the church terrace and leaned against the balustrade. The church stood on a ridge, dwarfed by higher peaks. To the west, on the upper ridge rose the village of Exogi and behind him, to the south, Mount Neriton. On the cliff path above Afales Bay, a villager was herding his goats towards the crest of the mountain. Like so many Ithacans who had stood here after visiting the cemetery, Andreas was struck by the contrast between the serene setting, and the proximity of death.

The following evening, he descended to Frikes Bay. From the upper slopes he heard the chatter of villagers on their way home from the groves. Hessian sacks, bulging with recently picked olives, were lined up on the roadside in readiness for the mills. Night had fallen by the time Andreas readied the caique.

He lifted anchor, guided the boat past the breakwater, and voyaged clockwise from Ithaca to Zakynthos, Kefallonia to Lefkada, waters he and Manoli had sailed many times. He anchored in harbours and coves on which they had beached *Brotherly Love*. He sailed for seven nights and, despite the winds and swells, the Ionian calmed him, as did the sight of the smoke rising from shepherds' huts on the Marmakas on the morning of his return.

On the anniversary of his brother's death he had Manoli's name inscribed on the family gravestone beneath the names of Stratis and Melita. He would return once a year, not on the date of Manoli's death, but on the anniversary of the day he left the island. All this I learnt years later, when I finally embarked on the journey that my father should have undertaken.

BOOK VI

The first return

I T IS autumn and the springtime of revolution, and a burden has been lifted from the polis. I lie in my room off Syntagma Square, in central Athens, and listen to revellers passing by in the early hours, scattering laughter.

It is eight years since the tanks burst through the gates of the Polytechnic and the ageing colonels massacred their young; seven years since the junta was overthrown. And many decades since the dark times began: sending waves of Greeks in search of new worlds.

I have relatives in the suburbs of Athens, but I have chosen to stay on my own. Despite their generous pleas I stand firm. I visit them frequently but return to a room far removed. I wish to come and go as I please.

I observe the city with the eyes of a lover in the first weeks of romance. I am drawn to the flowers on balconies, rather than the rusting tin cans from which they grow. I strain my eyes for a view of the Parthenon and ignore the fissures in the pavements on which I walk. I sit in cafes and take photos of the old lottery seller who approaches my table, and barely register the poverty that lies at the heart of his quest. I am more taken with the poles festooned with tickets than by the trembling hands that clasp them.

I attend concerts with my Athenian cousins where poets recite to capacity crowds. The audiences ride the lyrics like surfers wedded to waves. We sit in nightclubs and listen to the music of the *rebetes*, whose banned songs helped sustain those in exile during the time of the colonels. We party into the early hours, and stumble out arm-in-arm with strangers who mirror our lust for romance.

I move about the city with a sense of urgency. I am making up for lost time. A country I have never known has become my passion. I now understand why some who have been away from their home-lands for years, kiss the earth on their return. I have years of ignorance to make up, many gaps to fill. I sit at the edges of conversations and listen intently.

The talk returns to the fall of the junta. One moment is singled out: the July day in 1974 when Constantine Karamanlis returned from his Parisian exile to become Prime Minister of post-junta Greece. Radios broadcast the news throughout the city. Even weary cynics allowed themselves a moment of hope. Perhaps, at long last, brother would no longer kill brother.

I recline on a bench in a neighbourhood square as Athenians rush home for the siesta. The streets are gridlocked with busses, automobiles, pedestrians and motorbikes. Then, for a few blessed hours it is over. Blinds are being drawn. Shutters are closing. The city is falling into a collective slumber. The frenetic pace of my first month is slowing, and for the first time I register the rustle of citrus and mulberry trees, and the voices of women engaged in conversation over balconies as they air blankets and sheets.

I begin to see that beneath the chaos, Athens is a city of villages.

Neighbourhoods are built around intimate squares, and each apartment, I imagine, is a haven from a bloodstained past. Is that how it is on the island?

Days later I observe the city from the slopes of the Acropolis. The still point between day and night is giving way to darkness. Below me the lights of Athens spread over the plains of Attica to the mountains. I begin to comprehend the essence of journeying: a sense of unfolding. '*Siga. Siga.* Slowly, slowly,' say those who know what it is to wait. 'Make sure the journey is long, full of adventure,' recites the poet of Alexandria. Now that you are finally here, take your time.

Tomorrow I leave for Ithaca, where Uncle Andreas is expecting me. 'Andreas? He is the one who knows the winds,' a cousin has told me. 'When he is away from Ithaca, his thoughts stray to the island. Wherever he sleeps, he hears the beat of the sea against the cliffs of Afales. Whenever he hears the radio, it is the weather of the Ionian he listens for. Whenever he sets out on a journey, it is the first sight of the *patriko* he longs for. What can I say? He is afflicted with the Ithacan madness.'

———————

It is a four-hour journey by ferry from the port of Patras to the island. I stand against the rails on the upper deck and watch the crewmen. They fasten the winches, secure the cables, and when the boat is well clear of the dock, pause to draw on well-earned cigarettes. I cut off attempts at conversation and maintain my watch. I wish to savour my first voyage on the Ionian, to absorb the illusory movement of passing islands.

I scan the horizon for the first sign. That blue outline is Ithaca, a passenger tells me. An hour later it has grown into a massive presence. It takes time to realise I am looking at two islands. Ithaca and Kefallonia. Only when the ferry draws close, do I discern Ithaca's true form.

Mount Neriton rears dark against a falling sun, and just as we seem set to collide, the ferry bends into a hidden bay and sails towards Aetos, the Eagle Mountain. A fishing caique at anchor in the centre of the harbour is as still as a curlew poised over its prey. I observe the first signs of life, a scramble of goats on the lower slopes, cars flowing beside the coastline.

The ferry spirals from the Gulf of Molos to Phorcys Bay, named, say lovers of Homer, after the Old Man of the Sea. The labyrinth tightens and, as if irresistibly drawn into a vortex, the ferry rounds the narrow entrance into Vathy, the inner harbour. Houses tumble like vines over the lower slopes to the esplanade. Shutters are opening to the coming of the boat. Figures drift onto balconies. Two women stand beside the seawall and pick over the catch of the day. Cats wait for morsels that may be cast their way like manna from feline heaven. Damp nets lie in tangled heaps over the seawall.

The limestone escarpments above the town lean over us, Mount Neriton now looms behind us. The engines are easing down. The captain is tense, the crew focused. One error of judgement will damage their craft. The ferry slowly turns its stern towards the berth. I follow the flight of the ropes over the ramp. As soon as they are secured, the passengers disembark into a whirlpool of embraces and conversations that seem to have resumed where they left off, long ago, at the moment of departure.

Then abruptly it is over, sorted out, the luggage removed, the welcoming parties dispersing to all points of the island. Cars disgorged from the belly of the boat are well on their way to their destinations, and my taxi is on the isthmus. All day I have been in the hands of ticket vendors, shipping agents, stewards and seamen, masters of movement and change. I am now moving on firm land, tracing roads I had viewed from the upper deck of the ferry.

We scale the lower slopes of Neriton in a succession of hairpin bends from the east to the west coast. The sea bursts back into view. The mountains of Kefallonia, three kilometres distant, tower over the strait. I am sedated by the hum of the motor, and my dream of arrival.

The taxi slows on the approach to the village of Stavros. Old men raise their heads from their cards on the patio of a *kafeneion*. A bearded priest in a black cassock is crossing the square. A crowd surges around the tray of a utility heaped with fish. We break clear of Stavros into the northern heights. At the edge of my vision there is a sweep of mountains, and a hamlet beneath the highest peak. The falling sun sparks quivers of silver through rustling olive groves. It is too much to take in. The landscape is inextricably linked to other places, other times.

Ithaca. I cannot recall the first time I heard the word. It has always been there like an ancient longing welling up from the sea. And now that I am here, I am elsewhere: on the veranda of the Carrum house, the company dreaming into the night; and with Mentor at a Brunswick tram stop, waving for the final time, before he turns to stroll home. I am held captive by Fotini's face, growing smaller in a hospital ward.

And I am mesmerised by Manoli. He is overturning the kitchen table, lifting it high on two legs. Plates, cutlery and food crash to the floor. He stalks out of the house and, within an hour he has cast off. He is steering the boat through the river mouth. Ithaca: perhaps this is where Manoli goes when his boat dissolves in the dark.

I am jolted from my reverie by a roadside sign: *Ageii Saranda*, Village of the Forty Saints. The taxi stops on the gravel beside the road. Uncle Andreas is seated on the veranda of a stone house. When he sees the taxi he clambers up the embankment. His walking stick points the way as he makes it onto the road. He kisses me on each cheek, and I am taken by the similarities and differences between Andreas and Manoli. I register them both at the same time.

At first I gravitate towards the differences. Uncle radiates affection. It takes time for the similarities to become evident. They reside in the placement of the eyes, his pointed nose and hardened body and, for an anxious moment, in the intensity of his gaze. They are proof that the umbilical cord drip-feeds ancestral likenesses.

We have not yet paid the driver, but he is in no hurry. He has witnessed the scene many times, the instance of the first meeting, Ithacans returned after years away. He stands to the side and chats to passers-by as he unloads my luggage. Aunt Ourania has remained in the kitchen. She waves through the open shutters. Only now do I take notice of the small crowd that has gathered about us. One by one they step forward and introduce themselves. Those old enough to have known Manoli, scan my face for resemblances.

Many eyes are watching. I have been seen. Everyone is seen. From windows and doorways. I have my first suggestion of the paradox. There is intimacy and love, but also, intense scrutiny, and there is nowhere to run. Except for the mountains, and they are far greener than I expected. It is autumn, yet the slopes are dense with pine and cypress, wooded with groves and orchards.

Andreas ushers me in from the rising chill. A fire is burning in the lean-to kitchen. A stream of villagers arrives after nightfall bearing gifts and gossip. 'Manoli was a *levendi*,' they say, 'a beautiful boy. But he was nervous. He could snap at any time.' It is a common refrain. 'It runs in the family,' Ourania laughs.

She delivers a feast of roast lamb, vegetable stew and wild horta soaked in oil. When uncle eats he does not talk. He attends to the business at hand. He hunches over the food and shovels it in. He eats every morsel, wipes the plate clean with strips of bread, and washes it all down with a glass of wine.

'That was a good meal,' he says, rubbing his hands.

He seats himself by the fire, leans over towards the dying flames, and pokes the logs with his walking stick. The flames rear back. 'The fire is burning,' he says, 'and the fire loves us.'

Outside the wind is gusting. The weather has turned. The guests have departed and Ourania has gone to bed. 'It is going to storm tonight.' Andreas announces. 'The fishermen are praying to St Nicholas.' On his face there appears a mischievous smile.

'One of my boats carried a statuette of St Nicholas. Once, with the approach of a storm, as the seas were beginning to threaten us, I grabbed the statuette and hurled it overboard. We survived the storm, of course, and the statue is still swimming somewhere.'

'Manoli,' says uncle, his attention abruptly shifting. 'Why didn't you write? Every morning Stratis would get dressed in his best, button his waistcoat, and adjust his cravat and tie. He would sit down at the kitchen table, and eat a slice of bread and two cloves of garlic, to which he swore he owed his good health. He would rise, put on his hat and jacket, take up his walking cane, and with a posture as straight as his ageing spine allowed, he would walk to the all-purpose store.

'"Are there any letters today?" he asked.

'"Try again tomorrow," the shopkeeper replied.

'When Stratis walked back to the house, his steps were a little slower, his back further stooped. He would make for the bedroom, undress, and lie down for an hour. Then he would rise, dress again, and begin the day anew.

'I often wrote to Manoli and pleaded. "Send a letter to the old man. Just a few words will do. He thinks of you all the time. He wants nothing out of life anymore. Let bygones be bygones. It will make your father content."'

Andreas stands up. 'It doesn't matter,' he says. 'What is done is gone.' He walks to the door, and announces: 'We have many days in which to talk. I am going to bed.'

<hr />

My bed is covered in a spread woven in crimsons, ochres and blacks; the wrought iron frame leans against the bare plaster wall. I fix my eyes on the ceiling and count the cypress beams supporting the roof. The six beams are infested with white ant. Yet they hold fast. This is a patriarchal house, built to last. I am lying where Manoli was conceived, and where he slept beside his mother. It has been many years since he last slept here, far longer than Odysseus' twenty years of absence.

I have come to Ithaca in October, when the island begins its slow descent towards winter. Winds flare in and out of silences that guide me to sleep, and I am woken, hours later, by a rooster's crow. One crow begets a chorus of crows. The school bus is labouring up the steep incline from the lower village. It moves past the window and comes to a brief halt. I hear the chatter of children as the bus moves on. I become aware of a steady beat. The rhythm is hypnotic, a firm movement forwards and back. It rises from the *katoi*, the storehouse, directly under the floorboards. The day has barely begun and Ourania is at the loom.

I open the shutters. The eastern skies above the Marmakas are alight, but the rays are yet to rise over the ridge tops. The second window opens to the south, towards Neriton, the island's highest peak. At this hour it is a black presence. I enter the living room, open the double doors, and step out on the balcony. The village is perched on a ridge opposite the Marmakas. On the higher reaches, the woodlands give way to exposed limestone.

It is forty years, two times Odysseus' twenty, since the day Manoli left. Such calculations remind me of my limitations. I am not of this island, but a proxy, a second-hand version of the return. I cannot identify specific landmarks. All is new to my eyes.

What would Manoli have recognised on his return: the olive trees beside the house, the cypress that threatens to topple from the cliff into Afales Bay? Which landmarks would have moved him? The lean-to kitchen he and Andreas built? The groves once filled with voices? What would have dismayed him? The termites devouring the foundations of the house, the dead windmills on the heights?

I return to the bedroom, churning with questions, speculations. The beat of the loom is a counterpoint, a tranquilliser. 'Give yourself to the island,' it demands. 'Walk its roads. Follow the coastlines. Crest the summits and explore the leesides. All will be revealed in its own time.'

Andreas is up early.

'*Buona mattina*,' he says when I enter the kitchen.

He is proud of his few words of Italian.

'The storm is over, the sea, smooth as bone,' he says.

He perches by the stove, brings the coffee to the boil and stokes last night's embers until the fire re-ignites. Everything about the kitchen is small: the window frames, the door, the fireplace and sagging walls. The ceiling curves down from the main body of the house. The walls are white, the shutters painted in dark green. It is the kitchen built by the brothers.

'What do you plan to do today?' Uncle asks.

'Walk.'

'Go on your good way and when you return, tell me what you have seen.'

And so it begins, my incessant walking. Soon I will be known by the nickname, *Me ta podia*, 'with the feet', the mad one who walks and refuses to take lifts, the latest addition to the island's gallery of the insane. I descend from the village to the port of Frikes. In the lower village an old woman limps from her cottage. The smell of frying fish drifts through the open door. Emaciated cats are lined up on the wall by the gate.

'If I leave the fish for more than a minute, the cats will snatch them,' the woman complains. 'The mangy scoundrels are desperate for a bite.' She limps towards the cats and raises an arm to shoo them off.

'What does it matter?' she says, on second thoughts. 'I have no one but myself to feed anymore.' Her husband lies in the village graveyard, she tells me, and her sons and daughters are long gone. 'When their time comes, they will lie in graveyards scattered over godforsaken lands. Let the cats have their fill. Who cares? They can do what they like.'

I continue beyond Frikes, three kilometres by road, and scale a steep pass into the village of Kioni. The houses rise on steep slopes encircling the harbour. Three disused windmills line a peninsula that all but encloses the water. I follow a bayside path to a grave-yard. Bas-reliefs of crossed anchors and seagulls mark the tombs of seamen. On one stone there is an oval-framed photo of an eighteen-year-old boy. 'My Yorgo, please come into my dreams so I can tell you of the pain in my heart,' reads his mother's words.

'How did he die?' I ask a widow tending her husband's grave.

'How do you think?' she says. 'He dived one time too many. The sea killed him. Do not let its beauty deceive you. This is what I warned my sons. Of course they did not listen. The sea took them from me. They live on the other side of the oceans while I remain here, tending their father's carcass like an obedient fool.'

The conversation is over, cut short. Like the white granite soldier of Carrum, the widow turns her back on the harbour. She is possessed by a compressed anger. She lights a lamp, removes weeds, and walks from the grave with measured steps. As I move off for the long walk home, I sense someone is following me. The black widow is closing in on my shadow.

'No one cares about family any more,' she shouts. 'Everyone

goes their selfish way. Our young have withdrawn like crabs into lives of their own. Have children!'

I quicken my steps, but she is tough. She has trekked up and down these slopes for seven decades. She draws alongside and lunges towards me. 'Have children,' she shouts. I smell her breath through her blackened teeth. She is tiring, and I draw away with the advantage of youth. 'Have children!' she repeats as she drops back. 'Have at least three.'

I walk back to Frikes by the sea-road. Fishing caiques strain at their moorings. The cafe awnings have been dismantled, and umbrellas removed from their outdoor placements: the summer consigned to dark cellars. In the one coffee shop still open, a priest is seated with three men playing cards. An old dog sprawls at their feet. A man shuffles from the foreshore, clutching a fish trap in his right hand. He draws alongside, and without introduction, asks, 'What is the sea thinking today?'

There is something indeterminate about his age. His hair is white and unkempt, but when he smiles he looks like a child. When the smile subsides he assumes the expression of a perplexed man.

'Omeros,' he says, pointing at himself like an infant who has just learnt to say his name. He glances furtively up at the mountain and shuffles beside me as I begin my ascent from the waterfront. Fifty metres on, he stops by a two-storey house. The upper windows are boarded. The door creaks on its hinges as he pushes against it. He glances back at the port and lifts a hand to his chin. 'What is the sea thinking today?' he asks with a parting smile.

At this time of year and time of day the road is deserted, apart from an occasional motorcycle or truck. I detour to cousin Andonis' house. He sits in the courtyard, bent over a fishing net. 'The weather is boss,' he says. 'There is not enough breeze for fishing today.' He lets go of the needle and invites me inside.

His wife Jovania is four months pregnant, he tells me as he pours me a cold drink. She is away, visiting a doctor in Vathy. On the walls hang the spoils of voyages past: an elephant carved in ivory purchased in the Congo, wooden masks crafted in Brazil, a ceremonial dagger from Istanbul, and a photo of Andonis arm-in-arm with uniformed sailors posing in front of the Pyramids. On a chest of drawers sits a ceramic doll from Japan and a statuette of a fat laughing Buddha.

'I once loved working on the boats,' he says. 'But the excitement of new places wears off, and each farewell is more difficult than the last.' Andonis had decided to remain on the island, but spends many months at sea each year on oil tankers as ship's engineer. 'The work is more dangerous, but the pay better,' he shrugs. 'I want to stay on the island and fish, but there's not enough money in that.'

Andonis' words erupt and die back, like the wind gusts that had disturbed my dreams the previous night. His youthful enthusiasm is giving way to a sense of irony I will come to know well. When we finish drinking, he returns to the courtyard and takes up his seat over the nets. He can no longer be reached.

———◆———

'What have you seen today my child? Andreas asks.

'Ghosts.'

It is a warm night and we sit on the balcony. A half moon hangs over the mountain. I glimpse Afales Bay through a gap in the lower houses, and beyond it, the lights of Lefkada.

'Where have you been today?' Andreas asks, not registering my answer.

'Frikes and Kioni.'

'On the day we launched *Brotherly Love* the entire village accompanied us along the route you walked,' Andreas replies, on his own tangent.

'At the head of the procession, a step ahead of us, walked Stratis, and behind us came the boat, tied to a horse-drawn cart. Manoli designed it. He had a better eye for such things. He sketched designs for boats on scraps of paper, the backs of envelopes, and the wall above his bed: any blank space. And he was a better carpenter.

'We climbed the Marmakas and cut the wood on full moon nights, up there,' and Andreas points to the woodlands on the higher slopes. 'The wood is stronger at that time my child. We tried to build the boat quickly. We lit an oil lamp in the *katoi* and worked through the nights. We wanted to take it out fishing. We couldn't wait.'

I want to know more about the boat, but Andreas has moved on. He does not like to dwell on personal tales. He smokes incessantly despite long coughing bouts. His thinning voice crackles in the dark. He leaps through centuries, tears apart myths, and reassembles them in his own way. He is like a sparrow pecking over the same patch of earth. He circles recurring themes that inevitably lead back to his trinity of personal gods: Christ, Marx, and Buddha.

'These are the big three,' he says. 'Other philosophers said a few good things here and there, but these three changed the way we act.'

'Kazantzakis added Odysseus as the fourth member of the pantheon,' I say.

'Odysseus was involved with too many gods,' Andreas shoots back. 'At least the Hebrews got it down to one, even though they put him somewhere in the sky, but the ancient Greeks had a whole company of them, apparently living on Mount Olympus. Who can live on Mount Olympus? It's too cold,' he laughs.

As for Christ, he had spent fifteen years in the East, Andreas claims. There he had acquired the arts of healing. 'The true Christ,' he says, 'was not the Son of God, but a man who cared for the downtrodden. Read the Sermon on the Mount. He was not a saint, but a socialist. People told many lies about him.

'This is how it is everywhere my child. This is how it has been in our country in recent times. People turn on each other. Many were locked up. They endured years of beatings and torture after being set up by the people around them. Some people went mad from the beatings.'

I try to steer Andreas back to questions about family, but he clings to his obsessions. 'It has been a long night.' He lifts his fingers and ticks them off: the Balkan Wars, the Great War, the Turkish-Greco war, the fall of Smyrna. He stops at Smyrna for a while.

'I saw a ship full of *prosphyges*,' he says, 'refugees from Asia-Minor, in the summer of 1922. I watched as the ship berthed in Piraeus. Stratis was in Australia at the time. An uncle, Theo, had taken me with him to Athens. It was my first long voyage. I took in everything with my eleven-year-old eyes. Such scenes you never forget.

'The bible thumpers talk of eternal damnation, but they do not have to look far to find it here on earth. There were seven thousand passengers crowded on a boat fit for five hundred at most. They dozed on their feet, and pissed where they stood. What choice did they have? There was not enough room for them to lie down. They came ashore in rags. Puss oozed from their wounds. When they lifted their heads, I saw no light in their eyes. They had become the walking dead. I know all about it.'

Andreas pauses, stares straight ahead, lost to other worlds.

'I accompanied Uncle Theo on business,' he says, 'and walked with him everywhere. He took me to the camp where the refugees had built dwellings out of sacks and branches, and five-gallon drums. Families crowded into backyards where they lived like stray dogs. They carved shoes out of tyres and sloshed through the stinking mud. They peddled goods from handcarts and cooked their food in tin cans. They picked over rubbish dumps and scavenged anything of the slightest worth.'

'Theo took me to a city of tents at the feet of the temple of Zeus, in central Athens. The newcomers were strange creatures in their tattered clothes. The greater number were women, because many men had been killed or enslaved. I sat with my uncle in the coffee houses of Piraeus and listened as Theo talked to strangers. They spoke dialects of Turko-Greek, and told tales of the Massacre. My uncle beat me when I mimicked their accent. "Do not make fun of your brothers," he shouted.

Andreas stops and lifts his eyes towards the mountain. It is a gesture I will come to know well. 'After the beating I strained hard to understand what they were saying,' he tells me. 'I recall little fragments. How can I forget them? They spoke of the events their descendants call the Catastrophe to this day. The city of Smyrna had been burnt to the ground. Men searched through the flames for their sons and daughters. Women who had been raped wandered the streets with the eyes of the dead.

'There was nowhere to run but the harbour. When people swam out to the British ships they were pushed back into the sea. The British had encouraged us to make war with the Turks, and when the tide turned, they wiped their hands of us. For many months I dreamt of seas on fire. Between the two damnations, sky and harbour, there was nowhere to run. Why do priests talk about the fires of hell when they burn well enough here on earth?'

Andreas extracts a pack of cigarettes from his jacket, and lights up the next as soon as the last is out. I see the years of his country's agony embodied in his shrinking frame. 'It did not end there,' he says. 'Before we had drawn our next breath, the Second World War was upon us, and Manoli was gone. I wished him good luck and sailed the boat home on my own.'

I seize my chance. 'Why did Manoli leave?'

'Stratis thought of him all the time,' Andreas continues. 'On the day he died he lay in bed, very ill. He could not speak. He used his hands to ask for paper and pencil. With trembling hands he wrote down one word: "Manoli".

'I helped him out of bed and he walked to the toilet. He wanted to maintain his dignity to the end. When he returned he looked at each of us, lay back and died. The scrap of paper lay on the table beside the bed, and on it just one word.'

Andreas falls silent. Beneath us, the *katoi* door is being unlocked. Minutes later the beat returns. Ourania is back at the loom.

'It doesn't matter. Let the dead remain in peace,' says Andreas.

His eyes are fixed on the mountain; and beneath us the weft and warp, the infernal beat, back and forth.

———————

I lie in bed after my first full day on the island and cannot sleep. My thoughts return to a tale of a boat called *Brotherly Love*. It is the first time I have heard it and I am seduced by its elegance. Yet I am suspicious. The tale's perfection obscures more than it reveals. Something eludes me. Women clad in black pursue me. 'There is nowhere to run, nowhere to hide,' they hiss. 'All is *stenos kiklos,* an enclosed circle. All is written. All is fate.'

By eight the following morning, I am climbing a path that branches from the road to a forest, by the stream of Melanydros. I pause at Homer's School, the site of excavation where, as village folklore has it, the poet learned the alphabet. There is something about this site that detains me, perhaps its intimate tangle of plant and rock, the worn stairways leading nowhere. The ruins are equidistant between my two ancestral villages, and far more ancient than both.

I return to the path and continue my climb between perimeter walls. The path widens and becomes steeper. I see the dome of St Marina and scramble into the lower reaches of Exogi. I begin my search for the remains of the house Mentor grew up in: it is a pile of rubble. As I inspect it I hear a rustling behind me, and turn to see a woman pottering in an adjoining block.

She is plump and slow, yet sure-footed and tough. She clears away the weeds despite her laboured breath. 'Your grandfather's family is long gone,' she says, 'and the house is little more than dust. You will find nothing of Mentor here.

'So what?' she continues. 'Here, where I am standing, stood the home of my childhood sweetheart. He was a *levendi* with a rascal's smile, a young man with the devil's spark. And one day he left. What could I do? Stop him from going?'

'Two years later I married his best friend,' she says, bending over to remove some rocks. 'He was away at sea for many months and, in one stretch, for years on end. We had three sons, and each one joined him on the boats. What could I do? Stop them from going?

'Now my husband has left for the other world. His time was up. I observed the forty days of mourning,' she says, 'but as soon as they were over I took the bus to Vathy. I made my way to the hardware store, chose the brightest colours, and repainted every room: the kitchen yellow, the parlour sky blue, and the bedroom, I will keep as a surprise.

'Now I write letters to my childhood boyfriend. "Return to Ithaca. It is not too late," I tell him. He lives in Brisbane. His wife has recently died and he too is now free.' Her voice drops to a whisper, although no one is within sight.

'I tell him his land is being stolen, and that neighbours have shifted the boundary stones, a few metres here, a few there. I tell him I am building a fence around what is left. "Come home," I write. "I'm keeping an eye on your property. I have visited the offices in Vathy and looked over the deeds. All is in order. Come and claim what is yours."'

The woman invites me inside, and guides me through her house. 'While my husband was at sea I hauled the grain to the mills and waited. I planted my feet on the mountain and bent my back to my fate. I wove linen sheets, and bedspreads, and waited. I waited so long that my womb ran dry. Now I say, screw Penelope,' she laughs, as she shows me into the bedroom, painted a lurid red.

'When you return to Australia go and visit him. Perhaps he did not receive my letters. Tell the *levendi* that my husband is dead, and the house is freshly painted. Tell him the bedroom is red, the blankets and pillows crimson. Tell him I may be old, but I am soft and ripe.'

As I retreat from the house, she shouts, 'Tell the rascal that the bed is made, and the sheets are scented. Tell him his plot of land is well protected. Do you hear? Tell him it is not too late. Tell the *levendi* that the *levendissa* is waiting.'

———

I walk to a clearing in the woodland. Within the clearing stand two obelisks. The structures are so large they can be seen from the valley. I look back at the village. For each intact house there are two that have collapsed. Exogi is a village of the departed.

One derelict house is a mere doorframe to a single room. The roof has fallen in, the sky is framed by four walls. A lizard basks in a patch of sun. It eyes me for a moment, and darts under a pile of tiles. The winds have worked their way inside and the walls have been stripped. They lean precariously, as if frozen at the moment the earthquake struck. Or perhaps the house has succumbed to the slow death of abandonment.

When a house collapses the fireplace is the last to go. It remains, shattered but defiant. Beside it lies a decaying trunk filled with bedspreads stinking with damp. Beneath the top layer I uncover a scattering of photos. I look behind them for the names of the studios in which they were taken: London, Athens, Sydney, at various times between 1922 and 1958.

Two women walk by. 'What are you looking for?' one asks. 'There are only ghosts here. *Vricolakes. Kalinkantzari.* Bloodsuckers. Demons. You can choose which ever you like,' she cackles.

'*Trelli ine,*' I hear her companion saying, nodding towards me as they walk on. 'She's mad.'

———————

As I step from the forest back onto the road, mid-afternoon, Andonis speeds by on his motorbike. He skids to a halt, wheels the bike round, and doubles back. 'It will be a perfect night for fishing,' he says, when he stops alongside. His face is animated and flushed. We arrange to meet outside the house at two in the morning. He skids off the gravel and resumes the descent to Frikes Bay. The bike is weighed down with nets and supplies. He careers towards the port like a man possessed.

———————

'Where have you been my child?' Andreas asks.

'Exogi.'

'What did you see?'

'The obelisks.'

'We call them the pyramids. I know all about it. Our little island is full of such stories, each with many versions, and we are all convinced ours is right. Of course my version is the only one you can trust,' he laughs, and lights a cigarette. Andreas needs little prompting to launch into a tale.

'Ioannis was born in Stavros in the last decade of the last century,' he begins. 'He left Ithaca many years ago. He was perhaps fifteen at the time. He was not heard of for forty years, although one rumour has it that he may have returned from time to time in disguise.

'Some said he spent the years of the Great War in Paris. Others say he worked for years in the Congo. Some contend he worked as a spy, though no one seems to know for whom. Ithacan seamen claimed they had sighted him in Amsterdam, Alexandria, in Shanghai or Singapore. Some say he lived in New York, where he joined a Masonic lodge after making a fortune as a cloakroom attendant for theatre patrons. Others claim he was involved with shady dealings and fled back to Ithaca in fear of his life.

'His mother would sit every evening, waiting on the front steps of the house. She waited so long she forgot why she was waiting, but she kept sitting, on the same step, each evening, at the same hour.

'One evening a shadow fell over her. When she looked up she did not recognise the stranger. He told her that Ioannis was a friend of his and had sent him with money to make her comfortable in the last years of her life. She finally recognised the voice that had barely broken when he left.

'Ioannis settled back in Stavros. He was a small man who walked with a stoop, and drank only lemonade. It is said that he sat with his mother on the steps every evening at the appointed time. He promised the people of the village a share of his wealth. He donated money to the building of the square and a community hall. There was one condition. They were not to cut down the plane tree under which his mother sat with him when he was a child.

'All was well until a rumour spread that Ioannis had died. One of the villagers stole out and cut down the tree. "He's gone. What does it matter," he said. "Life goes on, and we need the land." When Ioannis heard what had happened he flew into a rage. He left the village and never returned.'

Andreas pauses, lifts his eyes to the mountain.

'Where does a man go when he leaves his home?' he asks, lighting his next cigarette. 'On Ithaca there are two choices, the sea or the mountains. Ioannis made his new home in Exogi. He built the pyramids in the final years of his life. He died alone, and it is said that he is buried there alongside his mother. Some say he erected the pyramids in her honour. Others say they contain the codes of a Masonic cult.

'The people of Exogi were great drinkers,' Andreas continues, without pausing. 'They had a dialect that concealed their secrets. They were forever drinking and singing, and produced the best musicians. I would bring back wine from Patras, in barrels that weighed down the caique, and they purchased them all; and when the barrels were emptied they called on a black wine of their own.'

'Stratis once told me that he preferred the village of Exogi to his own. He spent much time up there with Mentor. They were close friends my child. They wrote to each other for many years after Stratis returned. We were not surprised when Manoli married Mentor's daughter. Such arrangements were common. We are so inbred on Ithaca we are dancing under the tables.'

'My mother, Sophia, would often say the same,' I remark.

'Mentor would send Stratis photos of Sophia when she was a child,' Andreas responds. 'He took her to the same Melbourne studio, on the same date, each year. Sophia stood, holding a violin, against the same backdrop of trees on the banks of a stream. Stratis kept a collection in his wallet. He kept them until the day he died.

'It was a grand tree,' says Andreas, shifting tack. 'It should never have been cut down. Manoli would meet his lover, Stella, underneath it. Stratis did not approve of Stella. The couple saw him approaching during one of their trysts. They edged their way around the trunk as he drew nearer. Many people saw it. We knew all about it. The people of Stavros stood in the square and laughed. But Stratis was so proud he did not notice. Everyone knew about it except Stratis.'

'Who was Stella?' I ask.

'A woman from Corfu.'

'What did Stratis have against her?'

'It is a long story my child.' Andreas replies, and sidesteps to a recurring concern. 'Stratis died peacefully,' he says. 'He was in good health at the time. He grew old and died a natural death. The doctor came and said, "The fig has ripened, and has dropped off the tree. There is nothing we can do now."

'The day before he died he grasped a pen in his hand and wrote down just three words. "No letter today," and on the next day, just one word: "Manoli". My brother never wrote to him. I do not know why. Every day he would ask the postman if there was a letter, and the postman would say, "Try again tomorrow."

'Stratis was not the only one with this affliction. There were many others who did not hear from their children, and there were those whose children disappeared without trace. Old Kalliope had a son who rarely wrote to her. Her home is not so far from here, and is now boarded up. Soon it will fall in. Like Stratis, she returned from the post every day, empty handed. 'She would say to Stratis as they waited in the store, "What business do we have here? Let others come and wait," and she would hurry away muttering to herself.

'One day she ceased coming. She became a recluse. Few people saw her for months, and those who did said she had gone mad. All day she sat by the kitchen table, and sorted and read the few letters she possessed, and when the pile was full, she started all over again. I know all about it. Every house has its ghosts.

'Manoli was very determined. He was stubborn from an early age. He clung to his own thoughts. He was clever, and what he said, he meant, but he was nervous. And he bore grudges. We all have our slants, but some are steeper than others.'

'Why was Manoli so stubborn?' I hear myself ask. There are times, as Andreas' voice meanders on, that I feel like a disembodied presence, suspended between mountain and sky.

'It is a long story,' uncle replies. 'He was a good worker, but he was a driven man. That was how it was. He did not always do the right thing, but I loved him. I know all about it my Xanthe. I know all about it.'

Andreas shakes his head. His voice is tired, almost bitter.

'I never asked him for anything,' he mutters, as if interrogating his conscience. 'When he left, I had my boat. I was making a living. Manoli did not write to Stratis, but he sent me a few letters. He wrote one when you were about to be born. He said he wanted to return to Ithaca.

'I wrote back and said: "We will help you establish yourself. You can work on the boat, or set up a little business." The next letter he wrote arrived after you were born. For the first time, he seemed content. He said he was anchored in Australia and happy to stay.

'The final letter arrived not long after Stratis died. We did not know how sick your father was, my child. We had heard from other relatives that his condition had stabilised. His mind was wandering. It was hard to understand his writing. He wrote, "I am coming. They are sending me home." I did not understand. They say he gambled before the end and died of a lost will. Never mind. What is past is past.'

I want to know more. Many things remain unsaid, and Ourania is back in the *katoi*. The weft and warp punctuate my thoughts.

'It doesn't matter,' Andreas insists. 'Let the dead lie in peace.'

Andreas' eyes are fixed on the mountain.

Ourania's are cast down, fixed on the loom.

And for tonight, the conversation is at an end.

———

I wait for Andonis by the house well past two in the morning, the appointed hour for our fishing trip. Just as I am about to return to bed I hear the motorbike. He comes to a halt barely long enough for me to hoist myself onto the back. Andonis is in a hurry, and rides full throttle towards the port. I think of the abrupt transition from indifference to passion, from stoicism to childlike anticipation, in Manoli, obvious from the change in his gait as he left the house for the boat. He would stride from veranda to jetty with a sense of purpose. His face was alert, his entire being in harness.

I help Andonis transfer the provisions in Frikes, from the motorcycle to the boat. Even at this unearthly hour Omeros is about, empty fish trap in hand. He paces the waterfront, mumbling to himself. He watches while we make our final preparations.

'He spends his days by the quay from dawn well into the night,' says Andonis. 'He places his fish trap here and there, and does not care that it's faulty. He follows each boat that arrives and each boat that sets out. He stares at the water and claims he can fathom its thoughts. It is a madness that threatens all who spend many years at sea.'

Once we have passed the breakwater we move north off the east coast. The slopes of the Marmakas are black except for a lamp in a shepherds' hut. We round Agios Ioannis, the northernmost cape, and sail towards Afales Bay. Just as we are about to drop anchor at the fishing grounds Andonis decides, on an impulse, to pursue a different course.

He turns the boat about and heads west. The villages on the heights are huddles of lights, now visible, now hidden, as we move across the strait. Andonis' reserve is gone. It is night, the boat is his kingdom and he is in sole command. What more could an Ithacan want? He sings, out of tune:

> *Ah, if I die, what will they say? Some fellow died,*
> *A fellow who loved life died. Aman! Aman!*
> *Ah, if I die on the boat, throw me in the sea*
> *So the black fish and brine can eat me. Aman! Aman!*

We round the northern cape of Kefallonia and motor south, one hundred metres offshore. The outlines of the mountains rise and dip like the vertebrae of an arthritic back. Villages are marked by concentrations of lights, but the darknesses between them are far greater.

Due west, beyond the horizon, juts the heel of Italy, well beyond sight. And south, beyond the Mediterranean, rise the desert winds of North Africa. We have left the intimacy of the coast. I am out on the open sea in a small caique for the first time. Manoli did not take me out on his boats. I spent my childhood on the shore-line, my feet swept by the rind of the tides.

Andonis stands at the tiller, his gaze fixed on the sea. He belongs in the company of men, and the fetid bowels of engine rooms. He smells of diesel and brine, and prefers to sail alone. He is kin to Manoli, both in blood and kind, far closer to him in spirit than his cousin, Manoli's daughter.

'Directly beneath us,' he says, breaking the silence, 'runs a fault line that passes through Sicily. It continues east over seabed valleys, cuts between Zakynthos, Kefallonia and Ithaca, and slices through mainland Greece like a subterranean wound. Quakes can erupt at any time. Perhaps that is why we are such a nervous people,' he laughs.

The stars are fading, the skies giving way to the first hint of dawn. Andonis turns for the shore and heads for the bay of Assos. He moors the boat by the waterfront, and we cross a strip of land to a steep promontory. The ascent to the fortress is lined with carob trees dripping with the bread of St John.

'I came here when I left the shores of Ithaca and sailed alone for the first time,' Andonis says as we lean against a stone balustrade near the summit. At that moment his fate was sealed, he tells me. He wanted it all, both the Ionian and the oceans. From these heights he imagined the island of Sicily, the shores of Libya and beyond the Ionian, ports and seas encircling the globe.

'I was seized by an impulse to run back to the boat and set out, just as others are inexplicably tempted to leap from buildings and cliffs. Andreas knew it as soon as I returned. He saw it written on my face, and he knew there was nothing he could do to stop me. Weeks later I left for Piraeus to work on the cargo boats.'

We stand on a landmass torn apart and reassembled over millennia by quakes and tremors. On one side of the promontory there are coasts and harbours, and on the other, the suggestion of yet another enemy on the horizon. The stories I have heard, and am yet to hear, are echoes of one refrain: Is there somewhere on Earth where I can find peace and prosper? Once the question is posed, the agony begins, the eternal dilemma: to stay or leave? To retreat behind fortifications, or cast our fate to the winds?

———•———

I arrive back at the house, mid morning, to disarray. Severed branches are scattered over the embankment. Pregnant Jovania perches on the top rung of a ladder. Olives ricochet on the ground-sheets. Ourania rakes the fruit from the pruned branches. Andreas beats olives from the leaves with his walking stick in an effort to be useful.

'What are you waiting for?' says Ourania, and tosses me a hand rake. Her voice has changed. She is brusque and direct. The welcome is over. The village is being wrenched from its slumbers. All hands are needed for work.

At dawn the following morning Andonis draws up to the house in his utility. I help load the saws, sacks and groundsheets, and climb into the tray. Ourania eases her ample body into the cabin beside Jovania, and we hurtle from the unpaved paths of the village onto the cliff road. I look down at Afales Bay from my perch on the folded groundsheets. The Ionian glistens with the crimson skin of dawn. A snake flits across the rock face, its scales flashing in the first rays of the sun.

We turn inland and come to a halt in a clearing by the family grove. After a snack of bread and coffee, we set to work. Our first task is to spread the groundsheets. Jovania adjusts the ladder and climbs. Andonis moves ahead, chainsaw in hand. He removes entire branches and cuts them into small logs fit for the fireplace.

Once a tree is picked and the fruit heaped into sacks, we roll up the groundsheets and advance to the next. Goats graze on leaves left in our wake. Mid morning we pause for a quick meal of tomato, cheese and olives. I trudge home late afternoon, exhausted.

And so it begins, the picking cycle: from deep sleep to rude pre-dawn awakenings, Andonis signalling his arrival with a resonant beep. Soon after, we unwind from the streets of the village onto the cliff road. Day after day we labour under an autumn sun, interspersed by sudden squalls. We work against the onset of the cold, our eyes fixed on the fruit, backs turned to the sea. Andonis moves ahead wielding the saw like a man possessed. Ourania directs operations, yet, despite her hours of toil, ends her day at the loom.

She is plump and heavy and over sixty-five years old. She makes her way with the same steady beat to and from the groves. She insists on going out even as the winds are rising. The seas are dark, the skies heavy. Groundsheets tear at the rocks. Olive branches fall from the heavens. Ourania raises her head and nods towards Exogi, perched on the ridge beneath the summit. Her tale unravels in a drawl that matches the pace of her work.

She was born in Exogi, Ourania tells me. The man who was to become her father left for the Antipodes when he was young, and sailed back in 1912 to fight in the Balkan Wars. He returned to the island, ill and wounded, and stayed long enough to marry and father a child. Within a year of her birth, he returned to *Afstralia*.

While he was gone Ourania acquired the steady gait of the

mountain people. She hauled wheat to the windmills, and planted flax and corn in the hidden valley. She descended to the springs of the Kalamo, and carried back water in ceramic jugs. She laboured in wood-fired kilns to extract powder from limestone, and when the picking season returned, she joined the daily two-hour trek to the groves.

The night was far from over when the convoy of women, children and mules set out. The slope bottomed on a lower ridge and ascended past the trees we are now picking. They crested the Marmakas by the windmill to the leeside where land-starved Ithacans had planted terraces far from their homes. They worked till dusk and trudged back at night: and by the time the three months of picking were over, night and day seemed as one.

At the end of the tenth season, Ourania's father returned. He stayed long enough to impregnate his wife a second time, and again set sail for Australia. Ourania's mother did not cease working as she neared the time of birth. She set out with the convoy when the picking season returned. As they climbed the final stretch to the village at nightfall, her labour pains began. Two hours later her second child was born, and the following dawn she resumed the trek to the groves.

Ourania's father issued missives from afar. 'Make sure that you retain enough oil in case of lean seasons,' he wrote. 'Use the money I send to buy a strong mule,' he instructed. 'He wanted to remain our boss even though he was absent,' Ourania laughs. She rises from the stool, adjusts the groundsheet, resumes her seat and, with it, her tale.

Ten seasons passed. Ourania's father wrote a letter announcing he was returning. On the day he posted it he received a letter from his wife. He sat on a bench in a park in Melbourne, unfolded the letter, and died of a heart attack. 'Just like that,' says Ourania. 'One moment he was alive, and then *tipota*, nothing but a corpse. He was clutching the letter in his hands when he was found slumped on the bench.' Due to the vagaries of the mail the two letters, the one saying he was coming home, and the other bearing news of his death, arrived in Exogi on the same day.

Ourania shrugs. There is not an ounce of regret, nor trace of sentiment. Her voice has maintained the same matter-of-fact tone throughout. Let your men roam distant lands. Let them do what they must. What choice do we have? Bend your back to the mountain. Sow and reap.

———

With the passing days my body begins to adapt to the mountain. I graduate to the ladder beside Jovania and lean into the branches to prune, and when I'm done, I heap the fallen branches in readiness for the fires. And on my days off, I walk. It has not taken long to acquire my dubious status. I am *Me ta podia*, the mad one who walks.

I make my way to the *kafeneion* in Stavros, and sit on the patio overlooking Polis Bay. An ancient city is said to lie beneath its waters. Inside, at felt-topped tables, the men are gathered over their cards. Old Yorgos parks his battered Toyota in the square, and strides to the cafe arms akimbo, body leaning forward. He orders an ouzo, extracts a pack of cards from a shirt pocket, and plays patience. 'We come, we see, and we disappear,' he says. He wears a baseball cap with Durban emblazoned on the visor.

The children at the primary school have been released for

morning recess. They chase soccer balls in the concrete yard beside the church. Spiro the fisherman crests the road from Polis Bay on his motorbike. His dog shares his seat, propped on its hind-legs, paws resting on the handlebars. A utility follows, filled with the morning's catch. As soon as it parks a crowd gathers to haggle over octopus and snapper.

Panos approaches my table and introduces himself. A well-built man of sixty, he is neatly dressed in slacks and a chequered shirt. He speaks a hesitant English, and chooses his words with care. He had lived in Melbourne for five years, and knew Manoli well. They hunted rabbits and ducks, tracked their prey on the shores of lakes and rivers, and slept in their cars overnight. By the time the hunt was over, their clothes reeked of blood and the swamplands.

'Manoli often took me out on the bay,' Panos tells me. 'At sea he was a different man. On land he was rough in his talk. Like many of us, he was a noisy know-all. Yet out on the bay he was, how can I say it, reflective?

'He once said, "These winds were strangers when I arrived. I am still getting to know them. Unlike our Ionian winds, they do not have personal names. They are known by the points of the compass, as westerlies and northerlies, and so on. A wind without a name cannot be trusted. It takes a long time to befriend."'

Panos journeyed back to Ithaca to nurse his sick father. When his father died six months later, he made plans to return. 'I would wake up with great intentions but whenever I set out, I lost my resolve,' he tells me. 'The island slowed me down and robbed me of ambition. Ithaca is an island of lotus-eaters,' he laughs, and glances up at the mountains. On his face I register an air of bemusement. Life has passed me by, it seems to imply, and has left me stranded.

'I was a shepherd when I was young,' Panos remarks, as if reminded by the mountains. 'I spent my days following my flock in search of pasture.' He lowers his voice further as if his love of nature would cast him in a negative light. 'I love the scent of mountain herbs, and the first blossoms of the almond tree. I collected *volvous*, a purple flower delicious to eat, and warmed myself by the fire while they boiled. I slept in shepherds' huts at night, content with my own company.'

He had spent the war years up there, he says, and nods at the heights. When the Germans came in search of partisans, they took to the mountains. The soldiers stayed in the village and threatened the children and the elderly. 'Even up there,' says Panos, pointing upwards, 'there was no way out. I herded my sheep to the most remote pastures. The island was being eaten bare. Shepherds fought over the diminishing feed. German planes flew low overhead, and the flocks panicked and scattered.'

Andreas materialises from the distance in his perennial grey flannel suit. Stick in hand, he moves with brisk steps in a crab-like crouch. He pauses in coffee shops to talk with friends. A van crammed with carpets comes to a halt in the square. A gypsy steps out, rubs his eyes, and looks about. 'Where am I?' he asks.

Dionyssios the priest hurries from the church, and stops to converse with all who come his way. When he is finally done, he enters the *kafeneion* and orders brandies for the men playing cards and drinks with them. He approaches my table, grips my right hands in his massive palms, and shakes it vigorously. His breath smells of spirits. The morning is drifting towards siesta. Shops are closing, cafes emptying.

The priest invites me home for lunch. Evriklia, his wife, is in mourning, he tells me, as we approach. A black ribbon is tied to the front door. Her sister had died, days ago, in Zimbabwe. The shutters are closed, the rooms dark. Dressed in widow's black, her face veiled, Evriklia sits in the gloom. 'It is hot,' she says. 'Very hot.' She lifts herself out of the chair, switches on the fan, and serves lunch.

She has one memory of her father, she tells me, as vivid today as it was five decades ago. He is stepping out of a shop in Stavros with a box of chocolates. She sits on his knees while she eats them. Then he is gone, vanished from the face of the earth.

The Second World War breaks out. He sends packages of food and clothing, and for the first time in her life, she eats pineapple jam. The Italians occupy the island. 'They thought only about food,' chuckles Evriklia, 'and when their stomachs were full, they took out their mandolins and sang songs about their mothers.'

Her veil is slipping, dislodged by her laughter, but her tone changes when she resumes her tale. 'The Germans were different. They wiped the smiles from our faces. They appeared suddenly as if rising from the underworld. Boats pulled up on our shores and disgorged hundreds of soldiers. I heard the tramp of their boots advancing closer.

'They came looking for the guerrillas. Women, children, and the elderly were herded against a wall. For many hours we stood there, with a mounted machine gun aimed at us. The soldiers fanned out into the mountains. Motorcycles sped in and out of the square. The schoolmaster pleaded with the commandant to spare our lives.'

As she talks Evriklia moves about the kitchen. She makes coffee, and settles back at the living room table. 'The storm passed and we were released from our terror,' she says. 'We returned to our gardens and grew tomatoes, potatoes, cauliflower and onions, garlic and lentils, white beans, green beans, grains and almonds. But it was not enough. The Italian soldiers grabbed more than their fill. I loaded a donkey with grain and set out for your uncle's mill on the Marmakas. I have known your uncle Andreas since I was a child,' she says. 'Mother did not want to send my older sister because she was too attractive and tempting for the soldiers.

'The mill appeared by the crest of the mountain. Its white sails were dormant. When I arrived the wind had not yet risen. Andreas said, "Do not worry my child. I will take your grain and give you some flour I have already ground."

'I saw Andreas recently and asked him, "Why do you think mother sent me, and not my sister? She was far more beautiful, wasn't she?" "I don't think so. You were beautiful too," he replied.

'Now it pains me to see how frail he looks. He was a handsome man, and I am becoming old. Life is a miracle, but I don't understand it. God has given us so much beauty. He throws it all down, but then, takes it away. When I was young, I never thought about such things. I climbed the mountains as if walking on level ground. I ran as swift as a deer and swam with the abandon of dolphins. Now it is all behind me. Why did my sister die? Why do we grow old? Why does God do such things?'

Evriklia's veil slips and uncovers a face lined with mourning, but her eyes burn with youth. 'I knew my father by his letters,' she says. 'The letters swirled from alpha to omega and assumed many guises. Sometimes they were stern and admonishing, and at others, warm and close. "With this money I am sending you, buy a new dress, a thick coat," he wrote. We were raised under the wing of our mother. She worked day and night, and we loved the days and nights, even though he was not here.

'One day there arrived a wonderful letter. It was twelve years since he had left the island. The war was over. I was about to get married. In Brisbane, father was going to cafes and clubs, wherever Ithacans gathered. "I am going home to give away my daughter," he announced, and ordered drinks for his compatriots. Days before he was to depart, he sat with friends, closed his eyes, and his heart gave out.'

Evriklia adjusts the veil and fastens it back in place. 'I do not understand why God does this,' she says. 'I do not understand why he creates so much beauty, but mixes it with terror. I do not know why he gives so much, only to snatch it away.'

———————

'What did you see today, my child?' Andreas asks.

'Octopus and the priest's wife,' I hear myself say.

We sit on the balcony, and gaze at the mountain as we talk; it is becoming a companion, a familiar presence.

'Evriklia often came to the mill,' my uncle responds, pointing up to where it still stands, sail-less and abandoned. 'Whenever I saw someone coming,' he adds, 'I would warn Paolo, a deserter from the Italian army. He begged me to hide him. He said he could not push around people who reminded him of his own. I hid him in the mill by day and the *katoi* at night.'

Andreas lights the first cigarette. There is little need for questions. I would gladly listen to him for hours, here, on the balcony, his staccato voice softened by the sky and its constellations.

'We allowed Paolo into the house when the village slept,' Andreas continues. 'We played cards and drank wine late into the night. Stratis sat with us. He came to regard Paolo as a son. I still have the cards in a drawer of the dresser. They are black with the stains of our fingers. Paolo did not stop talking about his fiancée. He was insane with longing. He saw the sea that surrounds the island as a hangman's noose.

'The Italian soldiers ate everything,' Andreas laughs. 'Cats, turtles, snakes, old mules: anything they could lay their hands on. When they were done, they returned to their garrison above Afales. They allowed us to take out our boats a certain distance, as long as we supplied them with a good proportion of our catch. In turn they handed out rations of rancid corn meal. They would often come up to the mill and ask for food.

'"We'll trade our pope for flour," they once joked.

'"You can keep your miserable pope," I told them.

'The regiment's captain wore a crucifix around his neck and crossed himself as he spoke. I told him that Jesus was a socialist. He replied that these were an apostate's words. I said if he wanted to meet me in the next life and ask for food, he would have to detour to hell.

'After the Italians satisfied their stomachs, they would eye off the village girls. It softened the boredom of their days. Our Delilahs robbed them of their strength and in return they received coffee, tea and sugar. It is an old story my Xanthe.'

Andreas' voice drifts into the night, and my thoughts drift back to the veranda in Carrum, the rare evenings that it was alive with Ithacan compatriots; and to the snatches of tales that Manoli could not tell me. Of what was taking place in the years of his absence. I am beginning to understand my father's agony, and the agony of all who are cut off from their homelands in times of war and famine: their sense of impotence and disloyalty.

'The mill saved us from hunger,' I hear Andreas say. 'It had been idle for some time. Fortunately there were older villagers who knew how to get it started. When the wind blew I worked the mill day and night. When the wind is with you a miller must stay at his post.

'On calm nights we stole out in three-metre barques. We avoided the patrols of enemy gunboats, and sailed to neighbouring islands in search of supplies. We crawled over the hills and gathered mushrooms and figs. When food became scarce we sailed to the mainland. We kept a close lookout for mines. A fisherman in Frikes collected them to blow up fish. One night he miscalculated and blew himself up.'

'We transported our oil in goatskin flasks,' Andreas says, after pausing to draw on his cigarette. 'The skins were noiseless compared to tin containers. We moved slowly through the night to Zaverda and other mainland hamlets, where we bartered oil and soap for wheat. One kilo of our oil could be exchanged for up to six kilos of wheat. Villagers were waiting when we returned. They tied sacks of grain to their donkeys and disappeared into the dark.

'One night, one of the barques was intercepted. It was searched and found to contain potatoes and tobacco. The commander of the patrol boat, an Italian, looked at the smuggler and said, "You are a black marketeer and I am a bastard. So give me half the tobacco and we'll be square."

'I sometimes smuggled partisans from island to island. We kept our boats hidden, and slipped into the water after dark. I once ferried the guerrilla leader, Captain Fortunas, the Tidal Wave, so called because he was a powerful force against the occupiers. He was a determined man with a strong presence. He hid in the mill overnight and stayed in the house. He moved about the mainland and Ionian Islands at will.

'There were Ithacans who were inspired to join him. They moved to Lefkada and Patras, and camped in mountain hideouts on the mainland from which they descended to ambush German convoys. Some fought in Kefallonia, within sight of their childhood villages. The mountains were their protectors. They attacked the enemy, stole their weapons, and retreated to their lairs. They also fought gangs of brigands who raided the villages.

'Ithaca was saved by its size. Our island is small and not suited to partisans. The enemy was concentrated in Kefallonia. Terrible atrocities were committed there my child. The Germans came here from Kefallonia in search of resistance members. Stratis hid in an orchard. An apple fell and hit him on the head, and he was certain he had been shot. He did not know if he was in this world or the next,' Andreas chuckles.

'When the coast was clear Paolo sat beside me inside the mill,' he says, retrieving the key thread of his tale. 'The tiny window by the grinding stone was our lookout. He was a socialist and ridiculed Mussolini, the Macaroni King. He once said, "Signor Andreas, your home has become my home, and after the war, my home will be yours." He told me he had a brother serving in Albania, a second in Tobruk. The third brother was a prisoner in Germany. He was crying as he talked.'

Andreas is still for several minutes, his face obscured by the dark; but his silence conveys a deep sense of regret. 'As soon as the war was over, Paolo left,' he says. 'He could not wait a single day. He sailed for Patras in search of a boat to Italy. He promised he would write to me when he arrived home, but I did not hear from him.

'One evening, not so long ago, in a cafe in Patras, I struck up a conversation with some Italian seamen. Among them was a sailor who came from the same town as Paolo. He told me that Paolo had never made it back. While sailing to Italy the ship hit a mine. He did not live to see his sweetheart. I had lost a second brother. Neither lived to see his homeland, and Manoli was not here when the dark times descended. I almost forgot he existed. We had enough to deal with.'

Andreas falls silent. The outside world is receding. Darkness inflates the distance between Ithaca and the neighbouring islands; and in the *katoi* Ourania has resumed her seat at the loom. All that exists is a balcony adrift in space. And beneath us, a relentless beat, back and forth.

———

The sea ripples with the crimson skin of dawn. Andonis veers from the cliff, and comes to a halt by the groves. He unloads drums of petrol and leaves me to tend the fires. I pour the fuel into smaller tins, and return to the pruned olive branches. I light the kindling, pour petrol on the flames, and circle the blaze to evade gusts of smoke and embers.

I run to a well nearby, draw water, and douse the windward flames, herding the blaze from the groves. When one pyre is reduced to cinders I light another. Patches of slope are fissured and blackened. It is the time of the burning, and there are fires scattered throughout the mountains. And when mine die down, I walk. I am coming to know the skin of the island, the movement between wind and flame, earth and water. And wherever I walk, doors open, tales unfold.

'Come in. Have a brandy. A person who does not take time to sit with friends falls prey to the devil.' He is known as the Professor and his secluded house overlooks Polis Bay. 'Nature is my stage,' he says, ushering me to the terrace. 'Earth, wind and sea are the lead actors, and the windows and balconies are seats in an amphitheatre with a ringside view of the drama.'

'The drama changes every day,' I say.

'Every ten minutes,' he replies. 'I have been up since six o'clock,' the Professor continues. 'To live here alone is wonderful, as long as you are a friend of your own thoughts. Like all who are well into middle age, I have made many bad decisions. But one decision I do not regret: returning to live on Ithaca. That has cancelled out all my bad decisions.'

He fills his pipe, tamps down the tobacco, and refills our glasses. The sky is streaked with slivers of nimbus, the sea with swathes of turquoise. 'I was born in a village that no longer exists,' he says, jabbing his finger towards a clump of cypress on the mountain opposite. 'The earthquake of 1953 claimed it. I was on Ithaca at the time, on leave from my university studies in Athens.'

We lean on the balustrade, drinks in hand, and take in the vista. 'Sea and sky have exchanged costumes!' he exclaims. 'You see! Every ten minutes, something is added, something subtracted. Nature is a world of chaos seeking an equilibrium that can never last. There are times when the earth rages and entire settlements are felled. And perhaps that is how it should be. Otherwise our lives would be boring, and boredom is a subtle version of hell.'

He relights his pipe, performing the task with unhurried

movements. 'There were three quakes in all that year,' the Professor says. 'The first, on August 9, a Sunday, at ten in the morning, shook Ithaca. I was swimming in Polis Bay. Birds ceased singing. The dogs that barked through the night were silent. The air was still, the water placid. As I swam, I saw dust rising over the village. Rocks were hurtling down the mountain. The water was churning. I saw houses leaning over like lovers about to touch each other. "Run to the sea," people were screaming. "The hand of fate is destroying our island."

'The second quake, on the Tuesday morning, destroyed many towns and villages on Kefallonia, and the third, the following morning, destroyed the town of Zakynthos. The entire township was burning. Corpses lay in the charred ruins. The streets were bent like cardboard. The opera house was in ashes. The earth trembled for twelve days; there were seven hundred and fifty aftershocks. Headlines at the time claimed that Ithaca, Zakynthos and Kefallonia were no more. They had fallen into the Ionian.'

'Yet the quakes had unexpected benefits,' the Professor observes. 'For a time, brother stopped hunting brother, tracking down communists as if they were vermin, forcing them to sign declarations renouncing their beliefs. For a time we were united against a common foe, but after years of war and famine, the quake was the final blow. We no longer trusted the earth beneath us. Many Ithacans who had held out finally succumbed, and left.'

The Professor steps inside and returns to top up our glasses. The vista of sea, mountain and sky, are spinning me towards elation. 'I resumed my science course in Athens,' the professor says, drawing me out of my reverie. 'On graduation I worked in universities far removed from my native land. I relinquished my ticket to the amphitheatre and spent years backstage.

'One day, I looked into the mirror and saw my pallid reflection. I surveyed the small room that was my office, stepped out and ran my eyes along the corridor that housed the identical rooms of my colleagues. I had spent the prime years of my life in a prison.

'I handed in my resignation and packed my belongings. When I stepped off the ferry in Vathy, I felt weightless. I acquired this property, camped in a tent and directed the builders. You have to keep an eye on them, otherwise the job will never be completed. Now I live out my years in an amphitheatre, and each day heralds the premiere of yet another drama.'

It is night when I leave the Professor's house. The air is scented with the lingering smell of the burnings. The seas are studded with the lights of ferries making their way on mysterious journeys. At this moment Ithaca is an eternity, a limestone rock rising from the Ionian, bearing witness to an endless drama of returns and departures. And I am elated.

———·———

I have strayed into winter. The time of the fires is over, and the earth lies fallow. Snakes have returned to their burrows, and with each passing day the island becomes more silent. For the first time in many weeks, I take leave of the village.

I catch the early morning bus to Vathy. Mid afternoon, hours after arrival, I climb the stone steps from the waterfront to the upper reaches, into a landscape of derelict churches and terraces. The remnants of pre-earthquake structures are falling into oblivion. Isolated chapels are tucked within the ribs of limestone ridges. I step into a chapel, and within its cool walls I retrieve the events of the morning, the bitterness that had flowed like a foul breath as soon as Adriani's door had opened.

My grand aunt Adriani, Fotini's sister, had stood before me, a stout woman dressed in black, unsmiling. She showed me into the house where Fotini had spent her childhood, before sailing to Melbourne to marry Mentor. The walls of the parlour were bare except for an oil painting of a clipper floundering in a gale. The waves reared over the decks like a multitude of serpents.

Adriani observed the formalities: served a spoonful of quince jam, a cherry brandy, a cup of coffee, and a glass of cold water set out on a white tablecloth. Everything was clean and correct, but her bitterness was palpable. She displayed no curiosity for what I had to tell her, no interest in my inquiries. I wanted to know about Fotini's early years, her life on the island.

My grand aunt did not converse with me directly, but circled the same infernal questions. Why had Fotini not sent more money? Surely she was rolling in wealth in a land of plenty. Why, after she left for Melbourne, had she abandoned her blood family? Why did she not care for her mother's welfare, and not provide for her when she descended into dementia?

Throughout her tirade she kept her eyes averted, as if addressing unseen forces. I wanted to scale the fortress, and wrest the tales I longed to hear. I wanted to deliver Adriani of long-held grudges and self-interrogations. I wanted to stand up and shake her, to tell her of Fotini's struggles, and of the eyes that held me the last time I saw her. Glowing. Growing smaller. Dissolving in an ocean of white pillows.

I had left the house, depleted. The harbour was a blaze of mid-morning silvers, but its perfection mocked me. After months on the island, I was not welcome. Even at this hour, the zenith of the town's commerce, Adriani's house was shuttered.

Yet, as I return to the port from the chapel I realise my efforts have not been entirely wasted. I now know the physical location, and that the youthful Fotini had stepped out daily to the sight of the harbour. She had seen the boys swimming towards the Lazaretto, the prison islet, and perhaps joined them. She had observed the clouds enveloping the summit of Neriton, and the bare masts of hibernating boats that crowded the water mid winter. She had known the daily returns of the fishing caiques, and their evening departures. Her childhood has entered the realm of my imaginings.

At dusk, townsfolk stroll the esplanade. In the town square speeches are being made. The municipal elections are to take place this weekend. Trucks, busses and cars, are queued up in expectation. The nightly ferry is due to arrive any moment.

For millennia it has been like this. When will the boat arrive? Will it come on time? Will my Odysseus be on board? Will I recognise him? And, now that I see him, is this ageing stranger the man I have so long awaited? Will he force himself upon me on the first night of our reunion? Will the unfamiliar odour of his body repel me?

The ferry approaches like an ageing hostess gliding to greet guests and escort them to the banquet table. Passengers are filing out to intimate welcomes. Travellers, rucksacks on their backs, step ashore anonymously. They pause, disoriented in that awkward interlude between the voyage and finding one's feet in yet another foreign port, the moment when the traveller longs for someone to greet them, and stares with envy at those who belong.

I stroll back to my hotel long after nightfall. A family of gypsies is encamped beside the harbour. They huddle outside their van and cook over a portable stove. A blind seaman taps his way past a succession of municipal buildings. He passes a wall with a bas-relief bust of Odysseus and runs his fingers over its face, as if seeking reassurance.

The chill is deepening. A motorbike hurtles into the backstreets. The sounds of the town band, in rehearsal, can be heard through a second floor window. Dogs roam the darkened alleys. The one waterfront coffee house still open is given over to old men and young travellers. An old drunk feeds his spaniel at a table. He lurches towards me, the spaniel at his heels, and sits down at my table, unbidden.

'I have a cousin living in Melbourne,' he says. 'Fotis Karapangis. The poofter lives near a hotel, not far from the station. The poofter still owes me a fortune. You don't know him? You have never met him? You live in Melbourne and you don't know the useless wanker?'

When I leave the coffee house for my hotel room the drunk stumbles after me, the dog at his heels, yapping, while his master sings his one line ditty, 'You live in Melbourne, and you don't know the poofter?'

———

I set out from the hotel the following morning for the southern tier of the island. Grand aunt Adriani's indifference has unnerved me. My uncle's evasive circling has disarmed me. The old drunkard's accusations pursue me. I have been on the island for three months and I am, after all, *xeni,* an outsider, despite my status as Manoli's daughter. I am *Me ta podia*, the mad one who walks.

I wish to walk out my separateness, but the black-clad women are calling, 'Come! Join us. Master the art of waiting. You are the mirror image of the mother, who is the reflection of her mother, and of her mother's mother, and of all who have gone before you. There is no way out. There is no option, but the waiting.'

I branch off the unpaved road onto a narrow path leading to the fountain of Arethusa. The wooded slopes are bristling with myrtle and junipers. The white cliff known as the Raven's Crag, scoured with veins of ochre, plunges forty metres to an isolated shoreline. I return to the road and approach the red soils of Marathia plateau. A dog trots towards me like a forward scout sent out to investigate. He circles, sniffs at my heels and, as if I have passed the inspection, leads me to a farmhouse.

As we draw closer I hear the frenetic bleating of sheep corralled in a stone shelter. The dog leaves me by the wood-slatted door and runs off as if having completed its mission. The pen is dark, and reeks of damp and manure. The sheep are suckling newborn lambs. A middle-aged couple sit on pile of fodder beside them like doting parents.

'I am the real Odysseus,' the man says, with a mocking smile, as if greeting yet another fool in search of illusions. He has been a shepherd on this cape since childhood, he tells me.

'My mother was a sheep,' he laughs.

'The landscape is beautiful,' I say.

'Yes, very beautiful, at first sight,' he says with indifference, 'but I have seen it too many times.'

I pierce the veil of mist that separates Vathy from the northern heights and arrive back at the hour of siesta. All is quiet except for the beat of the loom. I descend the steps to the *katoi*. The door is wide open, the storeroom lit by a single globe. I stoop to avoid the thick lintel. When I adjust my eyes, I see it is not Ourania who sits at the loom, but a wisp of an old woman, my grand aunt Irini.

'Ah, Manoli's daughter,' she says, when she sees me. She stands up and runs her hands over my face. 'Manoli's daughter,' she repeats, as if in awe of my presence. 'You have come so far to see us.'

Thin as a sapling and growing smaller, Irini's skin is stretched so taut her cheekbones are transparent. She is visiting from her home in Perahori, the Far Village, on the southern tier of the island. Like many women who come to the house, she makes use of one of the few looms that remain intact on Ithaca. Follow the story carefully. This is how ancestors meet and form their unions. Irini is in her seventies, but in an instant she is five, boarding a boat from the mainland town of Zaverda.

'My sister Melita, your grandmother, was seventeen when Stratis came for her as arranged by their families,' she says, 'and he was not much older.' She pauses to retrieve the memory. 'Melita had looked after me since the day I was born. She was twelve years older. I did not want to be parted from her.

'I ran to the boat, as she was about to board, and clung to her skirt. I bit any hand that tried to tear me away and spat at anyone who tried to dissuade me. I finally got what I wanted, and was allowed to go with them. That is how I came to be on Ithaca.

'And I did not mind at all. Three years later, your father was born' she says, and again, reaches out to touch me. 'Stratis was away in *Afstralia* at the time, and Andreas was not yet two. I heard Manoli speak his first words, and saw him take his first steps. I helped look after him in his early years, and I was the first to see him after Melita's death.'

Irini returns to her seat and adjusts the thread. The *katoi* is quiet, except for the sound of her working. Now that I am fully adjusted to the dim light, I see that my grand aunt's eyes are alert with an inquisitive clarity.

'Melita died on an Easter Sunday,' she says, resuming her weaving. 'The bells were tolling the resurrection. Within the hour they were tolling the death of my sister. Manoli woke at dawn and found her cold body beside him. He was ten.

'They would sleep together in the bed that you now sleep in,' she says, and points up at the cypress beams that serve as both a support for the *katoi* ceiling and the floor of the room above us. 'She smelt of lavender and sage, and of sweat and the rocky earth. And on that Easter morning, she smelt of death.

'Manoli ran from the house, screaming. He hid in the chapel of St John, beneath the summit, and did not return until nightfall. From that moment I became Andreas and Manoli's mother. I looked after them for the two years it took Stratis to return from *Australia*.'

Irini pauses. Her bony fingers grasp the yarn she is threading. I am impressed by their agility. She bends to the loom, and, regaining the threads of her thoughts, continues. 'Stratis married again. His second wife was lame. Despina limped into the house on the day of her wedding and stayed there until the day she died. She bore him no children, but looked after the boys. She was pleased to have found a home and a purpose in life.

'In Stratis she had the ideal partner, because he limped to the other side. When they walked the streets together they dipped in opposite directions, then flipped back together like springs.' Irini cackles at the memory. 'Two little springs,' she laughs, 'bobbing side to side.

'After Melita died Manoli was never the same. He fled the house on the day of the wedding, and walked the many miles to Perahori, where I had gone to live with my husband. Manoli wanted to stay with me but Stratis insisted he return. He came all the way to fetch him.

'It was Stratis who had arranged my marriage,' Irini digresses. 'He saw it as his duty to find me a husband before he was free to remarry. The impatient devil wanted a warm body beside him as soon as possible,' she cackles.

'Stratis made inquiries among returned émigrés and presented me with a photo of a young man taken in a Chicago studio. He had amassed a fortune, it was said, as an odd-job man, and was returning to Ithaca to settle in his native village, Perahori. One evening, Stratis and I were out walking when two men appeared, one older, the other younger. Stratis nodded at them and told me one of them would be my husband.

'I liked the look of the young man, but he did not resemble the gentleman in the photo. I followed Stratis' finger closely and saw that he was pointing at his companion. I was to marry a man who was twenty years older. The fortune he was said to have amassed proved to be an illusion. He had squandered much of it playing cards with compatriots. No matter,' Irini shrugs. 'We made a good enough life together.'

My grand aunt stands up and walks towards me. She treads lightly on the rotting boards. On her feet she is an elf who moves like a puff of smoke. 'I saw your father the day he left Ithaca,' she tells me. 'I made my way from Perahori to Vathy to farewell him. I stood on the waterfront with my two children and waved as the boat cast off. For a moment, Manoli looked towards me, but he did not wave back. His thoughts were elsewhere. That was the last time I saw him.'

That is all Irini wishes to say. She reaches up to embrace me. Despite her slender frame, I sense that she possesses the strength of a stem that bends without breaking. Her entire being is tough, but devoid of ambition. She is feather-light. And smells of lavender and sage, and of sweat and the rocky earth.

———

The sky is reddening. A half moon hangs in the mid heavens. The sun is yet to rise over the eastern escarpments. I climb the steep slopes of the Marmakas in the cold shade. When I am halfway up, the dome of the sun finds a gap between two ridges. The Village of the Forty Saints is singed violet. One by one the shutters are being flung open.

As I scale the path I hear the sound of urgent bleating. Costas the shepherd approaches holding a newborn kid by the forelegs. He swings it like a dead rabbit. The kid's mother follows them, distressed by the plight of her offspring. The kid is one day old, Costas tells me. The mother's bells had alerted him to its whereabouts. He is taking it to join the ninety kids enclosed in the stock house to be fattened for days of feasting.

The path narrows near the summit, and veers towards the chapel of St John. A stick of incense burns inside, and I wonder who had made the trek before dawn to light it and decorate the altar with sprigs of sage and basil. A portrait of St John hangs on the wall directly opposite. A shock of black hair tumbles to his shoulders. His eyes are intense, his brows severely arched. He holds a bloodied platter bearing a replica of his head, severed.

Blood begets memories of blood. Manoli is in the backyard slitting a pig's throat, guiding its blood into a bucket. Blood runs from the wounds of beatings, sustained in fratricidal battles. Blood flows in the streets of Athens as the colonels of the junta slaughter their young. And Manoli wakes to the sight of his mother dead in the dawn light. He is running from the house. He leaps over boulders as he scales the steep path. He is running for the white eye of the mountain. He takes refuge beneath the portrait of the saint and, years later, I hastily step into the morning light from the dark chapel.

On my return to the village, the bells of the church begin to toll. An hour later, seated by the fire at breakfast, Andreas tells me, 'Another one of my comrades is gone. Soon there will be no one left. We know nothing about the beginning or the end,' he adds. 'So we should leave them alone.'

———

'When does the Maistros blow?' I ask.

'When it wants to,' says Andreas.

And today it storms. The water rushes through the village. One shutter, left slightly ajar, crashes hard against the window and shatters the pane. The entire island is swaying. Shrubs bending. Trees flailing. Skies moving, changing minute by minute, now black, now thinning to pale blues, returning to black. Dry wells are being replenished. The waters of the Ionian are racing, swelling from island to island, currents charging, splitting, regrouping.

Cousin Andonis has long departed for the oil tankers. Ourania has left for Athens. The *katoi* is silent, the loom covered. The streets are besieged with water. For days on end the storm rages. The house becomes elemental, a shelter. Despite the rot, the beams hold fast. The ancestors built a house, and centuries later it withstands the storm's fury. And two brothers built a tiny kitchen, and decades later its fire holds out against the cold.

> *When does the Maistros blow?*
> *When it wants to?*
> *And when does a man die?*
> *When it is time.*

Andreas' time is not yet up. He moves about the house, from kitchen to living room, from the fire to the bedroom. He lies back and hisses at the ceiling, curses ancient enemies. He dozes, wakes, and returns to the kitchen. His legs are bowed and thinning, his arms shrinking to reeds, but like the house, he holds fast.

Emaciated cats have gathered by the roadside. On the mountain heights newborn kids and lambs huddle at the teats of their mothers. The kids will soon be shepherded into enclosures for slaughter. In a ravine on the upper slopes, a litter of puppies stumbles about blindly, in search of nipples. The bitch searches for them through the streets of the village, her teats bloated.

And Andreas yields. He raises his voice to the edge of anger. 'Why was Manoli so stubborn? Where was he in the dark years of our struggle? Why did he leave me to sail alone? We built a boat called *Brotherly Love* my child, but the love soured. Why does the Maistros blow, because it wants to. Why did Manoli leave? I don't know. How can I know the ways of my brother when it is hard enough to know my own?

'All I can do, is tell the tale:

'Once upon a time there lived two brothers. Manoli and Andreas. When they were born, times were hard. The rocky soil of Ithaca mocked them. Their meagre crops of wheat and corn died of famine. Warring armies cut off the island's trading routes and destroyed its markets. Their father, Stratis, had no choice but to voyage in search of new pastures. He left the oceans far behind him and travelled to an inland city built on red dirt. Three years later he was reunited with his friend Mentor, and together they journeyed east from the desert city, the entire breadth of the land…'

BOOK VII

Mentor's manuscript

MELBOURNE 1917–1967

As I stood with Stratis on the steps beneath the clocks of Flinders Street Station, on a summer morning in February 1917, I was taken by a premonition that I would spend the rest of my days in the city in which I had just arrived.

I had journeyed far enough to know that each place has its peculiar melody, its distinct beat. And on that first morning, it was the tread of many feet—men and women crossing crowded streets, disappearing into arcades, turning into cobbled lanes, vanishing around corners, unbolting shutters, unlocking doors, clattering into emporiums and offices, descending to basements and cellars, taking lifts to upper floors and garrets, on their way to mysterious assignments—that marked the beat of the new song.

I wanted to lose myself in the crowd, to fall into its collective stride, propelled by the momentum of a journey that had conveyed me from the Ionian in blacked-out ships across the hemispheres via war-torn ports, to within sight of a desolate west coast. Then by rail to an inland city built on foundations of red dirt, where the raging mob bayed for our blood, 'Go back to where you fuck'n come from,' forcing us east beside the newly laid tracks of the trans-continental rail. And after many diversions and detours, chance encounters and miscalculations, I now stood on a summer morning on the threshold of a bustling metropolis, and envisioned possibilities I would never have imagined when I scanned horizons from the summit and awaited my father's return.

I glanced at Stratis and knew instantly he had similar thoughts. We burst out laughing and once started, found it difficult to stop. It was Old Niko I recalled as we laughed, leaping to his feet, dancing about the hovel, hands cupped to his ears, bellowing, 'Listen! Listen to the voices of merchants climbing over each other like ants scrambling for air. Cosmos is the most beautiful of words. Cosmos is a straining for perfection out of chaos. Cosmos means harmony, but first we must enter the chaos and withstand the howling of wild dogs.'

The noise of the city brought us back to our senses. I dusted off my jacket, lifted my suitcase and violin, stepped onto the pavement with Stratis, and flagged down a horse-drawn cab. The Gambler was right. I should approach life as a game of cards, accept that all is decided by the roll of the dice, and allow myself to be conveyed through a frenzy of cable trams, hansom cabs, wagons and bicycles, automobiles and pedestrians, one block west, and three blocks north, to the corner of Lonsdale and Elizabeth Streets, where we stepped out, paid the driver and hauled our suitcases up a flight of stairs to the rooms of the Ithacan Club.

Put down your bags, take the weight off your feet, have a slice of halva, a cup of coffee, a glass of wine, the manager urged. The boys will soon be here for lunch. At midday they began to arrive. Compatriots we had last seen in Port Said and Patras, Piraeus, Kalgoorlie, and on the island working limekilns and terraces, making their way to the fishing grounds. Or sitting, as they sat now, among friends, free to curse and call each other wanker, to speak the familiar tongue, free to scheme and lay future plans in the reassuring arms of the brotherhood.

Among them sat Antonios Lekatsas, Mr Lucas, as the many waiters and chefs, accountants, kitchen hands, hostesses and cloak-room attendants on his payrolls, called him. And before the day was out we would be one of them, hired on the spot to work in Cafe Australia, one of the three establishments that Lekatsas owned within walking distance of the club.

Not one to waste time Lekatsas guided us down the stairs, two city blocks south from Lonsdale to Collins Street. Gone was the laboured walk of the mountain boy, and the bow-legged gait of the seaman lurching from port to port. Gone was Antonios Ioannis Gerasimos Lekatsas of Exogi, second child of Ioannis the priest, and his wife Magdalene, grandchild of peasants tethered to the Ithacan earth and fishermen confined to Ionian coasts.

In his place strode Antony John Jereos Lucas, fifty-four years old, hair receding from the temples, a man in his prime, dressed in a pin-striped suit, white tie upon white shirt, fob watch on a gold chain, black shoes polished to a silver glow, a man of many guises: entrepreneur, philanthropist, community dignitary, patron of the arts and orthodox churches, co-founder of the Ithacan Club.

To this day I do not know which of his names to employ. Each has its connotation, each resides in its own universe, and on this first morning as he rushed before us, he alternated between Lekatsas and Mr Lucas, Ithacan compatriot and patron, fellow villager and boss. Stratis and I hurried to keep up as we turned left from Eliza-beth into Collins Street and came to a halt at an arched entrance of white quartz. Lekatsas urged us through glazed-doors into the portal, where we stood in astonishment before a corridor of light.

The light drew us on through the Fountain Court, flanked by three piers with reliefs of bare-breasted Echo, Daphne and Persephone, named in Greek lettering on the pedestals. Before we could take a second breath, Lekatsas was ushering us into the Fern Room, where we sat at circular tables flanked by three columns clad with gold delft tiles, encircling tubs of greenery. Goldfish darted about pools glowing with coloured lights, but before our bums had time to settle, Lekatsas was up and moving, urging us up a marble stairway to the grand Banquet Hall, where the last of the lunch diners sat over the remnants of their meals.

'Tomorrow you will be working,' he said, 'but for now you are my guests. I want you to know what it is to be served, so that you will serve our diners with care and respect.' He clicked his fingers to summon a waiter who relieved us of our jackets and helped us into our seats. He had started here as a waiter, Lekatsas recounted, when the cafe was known as Gunsler's. In 1908 he had bought out the owner, and renamed it the Vienna, a name he would have preferred to retain since it evoked refinement.

The cafe had earned a reputation as the city's choice venue for coffee and dessert. Alas the adopted country was at war with Austria, and in the previous year, drunken soldiers on leave had stoned the entrance and cursed the patrons for dining in a cafe that bore the name of enemies who, at that very moment, were slaughtering their mates.

A master at transforming adversity to advantage, Lekatsas had seized upon the enforced closure and hired the world's best architect, no less, a Mr Walter Burley Griffin, to remodel the cafe. He had spent fifty thousand pounds to make this the premier cafe in the city. The work had been completed the previous November, and the elite of the city had attended the gala opening: politicians, councillors, architects and designers, artists, sculptors, the bohemian set and their entourages. And Nellie Melba, the opera singer, in person,' added Lekatsas, still in awe of the fact.

He had named his new establishment Cafe Australia because, as he now reminded us, we lived in patriotic times and must not bite the hand that feeds us. We should be thankful that with hard work and daring, and by adopting a polite and restrained demeanour, a newcomer could make his way to success.

At two o'clock sharp, as arranged, the Griffins arrived. They strode to our table and, in response to Mr Lucas' introductions, shook our hands. Marion Mahoney Griffin was taller and five years older than her husband, slim and straight-backed, with a sharp nose and an elongated neck. She walked head tilted forward like a spindly waterbird in search of prey. Her eyes were close set and flashed when she spoke. In contrast, dressed in a loose-fitting flannel suit with wide lapels and a knitted silk bow tie, Walter Burley Griffin was quietly spoken, with considered opinions, and at ease with his place in the world.

Despite their differences the couple spoke as one. Ideas poured from them like the spring waters of the Kalamo. I strained to understand their Chicago-accented English, even with Lekatsas' whispered translations. They were democrats they affirmed, and true democracy meant independence of thought. They sought their authority from within, rather than from an imposed external source.

Their preferred clients were people of vision, and the best of clients were newcomers, immigrants willing to take risks.

Adventurous souls like Mr Lucas, who could appreciate beauty, though he had to be cajoled, mind you, over long nights of discussion, until he was won over to their designs.

While war raged their task was to keep the flame of creativity alive. The flame would not, said the Griffins, be extinguished in dark times. Their life's work was the creation of an architecture that would elevate the spirit. We were, despite it all, living in exciting times. Great discoveries were being made in atomic physics, the newest science. Did we know of Einstein and his theories? Everything was interconnected, everything alive: from the human spirit to the raw material of the natural world.

The architectural styles of the past could be adapted to the new world. They had applied these principles, the Griffins claimed, in their grand vision of the nation's new federal capital, Canberra, and this vision had brought them here from Chicago, two years earlier, as winners of an international competition for the coveted job.

Light was the word I heard most frequently in that first encounter. The Griffins were obsessed with light. Light united exteriors and interiors, and allowed the commerce of the streets to flow inside. Light created space, and shed new meaning on the Banquet Hall mural depicting gum trees shrouded in mist. Light filtered through the patterned glass ceilings on the lower level, creating the effect that had so astonished us when we first stepped inside. And the city was cast in afternoon light as Lekatsas ushered us through the arched entrance back into Collins Street.

Within minutes we stood on the threshold of the Paris Cafe. Among the waiters who greeted us were men we had met hours earlier in the Ithacan Club. They glided from room to room, and from table to table, dressed in tuxedos and bow ties. They hovered attentively over the guests in vast dining halls where, said Lekatsas, luncheons, afternoon teas, and three-course dinners were served in the Continental style.

Lekatsas conducted us into rooms reserved for private suppers, where waiters were laying tables for the pre-theatre guests. The walls were lined with mirrors to create an illusion of spaciousness. The silverware, said Lekatsas, had been imported from London and Paris, and the cuisine prepared by a French chef.

Like a man running on needles Lekatsas plunged back into the evening rush. We hurried past the town hall in Swanston Street and extricated ourselves from the throng at the three-storey building directly opposite, emblazoned with letters proclaiming Lucas' Town Hall Cafe. Years later I can still see the displays in the shop-front windows: pyramids of peaches, plums and nectarines, mountains of boiled sweets and chocolates.

The guests were greeted in the foyer by tuxedoed attendants, hostesses in black skirts and white blouses, and by Mrs Margaret Lucas nee Wilson, co-founder and manager of the cafe. A shrewd businesswoman, and the formidable force behind the Lucas empire, she supervised the staff of seventy with a firm hand and a flair for elegance. The Town Hall Cafe was the couple's first venture, opened in 1894, a year after they were wed.

Lekatsas guided us from the foyer into the ground floor cafe in which fruit platters, tea and coffee, ices and summer drinks were being served. A staircase rose from the cafe to the first floor dining hall. We glanced into rooms for ladies only and boudoirs fitted, said Lekatsas, with everything required for a woman's adornment.

We climbed to the top floor and inspected smoking rooms

reserved for gentlemen, and rooms that could be converted at a moment's notice into venues for euchre parties, soirées, club nights and banquets. The three-storey establishment, said Lekatsas, was a palace fuelled by a bakehouse and kitchen, fitted with gas stoves and vast ovens, alongside ice-rooms filled with fruit and provisions for 650 guests, no less.

The secret of his success, Lekatsas proclaimed, was a willingness to spend large sums on renovations that appealed to refined tastes. The Continental cuisine, the table appointments and service, chandeliers and carpets, the string quartets, the elegant attire of the waiters and waitresses, and their unobtrusive presence, said Lekatsas, had placed his three coffee palaces on a par with the world's best.

I could not sleep that night. I lay in bed and replayed the scenes of the past day: arriving on the overnight train from Port Augusta, where we had parted with the Gambler; Stratis and I laughing beneath the station clocks as we surveyed the morning rush; climbing the stairs to the Ithacan Club, its walls lined with prints of familiar hamlets and ports; Lekatsas guiding us through the streets to the gilded reliefs of ancient goddesses in the Cafe Australia; the Griffins' avalanche of ideas and the rapt attention with which Lekatsas listened while simultaneously keeping an eye on his staff; and the wall-mirrors in the Paris Cafe in which I caught my reflection beside Stratis, and saw two sunburnt peasants in weathered suits among well-heeled gentlemen and perfumed ladies out for a night on the town.

And Antony John Jereos Lucas, grandmaster of ceremonies, standing beside Mrs Lucas, his comrade-in-arms, at the door of the Town Hall Cafe, the couple waving as we left, and made our way to the boarding house where we were to spend our first night. As I drifted in and out of sleep, I saw him, Lekatsas, saw the village boy in the man: a triumphant bow-legged goat scrambling to the summit, scaling miraculous heights.

The meeting with the Griffins remained firmly in mind when I began work the following day. From time to time, the couple made their way from their offices in Collins Street to the Banquet Hall. They sat for hours with Lekatsas and discussed future plans. I was surrounded by their creations.

Every morning I stepped through the glazed doors and walked the corridor of light. Each object had been designed by the Griffins: the balustrades and chinaware, ventilators and menu cards, the high-backed chairs composed of rectangles, the tables of native timbers, dark stained blackwood in preference to oak; and the blue tiles and black granite that flanked the arched entrance.

The couple inspired me to learn English quickly. I strolled to the State Library after work and bent over the writings to which they had directed me. There were times when, frustrated by the limits of my untrained mind, I almost wept at not being able to decipher their meaning. I assembled Greek–English dictionaries and kept notebooks in which I scribbled new words and phrases. I studied lists of vocabulary by the kitchen table in the boarding house late into the night.

It was a fifteen-minute walk from the cafe to the wrought iron gates of the library. I ascended the stone steps from the forecourt to the columned portico, stepped into the foyer, and climbed a flight of marble stairs to the reading room. From the moment I stepped in I felt an uncanny sense of familiarity. I climbed the cast iron staircase that spiralled from the floor to the upper galleries, and leaned on the balustrades.

The room was laid out in a perfect octagon. Eight elongated spokes of oak, lined with desks, extended from the central rotunda to the book-lined walls. Three smaller desks made up the spaces between each spoke. The four entrances were equidistant, as if placed at the major points of the compass. The base of the dome contained sixteen portholes, two to each side of the octagon. Daylight streamed through the glass-panelled portholes, casting pools of light over the linoleum far below.

I lifted out books at random, took them to the oak desks, opened them out on black-leather writing-pads, and settled back in an adjustable chair. In time, sentences, paragraphs and entire chapters began to reveal their meanings. A new language was taking shape, a language that for many months had seemed beyond reach.

I moved from the few works written by the Griffins to volumes devoted to architecture. I battled through papers depicting the rise of the new sciences, elated with the idea that matter and energy were one. I leaned close to the books and sniffed the scent of times long past. I read as the sun streamed through individual portholes and rendered the pages golden. I read until day gave way to pools of amber cast by shaded globes, and, lifting my head, saw that the skylights were covered in night.

I left the reading room and wandered the streets of the city. I allowed myself to be swept along by the throng streaming to and from theatres and movie houses, coffee palaces and dance halls. I paused to listen to preachers who spoke of apocalypse and eternal damnation, and marvelled at their venom. I threw coins into the violin case of a street musician, and made out the motifs of ancient architectures woven into the buildings. The new city, I now understood from my reading, was composed of the accumulated visions of ages past.

Whenever I returned to the domed room I was assailed by the sense of familiarity I had felt when I first stepped in. One afternoon, as I lifted my head after hours of study, it occurred to me that the ascending galleries were an inversion of the terraced landscapes to which I had been born, and the shelves of books that lined them, pathways to the heights. The portholes were telescopes that illumined the oak and linoleum, just as the Ithacan sun spotlighted tiled roofs and bell towers in its daily passage over the slopes.

The ground-floor desks seemed as far from the dome's apex as the lower hamlets from the summit, and the bas-reliefs on the balconies as intricate as the impressions created by wind-blown olives. The entire dome was a giant brain vaulting to the heavens, and the panelled skylights the membrane of the summit. In that moment the idea, or call it illusion, took hold: I had found my way back to the mountain. I had returned home.

—————

Stratis and I moved to a rooming house in Gertrude Street, twenty minutes' walk from the cafe, and he occasionally read beside me beneath the dome. We were united in our passion for knowledge, but there was one vital difference between us. Stratis' wife and two boys remained on the island. It was his unspoken burden. His longing could be triggered at any time. The sight of a father playing with his sons, a family strolling on a summer night, or children at play in the alleys unnerved him. 'One more damned year,' he would mutter, 'and I will return.'

He moved from job to job, from building sites to restaurants. As soon as he accumulated capital, he set himself up in a small business: a fruit stand at the Victoria market, a milk bar in Fitzroy, a small cafe in Elizabeth Street. The pendulum swung between small fortunes won and small fortunes lost. There were times, after losing out on one of his ventures, when his eyes betrayed his panic. He would lie in bed for days before regaining his composure. 'One more damned year,' he slurred, like a punch-drunk boxer rising from the canvas.

He was not alone. Each of us separated from family approached it in our own way. Some lost themselves in the company of friends in the rooms of the brotherhood. There were those who kept mistresses and frequented brothels. There were those who disappeared with their second 'wives', and those who vanished without trace. There are details I do not wish to divulge. Why blacken the names of families who were later reunited? Why disturb the ghosts of those who did what many others would have done in their place?

I did not share Stratis' burden. In those early years I was a single man, free to roam the city. I walked to and from the library, as if weightless. I was addicted to the dome and to the Griffins, and elated whenever I saw them. Lekatsas allowed me to sit with them when most of the diners had gone. I rose through the ranks to chef and, as my English improved, doubled as a waiter when the dining halls were full.

The Griffins increasingly spoke of their disillusion with the Canberra project. While Mr Griffin retained his calm manner, and his wife, seethed with anger, the couple still spoke as one. Their battle with politicians and the bureaucrats of the public works office had reached boiling point. Her husband had been pushed aside, said Mrs Griffin, and his plans had been ignored in favour of jealous rivals, mediocre men.

As their frustration grew the couple turned their attention to a new project, to be financed by Lekatsas and his business partners. A theatre would be built on the site of Lucas' Town Hall Cafe, and housed in a ten-storey office building. They would name the building and theatre, the Capitol, as an act of revenge on those who had dismissed Griffin's centrepiece in his design for Canberra. It would be, as the Capitol was intended to be, a place of popular assembly in the heart of the city.

On a spring afternoon in 1921, the Griffins swept into the Banquet Hall bearing the first plans for the new venture. Lekatsas directed me to polish one of the tables and when I was done, Mrs Griffin unfurled the drawings with a flourish that brought to mind Old Niko unfurling maps on the rickety table in his hovel.

That first afternoon established the ritual, and over the following three years it was repeated many times: the couple striding into the hall, Mrs Griffin, eyes intent, leaning forward, in her gangly walk. Mr Griffin outwardly calm, containing his elation in his purposeful steps. The drawings unfurling over the glowing black-wood, Lekatsas and his partners surveying the latest plans.

Like sea hawks zeroing in on their prey, the designs targeted ever-smaller details: foyers, balconies, ladies boudoirs and men's smoking rooms, the proscenium arch and orchestra pit, fire escapes, mezzanines. And smaller objects: lamps of crystal, curtains and pelmets, glass insets, window frames and brackets. Each element, stressed the Griffins, was of equal value, an integral part of the whole.

I hovered on the edge of the inner circle, never quite of it, but an accepted presence, infected by the madness. The Griffins and their business partners were moulding a city, a cosmos. And I was journeying with them, shadowing their moves, absorbing their vision. My understanding of architectural terms expanded as my lists of vocabulary grew. I committed drawings to memory and sketched them at the oak desks of the reading room. It seemed to me that the plans were founded on pure geometries: triangle, circle, square and hexagon, arc and rectangle.

The drawings were a conduit between dream and reality, between the vision and its execution, and, a mere five-minute walk from the Banquet Hall they were being shaped into certainties. I walked past the site, to and from work, and saw the mystery unfolding. First the foundations and ground floor, then six massive piers rising day by day, the full ten storeys, terminating at the roof in elongated balconies capped by a cornice.

The concrete structure completed, the work continued within, spiralling back as I pictured it, through a maze of staircases, and foyers, corridors, lift wells and alcoves, to lounges and boudoirs, dressing rooms and box offices, and the many smaller spaces I had seen in the drawings. All this was the frame to the centrepiece, the outer garment to the building's inner climax—the grand auditorium.

The plans continued to unfurl in more minute detail: drawings of floor coverings, decorative doors, ornamented piers and column necking, with pencilled instructions prescribing colours and materials: copper strips, frosted glass, sheet metal, leadlight, plaster of Paris.

One design in particular caught my attention, a balcony escape to Swanston Street. At first I was drawn to the fine black lines of the illustration. Each step was numbered, and each flight curved from landing to landing. I sat at the oak desks and sketched them many times over, along with drawings of other stairways designed by the Griffins: rising from the foyer to the balcony, from street to foyer, from auditorium aisle to landing.

Then, as if superimposed on the architectural drawings, there emerged the outline of a flight of steps I had once known. It rose from the earth to the edge of a precipice. As I drew, the memory returned, and with it the fine detail. The stairway gave way, on one side, to the slopes of the mountain, and on the other, to a rock face.

I lay in bed that night and recalled the indentations, the slight twist in the steps, and the abrasive rock surface. I cannot remember at what point my waking state gave way to reverie, but years later, in the depths of my crisis, I would come to know what I experienced that night as lucid dreaming. I would understand that within us there exist labyrinths, inversions of staircases spiralling within, drawing us back to buried memories, and lost homelands.

I clambered over the steps and rediscovered their textures: the film of moss on the stone, an orchid breaking through the soil, mauve cyclamens sprouting from cracks in rock faces. The earth was ripe with the pulp of figs and the shrivelled skins of fallen olives. A lizard basked in the sun, tongue flicking, green scales throbbing. I slid down to the lower slopes and took in the entire site, the remnants of walled courtyards and ancient rock formations; the corroded remains of extinct civilisations.

On the detritus of the older city stood a church, recently abandoned. The roof was on the verge of collapsing, and the doorsteps sprouted a profusion of wild grasses. In the surrounds, jutting through the undergrowth, lay the moss-stained remains of three gravestones, and, within the dream itself, there returned my father's tale of the priest who was buried here beside his wife and son.

The priest, it was said, had unearthed many treasures buried beneath the church grounds, and had sold them on the antiquities market in Paris and London. Due to his illicit dealings he had damned himself, some villagers claimed, and was made to endure the death of his son. In telling the tale my father had instilled in me a fear of the price I would pay for acts of desecration.

I was now aware I was dreaming, and sensed that if I maintained the fragile balance between sleep and wakefulness, I would continue walking about the island at will, see what I wished to see, and encounter whomever I wanted to encounter. I knew also that with one lapse in concentration, one moment of overreaction or excitement, I would lose the fragile balance.

I willed myself to return to the stone steps and saw them anew, saw they were a continuation of steps buried. I willed myself to see the night falling, the crescent moon rising, until beside me, on one of the steps, stood Stratis. In one hand he held the Circassian dagger my father had brought back from his Black Sea voyages and, in the other, a bottle of wine he had syphoned from the barrel in the *katoi*.

With a lucidity that was clearer than memory, I saw the blade slice our thumbs, our blood oozing; and Stratis was ascending, pausing on the highest step, leaning over and daring himself to fall over the precipice, and I was dragging him back, drunk and doubled up with laughter.

We chased each other through the ruins, cut through the

undergrowth to the mule path, climbed to the village, and dashed up the steps between the houses. We scaled them in search of our homes, the concealed valley, and the windmills near the summit. Yet with each step upwards the stairway extended further, and just as I thought I had sighted their ending, another flight appeared in a never-ending escalation. In my frustration I lost concentration, and awoke to a sense of longing.

And decades later as I recall these events, the months and years are collapsing, and I am approaching the Capitol Theatre with Stratis, on 8 November 1924, the night of the grand opening. The city is alive with weekend revelry, the crowd thronging between the Melbourne Town Hall and the new building. Stratis and I are stepping in from the pavement, climbing the stairway beneath a glowing ceiling to the entrance foyer.

Each space flowed from one to the other, from the ground floor up a flight of steps through an archway into the stalls-lobby, from a gilt dome flanked by columns up a second flight of stairs into the dress circle foyer. For a moment, I was detached from the crowd, diverted by the gilded grand piano and bas-relief sculptures, the ornate fireplace and sofas. I was drawn back into the drift of collective chatter, and moved with the crowd up a final flight of stairs from the dress circle to the upper stall's foyer, and through one last entrance into the auditorium.

I will never forget the collective sigh of astonishment at the sight before us. The ceiling was bursting with coloured lights on the inverted steps of a ziggurat, inspired, as the Griffins had pointed out, by the hall of the two sisters, in twelfth-century Alhambra of the Moors, in the city of Granada. The upper walls erupted from the balcony piers in crystalline shapes; and the ceiling lights within recesses radiated the full colour spectrum. The lights finally dimmed to darkness, drawing our attention to the proscenium arch and rising curtain.

The Wurlitzer organ gave way to an overture performed by a live orchestra. The score rose from the pit to a screen bearing Cecil B De Mille vistas of the pyramids. The waters of the Red Sea were parting for the fleeing Israelites, before crashing down on the pursuing army.

Looking back on the night of the opening many years later, I see a continuous movement through civilisations, a contraction of time and space, from dreams of Ithaca and its buried cities, to the brilliantly lit foyers of the newly built theatre, from the auditorium and its pulsating ceilings, to panoramas of biblical Egypt and the austere mountains of the Sinai Desert.

And I see that the opening night marked the end of a time that had begun on the day of my arrival, when I stood with Stratis on the steps beneath the clocks of Flinders Street Station. Just days after we stepped out of the Capitol Theatre from the premiere screening of De Mille's *Ten Commandments*, Stratis received the cable that informed him of the sudden death of his wife, Melita.

I walked the streets that night with Stratis. The city was now cast in a darker light. The theatres and cinemas were long closed, the dance halls and tearooms barred and padlocked. Ghostly faces lurched in and out of the shadows. We had stumbled upon a netherworld of nightwalkers, a veiled city within a city peopled by a generation of lost souls: soldiers returned from the Great War, men old before their time, defeated.

Even as I write, years later, the anger returns, an anger first awakened by the death of my father and the ranting of Old Niko, anger at what is consigned to the margins, to fringe worlds peopled by the warped and wounded. Young men deformed by the dictates of war and the fateful decisions made by others. For hours Stratis and I walked with them, kindred spirits in a battalion of the sleepless, men on crutches, men trembling with the enduring agony of shellshock and gas poisoning. We moved through the streets of the inner city, back to the epicentre, the steps of Flinders Street Station where, sitting beneath the clocks, Stratis finally wept.

———

Stratis' grief was the prelude to a greater crisis years later. In the meantime I held on to the fringes of the brotherhood, sat in on card games in the clubrooms, played the fiddle at Ithacan weddings, and rose through the ranks to become a leading chef in Lekatsas' coffee palaces; while late at night I continued to walk the streets of the city with Stratis to keep him company in his time of mourning.

We came to know individual faces, regulars who clung to their haunts: a particular arcade, a wooden bench outside St Paul's Cathedral, a sheltered recess in a laneway, a stretch of lawn beneath Princes Bridge on the riverbank. And they came to know us, and responded with quiet acknowledgment or brief conversation, as we passed by on our way to our haunt, beneath the clocks on the steps of the station.

After one last year of labour, one last tilt at raising his savings, Stratis made preparations for his return. I have neglected my boys long enough, he announced. I helped him pack three wooden trunks with the books he had collected in his fifteen-year sojourn: encyclopaedias, almanacs, guides to animal husbandry, medical dictionaries, books that we had discussed and argued over, volumes that would, claimed Stratis, reform the ways of the village.

I accompanied him from the boarding house to the port, and stood beside the customs sheds on Station Pier as the ship departed. In the clarity that comes at moments of departure, I saw how much he had aged, his premature greyness, his resigned steps as he climbed the gangway. I also observed his proud bearing, hard-won from his journeys, and the sigh of relief that seemed to envelop him now that the ropes were being hurled from their moorings. He was regaining the oceans. Returning to Ithaca.

I returned months later, to the same pier, and stood with the crowd, waiting to greet new arrivals. Men paced the timber boards as the ship drew closer. They scanned the decks for the wives and children they had not seen for years, and for the first sight of brides they had never met. Among them, Fotini, the stranger I had, at the urging of a cousin, agreed to marry.

And despite the strangeness of our union, our unexpected passion and hunger for company deflected me into a new orbit. I abandoned the reading room, the book-lined galleries of the inverted mountain, and my single-minded pursuit of knowledge, in exchange for the euphoria that accompanied the births of my son, Demos, and daughter, Sophia.

Life was moving ahead of me and I hurried to keep up, to and from the cafe and the club, to and from baptisms, marriages and community gatherings, to the post office to receive letters from Stratis bearing news of his remarriage, and of his boys, Andreas and Manoli. And the rare letter from the Gambler.

He was still following his immigrant brothers, from Port Augusta to the opal mines of Coober Pedy, from the cane fields of Northern Queensland to the abattoirs of Darwin. From the eating-houses of Broome frequented by pearl divers, to gangs of itinerant farmhands moving from station to station. Wherever he journeyed he set up card tables tempting men to overnight fortunes or instant ruin. And he returned, every year or so to the gambling houses of Sydney and Melbourne, and to the rooms of the Ithacan Club where I saw him holding court, spinning the latest instalment of his journeys, filling in time between his seasonal wanderings.

To curb my restlessness, I built a workshop in the backyard and in my spare hours constructed violins. Every year, on their birthdays, I took my son and daughter to a photographer's studio, where they posed, violins raised to their collars, in front of a stream flanked by willows and eucalypts. And in the endless recycling of days I did not perceive the gravity of my five-year-old son's illness. I relied, instead on the reassuring words of the physician. He was suffering from one of the usual ailments, he claimed, a common cold, a touch of fever. He did not see that Demos' brain was on fire, his life ebbing.

Ti na kanoume? Ti na kanoume? the black-clad women chanted. What can we do? What can we do? And they drew Fotini to them to keep her from falling, and restrained her as she tore at her hair and howled over the coffin. And they returned night after night along with workers from the cafe, men from the club, compatriots from Ithaca and the Seven Islands of the Ionian, and from towns and villages scattered throughout the mainland. They commandeered the kitchen and living room, and filled the house with food and talk, and their constant presence. They sought to obliterate the dangers posed to distressed souls by prowling demons, the threat of solitude and melancholia.

Fotini and I moved about the crowded house as strangers. We could not look each other in the eye. We interrogated ourselves with the eternal question: why? Why? Why didn't we do more, why were we not alert? Why had we forsaken the island only to lose our first-born child? We were gripped by grief, unable to breathe, unable to sleep, barely able to ride out the night and withstand the mocking daylight. I saw Demos in a dream, and for a moment believed he was alive. I awoke to the sight of Fotini, burning incense at her makeshift altar, rocking back and forth in violent prayer, and did not know how to console her.

I left our Brunswick house and walked towards the inner city, by way of Sydney Road, through the darkened grounds of the University. The sandstone buildings were enveloped in silence, the residence halls concealed in shadow. I continued on Swanston Street, past the bluestone brewery where the smokestacks were still belching. The all night inferno marked the edge of the inner city, one block removed from my destination, and like a homing pigeon I found myself, pre-dawn, climbing the steps to the library forecourt.

I sat back on the cold stone against one of the columns, and gave way to a fitful dozing, interrupted by the sounds of the city awakening. Hours later, after the sun had risen and the doors opened to the public, I climbed the marble stairway to the upper landing, and, for the first time in years, stepped into the reading room.

Following a familiar script I picked out books at random, and leafed through the pages, but I could not bear to read them. Bent over the books I fell into a deep sleep for the first time in many weeks, and woke, hours later, disoriented. The dome was whirling, the book galleries spinning. On the podium in the rotunda sat an attendant, keeping an eye on the readers. I was back in the inverted mountain, free to silently weep and dream, propelled by an aching longing to retrieve Demos.

I resumed my search with greater deliberation. The books were an excuse, a cover for my real purpose. I kept them before me so as not to be ejected from the library as a vagrant. I looked at them as if reading, closed my eyes and took in the sounds: a door closing, the echo of laughter, the collective hum that graces public places. Soon I was descending, spiralling from wakefulness to dreaming, returning to the ruins of Homer's School. I surveyed the weathered walls, the stone stairway and the three tombstones jutting through the undergrowth. I had regained the state of lucid dreaming, that fragile balance between awareness and sleep, consciousness and reverie.

Heart pounding, I set out in search of Demos. I found him standing on the stone staircase, on the upper platform. I dashed up the steps to snatch him away from the precipice, and in my excitement, lost the fragile balance, and woke to the books open before me. Despite the brevity of the encounter, I was certain that with practice I would extend my conscious dreaming.

I left my job at the cafe and put my affairs in order. I had accumulated enough money to see my family through a year or two. I returned, day after day to the domed room, and as soon as I entered I followed the same procedure. I retrieved books from the shelves, opened them out on the oak desk, and bent forward as if reading. I closed my eyes, and soon I was descending, spiralling back to the illumined landscape.

On each descent I held the dream a little longer, and on each landing I located Demos a little sooner. The doors of memory had been prised open and I was overtaken by a whirl of images. I glimpsed Demos in the backyard shed, and saw him bent over on a winter's day, inspecting the stormwater drain, wondering where the torrent of rainwater had vanished.

I found him in the rooms of the Ithacan Club, passing from table to table, feted and embraced in the arms of the brotherhood. I stood by his side at the front window of the house in Brunswick and watched hailstones plummeting to the road and front garden. The sky was an eerie grey, the street lit by flashes of lightning. We hurried outside during a lull in the storm, gathered the hailstones and scooped them into our mouths before they melted.

As if detached from my own being, I observed him seated on my shoulders as I carried him through the streets, teaching him to count by the numbers of the houses, odd numbers on one side, evens on the other. I came across him sitting on the stone steps of the ruins and, moments later, on the doorstep of our house in Brunswick. As I had when he was alive, I sensed his solitude, his evolving awareness of life's mysteries and terrors.

The images lingered long after I woke and, like a film restarting, resumed as soon as I returned to the ruins. With each descent the images were more lucid, and with each awakening, the words in the books before me, clearer. My eyes inadvertently took in individual sentences and, in time, entire passages. My passion for knowledge edged back. I sought out books that probed the mysteries of sleep and dreaming, and I drew up lists of words that depicted states of the psyche: hallucination, fantasy, hysteria, apparition and trance, phantasm and delusion, automatism, delirium.

Again I agonised at the impossibility of becoming fluent in the new language, my limits as a self-taught man, but each term added a little to my understanding. I was regaining my will, propelled by an urgent need to know the workings of the mind, and the indifferent logic of fate. But as if mocking my efforts, with each successive descent the pain of longing intensified. The images of Demos were inextricably linked to the landscapes of Ithaca. There were times when I awoke short of breath and perspiring, and doubly cursed as I realised that I had been wrenched away from both my son and my childhood landscapes.

I made inquiries at the offices of shipping companies into the cost of passage to Ithaca. I wrote to Stratis and announced I would soon be joining him. I sketched designs of the marble I would lay on my mother's grave to replace the stone that Stratis was tending in my absence.

Fotini dragged me back to earth. Never before had she raised her voice in anger. 'Our son was buried in Australian soil,' she shouted. 'We are duty bound to tend his grave, to light the lamps and erect a stone, and to replace the wilting flowers. To leave him would be a betrayal. It is our sacred duty to preserve Demos' memory.'

With my way back to Ithaca barred, I panicked. Fotini and I were condemned to remain on foreign soil. I now understood that nostalgia was an infernal ache. 'We must dissect words to know their essence,' Old Niko had shouted. I located the word in dictionaries of etymology and traced its origins to a Swiss doctor named Johannes Hoffer. In 1678 Hoffer had coined the term after learning of the strange illness of a student from the city of Berne. While studying in Basel the young man began pining for home. His illness became so severe he was on the brink of dying. When told he was being sent back to Berne his condition improved, and by the time he was on his way home, he had fully recovered.

Hofer named the condition nostalgia, derived from the Greek *nostos,* the return, and *algos,* meaning pain: the pain of longing for the return. It was an affliction of the imagination, a disease of both body and spirit. Doctors identified the symptoms as a ringing in the ears, wandering pains in the body, palpitations, paleness in the complexion, severe headaches and high fever.

As the condition deepens, the patient is overwhelmed by involuntary images of the homeland. Some are driven to bouts of insanity and delirium. Soldiers fighting in foreign lands were said to have died from the disease. Entire battalions were infected, especially after incurring losses in battle, and recovered on being told they were to be discharged and sent home. Inmates of prisons, exiles and refugees, those who could not return to their native lands, were doubly afflicted.

There were some who saw it as a nervous disorder, or an aberration of memory. Others argued it was an indulgence, and urged the afflicted to fight against the invasion of their memories. I did not care for the disputes. My nostalgia was a living reality, and my lucid dreaming, a state more enticing than wakefulness. Resorting to forgetting, as some doctors advised, was an act of betrayal. I wanted to fuse the past with the present, and to move at will between them.

As in earlier years, I wandered the city after the library closed and allowed myself to be swept along by the evening crowd. Images of Demos and the Ithacan landscape invaded my waking state. I followed an infant walking hand-in-hand with his father, hoping he would lead me to Demos. The borders between reality and dream were collapsing. The sight of a bluestone wall gave way to lucid images of walls on the site of Homer's School. Flights of stairs to the entrances of cathedrals metamorphosed into the flights of stone steps in the ruins. In my delirium I saw the streets as passages, running between stairways leading from cave-like entrances to the hidden labyrinths of the city.

I stepped from the pavement into a vestibule, climbed a flight of wooden steps and found myself in a theatre foyer. I purchased a ticket and was ushered to a seat in the darkened auditorium. The curtains parted to an oasis of palms, hanging over the walls of an oriental courtyard. A train of camels was silhouetted on dunes rising on a desert horizon. The scene, stage-lit, appeared as luminous as the landscapes of my lucid dreaming. A magician, dressed in a robe stepped onstage to an oriental melody played by a flautist.

I cannot recall the acts performed that evening, nor the names of the performers. It was the first of many shows I would attend over the years. The acts have coalesced into a succession of crystal gazers and flame eaters, contortionists, card sharks, ventriloquists and vaudevillians, crooners, conjurers, clairvoyants and cancan choruses. Apparitions stepped in and out of elongated mirrors, and a woman in a white gown levitated in a horizontal position. The head of a girl was severed and restored, a silk scarf transformed into doves and parrots.

A magician danced with a skeleton, while a gold-eyed owl perched on his shoulders. A semi-naked fakir swallowed a length of thread and packet of loose needles, and regurgitated them neatly strung together. Flowers were propelled from paper cones, and single seeds planted in wooden boxes, grew before our eyes into trees dripping with oranges. Cards disappeared up sleeves and reappeared from vest pockets. Kings of hearts were transformed into jokers, and aces took flight and changed direction. Mind readers located nominated cards blindfolded, and exposed the thoughts of audience members.

At some point during that first performance I snapped out of my stupor. I shifted my focus from the stage to the audience, surveyed the spectators, and observed their varying states of scepticism and surrender. I saw how desperately they wanted to be lifted out of the ordinary. I saw how much they yearned to return to a state of childhood, and imagined Demos viewing the performance. He was seated on the front steps as I had so often seen him, in awe at life's mysteries, and I understood he had lived long enough to sense the wonder, yet not long enough to be disillusioned.

By the time I left the theatre I felt a sense of composure I had not experienced for months. The performance had broken the spell of my illusions, and hinted at my future vocation. It allowed me to discern the fine distinction between dream and reverie, appearance and suggestion.

One practice in particular drew my attention. From the moment I saw it performed I sensed that hypnosis, like lucid dreaming, was a means of accessing lost landscapes. I had climbed the stairs in a delirium and left, hours later, with the first inklings that I could help others afflicted by grief and nostalgia.

The following morning I returned to the domed room with renewed purpose. I located books on the art of conjuring, magician's manuals, performers' memoirs, entire volumes devoted to mind-reading and hypnosis. I was still assailed by attacks of panic at the loss of Demos. It could not be otherwise. Yet there were extended periods of clarity, and, moments beneath the dome, when the rays of the sun finding a way through a porthole fell on an open page. And in the glow there was warmth and sustenance, and the elation that accompanies new understandings.

I was particularly drawn to the writings of Robert-Houdin, the legendary father of modern magic. I devoured every line of his writings. He had founded a theatre in Paris in 1845, where he performed with the use of mechanical devices, called 'automata', that he had designed and constructed.

In his memoir he paid homage to his mentors, and the magicians who had preceded him, and in his manuals he passed on his experience and knowledge to future performers. He was an actor playing the part of a magician, he wrote, a showman as much as illusionist, the son of a watchmaker, who strove for precision. He elevated magic from the fairground to the theatre, and acted the role of scientific lecturer to distract the audience from his deceptions.

Inspired by his writings, I formed the delusion that I could make a living as a stage-performer. I bought juggling balls, silver hoops and trick ropes, and whiled away many hours in the backyard shed practising the deft movements required for sleight of hand. I attended meetings of the Australian Society of Magicians and met both seasoned performers and amateurs. I had deserted the Ithacan brotherhood for a fraternity of tricksters, lured by their passion for the mind.

Inevitably I met Will Alma, the most well-known of Melbourne magicians, an expert wood turner, electronics maestro, and perfectionist. Alma invited me to his business in South Melbourne, and took me on a tour of his props workshop.

He had been born to a family of magicians, he recounted. His father toured Australia as Pharos the Magician, accompanied by his wife, the Floating Lady. Pharos disappeared on tour and abandoned the Floating Lady and the infant Will. Alma's mother forbade him to follow in his father's footsteps, but the lure of the stage was far greater. He performed card tricks at the age of fourteen at a church concert and knew instantly that it was his calling. The Floating

Lady gave him a hiding, but the Amazing Will Alma was on his way. He toured the rural circuits, performed in the capital cities, and learnt many times over that an audience prefers to be mystified rather than enlightened.

All the while Alma was enticing me with his products. The display window of his shop was neatly arranged with meticulously crafted models of illusions: an electric chair, a guillotine, a woman suspended on the tip of an upright sword, a false-bottomed cabinet. By the time I left, I had placed orders for a kit of tools and Alma's levitation apparatus.

I stumbled out weighed down by books and manuals, a human skull, a disembodied hand, a magician's baton, and instructions on how to construct a performance. Alma had advised me to specialise in skills that matched my temperament. I should first adopt a stage name, and in choosing the name I would be able to construct monologues that cloaked my deceptions. I should order the sequence of acts accordingly, and complement the script with a matching backdrop.

I knew immediately what the backdrop should be. I drew outlines and commissioned a stage artist to paint it. I spent my dwindling resources on materials and worked for months on set constructions. Against the fierce protestations of Fotini, I trained Sophia as an assistant. She was seven years old, young enough to enter into the performance with a child's innocence, yet old enough to acquire the skills with practice.

After a year of preparation, I hired a city theatre and an assistant, and engaged a veteran vaudevillian, George D'Albert, to provide comic relief. D'Albert had not performed for years and was grateful for work at a time when, due to the rising popularity of cinema, vaudeville was on the wane.

The entire Ithacan brotherhood made its way from the club-rooms to attend the opening performance. Mentor has lost his senses they whispered, as they milled about the foyer. The death of his son has pushed him over the precipice. But I remained certain that even the sceptics would be impressed by the backdrop.

When the curtains parted, the theatre was plunged into dark-ness. Standing in the wings I heard the first gasps of recognition, as the spot-lit backdrop unravelled like a scroll of parchment. The artist had, as directed, painted a hamlet of stone houses, huddled on the slopes of a mountain, not far from the summit. A sea hawk hovered over the panorama, scanning the landscape. In the fore-ground, Hellenic walls rose from the undergrowth, in the shadows of a cypress grove. A flight of stone steps ascended against a rock face leading nowhere, and beyond the slopes, stretched the sea and the skies of twilight.

I allowed the audience time to take in the scene before making my entrance. Emulating engravings depicting Robert-Houdin in performance, I had oiled my hair and parted it down the middle. Dressed in tails and dark grey trousers, a light grey vest, and a bow tie over a starched white shirt, I attempted to assume his easy manner. I was acutely aware of my foreign accent and hoped that it would add, as Alma had assured me, an exotic touch to my stage persona.

Ignoring the undercurrent of ridicule I addressed the audience: 'Tonight we will witness the wonders of the mind. We will redis-cover the power of dreaming and come to understand that we live in a world of illusions. We will retrace our childhood landscapes and explore the wisdom of the ancients.'

I introduced my stage-name, Asklepios, the god of healing. For two millennia, healing sanctuaries known as Asklepeions were scattered throughout the Hellenic world. 'In times of crisis and illness,' I continued, 'patients undertook pilgrimages to the sanctuaries, and placed themselves in the care of *therapeutes*.

'The sanctuaries were a retreat from the frantic pursuits of daily life. Massage, bathing, performances of music and drama, quietened the soul and brought patients into a unity of mind, body and spirit. When the patients were considered ready, the *therapeutes* would usher them into sleeping caves known as *abatons*. The ancients understood the healing potential of dreaming,' I contended, 'but all that remains of the sanctuaries are the ruins you see behind me.'

Wearing a white dress, Sophia skipped onto the stage and lay down on the floorboards. I covered her with a silk sheet and at the command of my baton she rose horizontally. I kept her suspended on the silk sheet, waist height, for several seconds, parallel to the stone steps in the backdrop. As I drew the sheet away, Sophia vanished mid-air, as if propelled into the skies beyond the precipice.

Invented at the turn of the century by the Belgian magician, Servais Leroy, the Garden of Sleep, as the act was called, was an illusion dependent on wire supports and special lighting. I was relieved that despite the creaking of the wires, the illusion seemed to have been performed without mishap. I resumed my monologue, expounding the power of hypnosis.

'Hypnotism is a science,' I insisted, 'and as science it is subject to investigation and an ongoing exploration of the subtle distinctions between levels of consciousness. Recent advances in the science of hypnosis,' I declared, 'confirmed what has been intuited and practised by the ancient *therapeutes*.'

On cue, my assistant stepped from the wings with a caged bantam. When the bantam stumbled onto the boards, the audience broke into laughter. Undaunted, I hypnotised the bird by drawing a straight line before it. Within seconds the bird toppled over. The laughter grew louder. Observing my predicament George D'Albert bounded on stage. He launched into a routine of jokes and impersonations and made it seem that my act had been planned as a comedy.

When D'Albert completed his performance, the theatre was again plunged into darkness. A black curtain concealed the Ithacan backdrop and my assistant, dressed in black, to render him invisible, finalised the props for the next item. The stage was dimly lit with blue footlights. By my side stood a barrel. I rolled it forward and invited a member of the audience to confirm it was empty.

The lights were dimmed further, and with a wave of the white baton, I drew out the hypnotised bantam. Again, the show threatened to turn into fiasco. Working fast to stifle the laughter, I drew out a skeleton and danced it across the stage, followed by a succession of violins. The instruments floated to the wings and vanished. I upturned the barrel to show it was empty and when I placed it upright, Sophia jumped out and bowed to the audience.

After an intermission, I stepped back on stage and lectured on the science of mind-reading, then distributed six envelopes to members of the audience, and asked them to seal a small object inside them. 'Psychometry,' I intoned, 'is the art of divining facts about its owner from an object.' I instructed my assistant to blindfold me. He handed me the envelopes and I identified the contents of each one—coins, a purse, a business card, a page from a notebook—and described the person who had sealed it.

It was not difficult to perform the deception. I had long rehearsed the association-of-ideas method of remembering appearance, and the envelopes contained nicks in a pre-determined order that enabled me to deduce who had received them.

After one last interlude from George D'Albert, I returned to the stage for the finale. In my right hand I held the baton, and on the palm of my left, the skull. 'Since time immemorial,' I declared, 'mankind has struggled against the forces of evil.' My assistant appeared through a plume of smoke, in a red cape and black tights. Horns protruded from a mask. Flexing his muscles, the devil knelt down, and drew a pistol.

Before he was able to pull the trigger, there appeared a spotlight on the rafters. It followed Sophia as she descended to the stage dressed as an angel. I hoped the ropes were adequately disguised by their blackness. Sophia landed at my side. The devil wavered. I stood my ground. A shot rang out. The audience gasped. I caught the projectile in my teeth. Each succeeding shot was deflected until the pistol was emptied.

I took my bow alongside Sophia, and knew that my career as a stage magician was over. The evening was a farce interspersed with rare moments of competence. Only the backdrop received universal praise, though painted, my compatriots hastened to add, by a hired artist. I was not made for the arts of deception. I did not have the required audacity. And I preferred solitude to the glaring exposure of performance.

I had no option but to return to work. The era of the coffee palaces was over. Ithacans, ever adaptable, took to the simple cafes they had long established and served mixed grills, soups and coffee. We knew how to cater to the needs of the time, the austere years of the Great Depression. I did what I had to do to earn a living, but my mind was elsewhere. In the evenings I returned to my studies of hypnotism. After two years of practise, I placed advertisements in the pages of the Greek newspaper headed: 'The power of Science and Hypnosis'.

'To all Greeks,' I wrote, 'We announce that those who suffer from headaches and back pains, sterility, melancholia, stress and worry, insomnia and epilepsy, and all the ailments and pains of nature, hypnotism is a potential cure.' The cost of a consultation was three shillings, and would take place in the backyard shed, where I am now writing the final pages of my manuscript.

And they came, just two patients in the first month, but in time, a steady stream. I knew from the moment they stepped in what truly ailed them. In their melancholia and migraines, shortness-of-breath and insomnia, I detected the symptoms of a deeper malaise. It could be seen in their bent shoulders, and the defeat in their posture. It could be sensed in the tightness of the body, as I had sensed it in Stratis on a Fremantle wharf, on the day of my arrival. In their eyes I saw signs of the panic I had known following the death of Demos. The symptoms indicated an enduring nostalgia, a longing for idealised pasts that could never be reinstated.

The patients sat in a comfortable armchair, and I began my instructions. 'Focus on the sounds about you,' I intoned, 'the swish of a passing tram, the distant bark of a dog, the rustling of leaves on the vine. Detect the silence that lies at the core of all sound.

'Submit to your weariness. Conjure the image of a spiralling stairway. Descend and allow yourself to touch the earth beneath you. Open your eyes and observe the landscape: rocks bathed in white light, a lizard basking in the sun, eyes glazed with wonder. Raise your eyes beyond the precipice, fix them on the sky beyond it, and follow the flight of the sea hawk. View the island through its vigilant eyes, the boats returning to harbour, the terraces etched in the mountain, a shepherd driving his flock to pasture. Become aware of the weary voices lifting from the valley as you trudge home after a day of labour. Hear the excited barking of dogs as you step onto the familiar pathway.

'Pause for a moment on the threshold. Strip yourself of illusions before you enter. Recall the moment of decision, the last time you stood here, the shrivelled harvests on the blistered earth, the infertile soil of the hardened landscape. Recall the years of famine and endless warring, the enemy landing on your shores, marauding armies stealing across mountain passes. Recall the fratricidal feuds, brother informing on brother, son upon father, the fatal disputes over a few square metres of farmland. Recall your lust for a new life, your desire to flee the suffocating presence of ancestors.

'Now enter and close the door behind you. Rest your limbs after years of work. And when you are refreshed look about. You have regained the hearth and the homecoming. Now that you know you can return, retrace your path to the labyrinth. Climb the steps and return to the hum of the world around you. Allow the fragments of sound to draw out fragments of memory. We all have our fragments to assemble and make sense of. We all harbour the wish, like blind Homer, to take the lyre in hand, and recount the tales of our journeys.'

And seated here, I heard them, endless variants of the voyages we had all embarked on: re-enactments of the moment of leaving, the last trace of land sinking, the precise moment when the past was lost, and the future was shrouded in mystery. All that remained after years of absence was the recital of names. Of hamlets and villages, islands and cities, scattered throughout the homeland. Each name, a vital link in an ancient chant, each tale a variant on loss and separation, fortunes won and squandered, of aborted dreams and thwarted ambitions. And small triumphs: a son and daughter who had gained entrance to a university, a business grown to fruition, a family reunited, an enmity reconciled, the birth of the first grandchild.

In each telling, time was suspended, and in each tale, there resided the bitter aftertaste of life's ironies. Through each tale I relived my own, and came to understand that all we can hope to retrieve from our wandering and exile, is the tale of the journey. And in the silence that followed after the last words were uttered there was release, and in the completion of the telling, the temporary calm after the tempest.

<hr />

There is little more I wish to write. I know my end is coming. It is in the strenuous effort I must make to perform the smallest of tasks. It is time for others to take up the tale. I cannot speak for Fotini. She was a kind soul, and I regret I did not know how to give her comfort. And I have little to say of Manoli. Stratis wrote to me of his youngest son's departure.

I was there to meet him, in the summer of 1939, when the boat drew up to Station Pier. As soon he stepped out of customs I saw the resemblance to Stratis, the fatal brew of pride and stubbornness. When I embraced him on the stained boards of the pier,

I felt the same tautness in the body I had felt when I embraced his father on my arrival in Fremantle.

Within days, I saw the signs of the malaise that afflicts those raised by absent fathers, a dormant anger that could erupt at any time. And within months, I observed the symptoms of his overwhelming nostalgia, Manoli's manic obsession for the sea. And I loved him, as I had loved Stratis, and ached for Sophia, my daughter, when she fell for his charms. But I could do nothing but allow fate to take its course.

———

It is Sunday evening. I have returned from the station where I farewelled Sophia and Xanthe. This afternoon I walked with Xanthe to the park and taught her how to handle kites. When we returned I made sure, as I have in all her visits, that she saw the manuscript. I am certain she will read it. After all, the fattening of the mouse, and the presence of a skull were deliberate diversions, and diversion is the essence of magic. And the presence of the manuscript, beneath the skull, was a suggestion, and the art of suggestion is the essence of hypnosis.

I am surrounded by my books, the violins, the tools of many trades, the prints of the island, the cockatiel, the sayings glued to the walls, and the absurd skull—'my faithful comrades,' as Robert-Houdin said of the props he surrounded himself with after he retired from the stage. On the summit I was enveloped in sky and wind. And in this shed, I am enveloped by my eternal studies. This room is all I need. I have learnt to dance alone.

BOOK VIII

Andreas' tale

Xanthe: Ithaca 2002, 1981

It is approaching midnight. The *patriko* is silent except for the labour of rats and termites. Despite their stubborn endeavours, Martina sleeps soundly. One manuscript has ended, and the other is yet to be completed. I take up my pen to rework the tales Andreas recounted in that winter of tempests, punctuated by abrupt silences, interludes in the storm. Nature has taken her place by the loom.

As I write, I retrieve Andreas' voice, as it once flowed: from the balcony, the cafes of Stavros, by the kitchen fire, and, on feast days, by this walnut table in the living room. 'Once upon a time there were two brothers,' Andreas resumes, 'and we met our father for the first time when he returned from *Afstralia,* the Great Southern Land.

'Stratis did not announce the day of his homecoming,' Andreas recalls. 'He knocked at nightfall, and we did not recognise him when we opened the door. He had been gone fifteen years and smelt of foods we had never eaten. His one familiar feature was the thick moustache that men of the island were so proud of. There is a saying that a man without a moustache is like a meal without salt.'

'Stratis stood at the threshold of the kitchen that Manoli and I had built in his absence. He was afraid to move towards us, and we were afraid to move towards the stranger. He lifted his arms as if about to embrace us, then let them fall by his sides. His face was caught between bewilderment and a dismal attempt at a smile. He did not say a word, and this enraged Manoli. He pushed past him and ran from the house.

'It was the first of many escapades, my child. Manoli would trek to Perahori, the Far Village, to stay with Aunt Irini who had looked after us since the death of Melita. Or descend to Frikes to spend the night out on the fishing boats. He would depart at dusk and return as the sun was rising. Whenever he saw Stratis approaching he would step aside to avoid him. If Stratis tried to placate him, he would back away. There is nothing sadder than the sight of a father trying to reach out to an enraged son,' Andreas says. 'And I remained in the middle, not knowing which way to turn.

'In the weeks after his return, Stratis walked the paths of the mountain as if regaining his bearings. He inspected the family groves, and ran his hands over the lower branches like a physician. He bent over and entered goat houses, and busied himself with adjusting the timber supports. He stood on the cliff path and gazed for hours at Afales and the neighbouring islands.

'Those who knew him before he departed said he had returned leached of his spirit. Only when he met up with compatriots who had journeyed to far places, did he become animated. They were of the same clan. They sat for hours and spoke a dialect only they could comprehend. Their talk was threaded with the strange names of streets in foreign cities. They were like old soldiers who had fought in distant battlefields.

'Stratis was most at ease when consulting his books. They were his advisers, his ministers of state. He built sturdy chicken coops and kept accounts of the number of eggs each hen laid. He devised more efficient means of retrieving the olive harvest. He took to keeping bees, and in his hands the hives flourished. The best honey is made from the flower of the *thymari*,' Andreas tells me, 'but nowadays there is not enough nectar for the bees to feast on.

'Stratis knew much, but talked little. He went about his tasks with a dignity that drew neighbours to consult him about their ailments. Within a year he had gained the respect of all in the village, except Manoli. His return had thwarted our plans. Finally, we descended to the *katoi*, moved aside the looms and threshing bins, and set to work.

'When the boat was completed Manoli could not wait to be away. He was fully at ease only when he cast off. While I was as content to return as he had been to leave, Manoli's mood darkened whenever the caique approached home. A chasm was opening up between us.

'And it widened when Stratis announced he was to remarry. Despina was lame and glad to have found a husband. Like Melita, she came from Zaverda, the mainland town that provided many Ithacan brides, but unlike the straight-backed women of Zaverda, she walked with a limp. She was a kind woman and I did not mind her presence, but Manoli refused to have anything to do with her. He pushed away the food she served and sauntered out whenever she entered. He refused to attend the wedding, and spent the day in Frikes, by the caiques.

'He said that no one could replace Melita, and that to marry a second time was a betrayal. He accused Stratis of spitting on her memory. He did nothing to conceal his contempt and anger. I saw it all,' Andreas shrugs, 'and could do nothing about it.

'Manoli wanted to sail ever further from Ithaca. *Brotherly Love* was not big enough for his ambition. We used the profit we had gained from trading as a down payment on a bigger boat. Manoli was far more strong-willed. At his insistence we embarked on trading voyages east to the mainland port of Piraeus, and north to Corfu and the Adriatic.

'We approached Corfu town for the first time late afternoon. We rounded the old citadel into the harbour and drew up to the marina. It was dark by the time we finished securing the caique. We walked through the arcades in search of a place to eat. Strips of sky could be seen between the walls of narrow alleys. Clothes were flapping on lines strung from balcony to balcony. An operatic aria drifted through an open door, drawing us into an eating-house.

'As we ate, the young woman who had served the meal sat down at our table. We were the last customers. Stella was three years older than Manoli, a schoolteacher with modern ideas. Her father, who was once a fisherman, had journeyed to New York in search of a living. At nights she helped her mother run the eating-house and a *pension* on the floor above it.

'Where do such things begin, with a glance, a wink? Within days Manoli and Stella were seeing each other. Manoli was lost in a delirium. He insisted we take Stella when we set sail for Venice. As a child she had accompanied her father in his fishing caique. She knew the craft of seafaring well. She winched in the anchor, adjusted the rigging, and took her turn by the wheel. Manoli worshipped her.

'For seven days and nights, we traded our way north through the Adriatic. There was always cargo that required the services of a smaller caique: pigs bound for an offshore islet, local wines and dried goods that we sold in the bigger ports on the Adriatic coast of Italy.

'It was dark when the caique approached Venice. We moved between outlying islets as the dawn was greying. Not a word passed between us. Cathedrals and mansions, grand hotels and warehouses peered through the mist from the banks of narrowing channels. Facades were stained and peeling, foundations rotting, but the grandeur overwhelmed us.

'The caique was moored in Venice for five days, while we went about our business. I recall one thing above all others, the sound of feet tramping. Venice was as much a city of feet as a city of water. Manoli and Stella would leave me and stroll through the streets. I did not mind at all. I sat in cafes and listened to armies of feet treading the pavements.

'One evening I saw a band of black-shirts marching with fascist banners. In their tread I heard the march of armies through the millennia. They distributed pamphlets proclaiming the rebirth of Empire. They chanted slogans that spoke of days of reckoning. Their sullen faces were a portent of what was soon to come.

'On the return voyage we detoured to Corfu where Manoli farewelled Stella with the promise of returning. Months later, she arrived unannounced in the village and knocked on the door of the *patriko*. We were at sea at the time. When Stratis opened the door, before him stood a young woman in a tight-fitting dress and high heels. She looked him in the eye and asked for Manoli.

'Stratis was seized by anger. He was affronted by Stella's brazen manner. He slammed the door in her face. Stella knocked again. Stratis rushed outside, and drove her from the house. As she ran, he called her a whore and a foreigner. "May demons dance in your stomach," she shouted as she paused to kick off her high heels. Soon the road was lined with spectators. Those who enjoyed the performance say that she clutched a shoe in each hand, and laughed as she ran.

'When we returned from sea, Stella and Manoli were inseparable. They attended the weekend dances at *La Romanza*. A band from Vathy played tangos and waltzes, swing and sambas. Manoli dressed like a *levendi*. He doused his hair with pomade, and wore a light flannel suit and panama hat. The couple rowed out to islets for picnics on secluded beaches, and met at night for secret trysts. Everyone knew about it my child, except Stratis.

'Stella stayed on Ithaca for the three months of summer. She left on a fine day in September, as she had arrived, without forewarning. Manoli's rage knew no bounds. He blamed Stratis for his loss and cursed him for driving Stella from the island. He accused him of sending Melita to an early grave. He said he had forgotten about his wife and sons in his years in Australia. He claimed he had slept with whores while they were left to fend for themselves. He said many things, words that once uttered cannot be retracted.

'Stratis remained calm during his son's tirades, but there came a time when he erupted. Their quarrel thundered from the house and through the village. It spilled into the streets where they stood, face-to-face, fists clenched, hatred blazing. I separated them just as they were about to come to blows. My brother turned on me and said I had colluded with the old man. He descended to Frikes, and took out the boat for a week. When he returned, I knew that he would never trust me again.'

Andreas leans forward to grasp the poker, and stirs the embers.

The wind has temporarily ceased. All that can be heard is the wood hissing. 'Yes, we built a boat called *Brotherly Love*,' he says, his gaze on the fire. 'We worked the islands for twelve years. We built a kitchen and grew up under the same roof. We drew our boat up to secluded beaches and slept under the stars. We sailed the length and breadth of the Ionian, and knew its waters like the paths of our village. And when Manoli announced he intended to leave for *Afstralia*, I obeyed his final wish and did not tell Stratis.'

Andreas turns to me, in a rare show of anger. 'It was Manoli's parting shot,' he tells me. 'He arranged the journey secretly and left without a word of farewell or forewarning. He turned his face to the morning star and did not look back. I ferried him to Vathy and returned to Frikes. And for the first time I cursed him. "You have turned your back on the island," I shouted. I stood on the deck and hurled my curses against the sky.

'That sky would soon be buzzing with enemy planes, the sea I returned on would soon be littered with mines, and the famished earth on which we walked, would soon send me foraging in the hills of neighbouring islets. And that is all I have to say.'

Andreas stands up, paces the kitchen, and leans his forehead on the door. 'Life is a lie,' he says. 'Man is nothing. *Tipota*.' He steps out on the veranda. I help him sweep up the broken glass from the window, shattered at the outset of the storm. The upper slopes of the Marmakas are covered in black clouds. A gust of wind almost catapults him off his feet. Thunder rolls across the skies. 'The angels are fighting,' he shouts.

As soon as we step inside, he resumes his restless wandering. This is the final irony; the sea is within sight through the shutters, yet Andreas cannot reach it. He is marooned. He withdraws to his bedroom. I remain by the fire and hear the crackle of his transistor. He lies in bed thinking, thinking, and reappears abruptly.

'Stratis could never kill his animals,' he says. 'He did not have the heart. Do you understand? And Manoli was an honest man. Why spit on the dead? They have no chance to speak back. That is what I fear about death. I will no longer be able to speak for myself. I have told you one version of the story and tomorrow I may tell it with a different slant. Each word I utter is true and false at the same time.

'Why did Manoli leave? How can I know? I take back all I have said. I wish only to recite the facts. Stratis left. Melita waited. Melita died. Her sister Irini became our mother. Stratis returned. Irini departed. Despina arrived. Manoli left and did not return. Stratis waited. That is a tale you will hear on the island wherever you go. It is our book of Genesis. We do not say so and so begat so and so, on and on, page after page. We say so and so departed, and so and so returned. Or vanished. Perhaps the old women are right when they say that all has been written.'

Andreas is angry, and I am overcome by panic. I am a parasite, sucking the marrow from an old man, and from both the dead and the living. In exposing their tales I am betraying family, recasting their words with my interpretation. Retelling the story to serve my own ends.

'There are no ends to tales,' Andreas says, as if intuiting my thoughts. 'We tell them to ride out the storm when holed up in foreign ports. We tell them to while away our time as we wait for death. The slant I have put on them takes no account of that which bound Manoli and I together: our mania for the sea. My own son, Andonis, is infected, and you can see where it has led him. He is somewhere out there, who knows where, tending to a never-ending cycle of shit in the engine rooms of oil tankers. It has all come to this. Perhaps I should never have led him, hand in hand, onto the boats, when he was barely able to walk.'

Andreas retreats to his room, lies down, and lights a cigarette. I remain by the fire, and hear snatches of words: 'Wanker. Fascist. Fucking traitor. Go screw your Virgin Mary.' Interspersed by fits of coughing, and the incessant babble of the radio, issuing weather reports, news bulletins, gossip and song, always song in a land of song. Sung at family gatherings, projected through the speakers of busses and ferries, trailing through car windows, rising from the pavements, drifting from balconies, squeezing through shutters, crackling from radios in the holds of fishing caiques.

The word music, *mousike,* derives from that which is inspired by the Muses. And it is music in part, that has inspired my quest, songs I first heard on the veranda of a weatherboard house in Carrum, their power and beauty, their expressions of longing. Songs accompanied by a deeper music: the ebb of the tides, the whirr of sea-birds, and the voices of contemporary Homers sitting on terraces and balconies, in kitchens and coffee houses, domesticating epics, taming life journeys into rhapsodies.

From *rhapsodos,* 'singer of woven words'. Perhaps this is the heart of the Homeric quest, the rhapsodies the poet is said to have composed and refined, night after night, in the performing. Reflected in my clumsy attempts to capture the cadence of contemporary tellers: Andreas, weaving words in a cough-stained voice, worn down over the years to rapid-fire monologues tempered with endearments.

'Come here my child,' he says calling from the bedroom. 'Listen. They are singing *cantathas* from Zakynthos.' He lies on his back and conducts the song with a cigarette. 'Song makes a man forget,' he says. 'During the war we sang songs of resistance day and night. People fell in love with the Movement through song. Do you understand? Even in the darkest days of occupation, song lifted our spirits.'

And it has lifted Andreas now. 'They say that the Nidri ferry may resume its services tomorrow,' he announces. 'We must pack our bags and be ready to board when it arrives. We will sail to Lefkada and return to Ithaca the following day. I am sick of staring at the sea through the shutters.'

———————

We leave for Frikes mid morning. The road is littered with shattered tiles and rocks dislodged by the storm. An electrician is working on cables, downed by the winds. An hour before the ferry is due Omeros is one of the few souls about. 'I wonder what the sea is thinking today,' he says as he limps by, fish trap in hand.

Platon pulls up in his van soon after. A plump and balding man, who moves about the islands selling vegetables, he is anxious to return to Lefkada and replenish his stocks after being confined to Ithaca for days. 'The sea is as smooth as oil,' he says when he steps out, as if willing it to be that way.

The coastguard skids to a halt on a motorcycle and announces that the boat is coming. The news travels fast. Cars, motorcycles, gypsy vans, trucks and cars descend on the waterfront. The coffee shops are filling. There is an air of celebration. The waiting of many days is being released. An hour later, as we pull from the shore, the port empties.

The ferry rounds the breakwater and moves north into the strait between the islands. I observe by day what I had seen at night on cousin Andonis' caique. Through Andreas' binoculars I make out stone shelters on the wooded slopes of the Marmakas. The sun breaks free of the clouds and trails a wake of silver. 'The sea is far more treacherous than it appears,' says Andreas. He is alert, his restlessness gone. He sniffs the air and declares that the gentle swell will not hold for more than a day.

'There were times that we lost sight of all land,' he says. 'When the sea is calm and no shores are in sight, it is easy to believe this is all that exists, a caique manned by two brothers, a universe unto itself. Time bends and stretches. The horizon slips away and is replaced by an illusion of infinity. All day the caique drifts and when land finally appears it is a shock.' Andreas' voice flows with the swells, and I am lulled by the rhythm until the hoot of the ferry signals the port of Nidri.

At nightfall we eat in a restaurant on the ground floor of our *pension*. Entire families are out on the streets, taking advantage of the break in the storm. Coffee houses are overflowing with men watching televised soccer. A collective roar explodes through the doors whenever a goal is scored or averted, but Andreas takes no notice. He is focused on eating.

When he finishes he sits back, and lights a cigarette. There is no need for talk. I am Manoli's daughter, and he, my father's brother. We have been journeying for many years and tomorrow we are returning. We have ransacked history, and laid siege to memories. We are fully spent, and so close to our destination we need only scale the heights above the town to see the lights of Ithaca.

In the morning we are back on the waterfront for the return voyage. The skies are clearing, but there are doubts. Captain Aristides consults the coastguard and the ferry owners. 'It is the devil's calculus,' says Andreas. 'And lives depend on it.' Platon has restocked his van with fruit and vegetables and is impatient to get moving. A busload of devotees bound for the tomb of St Gerasimos on Kefallonia, are eager to resume their pilgrimage. A family of gypsies in a battered utility stuffed with carpets, queues between an oil tanker and a truck weighed down by a pyramid of fodder. When the order to sail is finally issued, the crew is galvanised into action.

Within half an hour the heavily loaded ferry is moving past a string of islets. It sails close to Skorpios, a forested isle owned by Aristotle Onassis, the shipping magnate. Two large dwellings, a kilometre apart, peer from clearings high above the water. A middle-aged woman disputes the claim. 'This is not Skorpios,' she shouts. 'It is too small. An island owned by Onassis has to be far bigger.' Passengers try to calm her by showing her the island marked on their maps, but she cannot accept it. It violates her hunger for myth. She is angry, distraught. 'Skorpios is far bigger' she persists, as we break free of Lefkada.

Ithaca is within sight. We are edging closer, sailing towards the Bay of Afales. Above the cliff I can make out the walk to the wind-mill. Through the binoculars I see sheep being driven to pasture. I follow the path down to the village, and single out our balcony. Our destination is tantalisingly close. The strait is calm, the return imminent.

'Do not believe it,' Andreas warns. And slowly it registers. The troughs between the waves are deepening. The winds are rising, tinged with bitterness. The seas have grown dark and forbidding. Water careers over the deck, and changes direction with the boat's lurching. The crew is worried. Their anxiety infects the passengers.

One of the pilgrims begins to dance. She sings as she whirls. There is something sinister in her shrill voice and movements.

The rain slants across the deck and into our faces. We stumble to the lee side of the boat and fall back onto a bench beneath the awnings. The woman still dances on the open deck. She allows herself to be deluged. The chatter of passengers has been reduced to urgent whispers. The coast of Ithaca, so close minutes ago, is receding.

'When does the Maistros blow?'

'When it wants to,' Andreas has insisted.

Now it blows and he is elated. It sweeps in and whips the swell into a fury. He conducts the ferry's awkward lurching with his cigarette. 'Kazantzakis may be right, after all, to include Odysseus as the fourth member of the pantheon,' he says, 'if only in one sequence.'

I know, instantly, the sequence he is referring to. Odysseus and his crew, shaken from their encounter with the one-eyed Cyclops, and grieving for the death of comrades, land on the floating island of Aeolia, home of the lord of the winds, Aeolus. The men are entertained and feted in Aeolus' palace but, after years away on the battlefields of Troy, Odysseus is anxious to resume the return voyage.

Aeolus agrees to help. He makes arrangements for the journey and presents Odysseus with a leather bag made from the flayed skin of a full-grown ox. The bag is stowed in the hold of Odysseus' ship and tightly secured with burnished silver wire to prevent any leaking. Within the bag Aeolus has imprisoned the wild energies of all the winds, bar Zephyr, the westerly, which he summons to blow the ships and crew back to Ithaca.

For nine days and nights the ships sail on, propelled by the fair westerly. On the tenth night the men are within sight of the homeland, so close they can see shepherds tending their fires. In his anxiety to speed the voyage, Odysseus had steered the ship without a break. Utterly exhausted and with landfall assured, he falls asleep.

The crew begins to discuss matters among themselves. Surely the bag contains a fortune in gold and silver. Why should they arrive home empty handed? They too had battled in Troy and endured the hazards of the journey. Did they not deserve a share of the spoils? Their evil counsel prevails and they undo the bag, allowing the winds to rush out.

In an instant the tempest is upon them, driving them headlong out to sea, away from the island. The distraught Odysseus and his crews are blown back to Aeolia. The lord of the winds is enraged by their folly. He condemns them to journey on without fair winds and divine guidance. They are destined to die, one by one, except Odysseus, and he will endure yet another decade of wandering until he is finally deposited on the shores of Ithaca.

'I do not hold with the gods,' says Andreas, 'but Homer understood the seaman's paradox, the allure of riches and conquest against the longing for the homeland. Even here, nearing the end of our journey,' he says, 'the seas are seething with blood and the watery graves of its victims.' And he recounts a tale I have heard told on balconies overlooking the seas we are now floundering on.

A convoy of German boats was making its way through these waters on 21 May 1941, when attacked by the submarine, *Papanikolis,* hidden in a cave by the cape of Agios Ioannis. The first ship hit, it is said, was blown clean in half. Soon after, a part of the boat rose out of the sea, as if taking one last gasp of air. Hundreds of soldiers leapt into the water. Their screams could be heard from the northern heights above the bay of Afales.

It was a wonderful day, I have heard said in the village. Hundreds of German soldiers were drowning and we were making sweets. They had pillaged and murdered, and now they were dying. Thiaks ran to the shores and tore off clothes and shoes from the corpses. One fisherman steered his boat to the wreckage and salvaged motorcycles, but in his greed he took too many, and his boat capsized. The captain of the submarine climbed up to the Kathara monastery to offer thanks for the victory.

Andreas takes a different tack. 'We saw them melting in the fires,' he says, 'choking on oil and water. Their vomit floated alongside the debris.' He spits at the memory and the waters that contain it. 'War is the wildest wind contained in the ox-skin bag,' he exclaims. 'Once released, you have no choice but to defend yourself against its fury. If you have not lived it, you cannot know it.

'There were Ithacans who took pity, and waded out to help the soldiers. Some villagers took the wounded into their homes and gave them food and shelter. They saw them for what they were, young boys polluted with hatred instilled by their elders.

'They were perhaps the same boys who would have obeyed the order to hoist the Nazi flag on the Acropolis,' says Andreas, 'the same boys who would strut through the streets of Athens, and starve and torture the people. Perhaps the same soldiers who, in December 1943, would march through the valley of Kalavrita, on the mainland, and murder fourteen hundred men aged between thirteen and eighty, before setting fire to the village. Perhaps among them were officers who would have massacred thousands of Italian soldiers on Kefallonia, among them men who had been stationed on Ithaca.

'Even as the war ended, the ox-skin bag was not yet empty,' Andreas tells me. 'The storm did not cease with the defeat of the Germans. Within months the time we call "the division" came upon us. It was worse than all that had taken place before it. At least then, the enemy were foreigners. Now men we had grown up with dragged us out for interrogations and beatings. There is nothing more terrible than waging war on your own people, my Xanthe. Nothing. Neighbours were beaten, imprisoned, driven into exile. I can point to houses in Ithacan villages that belong to those who did the beatings, and to those who were beaten.'

The ferry rolls and lurches. 'Manoli loved the storm,' Andreas shouts. 'He ran about tightening the rigging, bailing out water, laughing. He shook his fists at the winds and dared them to become wilder. He surveyed the skies and rejoiced when they were black and bloated. He would have ripped open Aeolus' ox-skin bag willingly, not for the imagined riches, but to release mayhem and chaos. He preferred wild winds to the hearth, the storm to the returning. Who knows what drove him?'

The mad pilgrim is still dancing, barely maintaining her footing on the wet timber. Her movements are increasingly desperate and frenzied. Only the momentum of her spinning saves her from falling. Our destination is within sight, but we are stranded. And I see him, Manoli, my father, in his final months, motoring beyond the estuary.

He is shouting above the din of the engine, shaking his fists at Aeolus, at Zeus the cloud gatherer, Poseidon the earth shaker, and the lord of the skies, Ouranos. He is baying at the entire pantheon of gods who, despite it all, he cannot believe in. The waters of the bay evoke memories of Ionian voyages. The lights of the city are winking, the return beckoning, but he cannot yield.

He sails through the night and his madness is growing. He cannot shake off the sight of his mother's corpse lying beside him. He inhales her scent of lavender and sage, of sweat and the rocky earth, and on that Easter morning, the odour of death. The bells are tolling, and he is running to the chapel of St John on the mountain, then hurtling down to the quay, exhilarated by the sight of boats departing.

I now know something of his tortured ambitions. He had left Ithaca, his spirit wounded. He had left like an enraged sea trapped within its own fury. He left vowing to shatter obsolete gods and superstitions. He left obsessed by ambition to surpass his father. He left lashing out at the brother he loved. He turned his back on the island, and did not dare look for fear of hesitating, breaking. And years later, before the final descent, his life crumbling, he understood, too late, that the winds would never cease howling. He had journeyed to far to have any hope of returning.

The mad dervish is spiralling towards hysteria. We are being driven further from our destination. The coast of Lefkada is again upon us. The lighthouse is issuing its warning. Though I have glimpsed the white cliffs many times from the balcony, for the first time I truly see them. They fall from the limestone promontory, cliffs known for millennia as Sappho's Leap, the site of a lovers' yearning. Here, legend has it, the poet of Lesbos threw herself into turbulent waters driven by her unrequited love for a seaman.

Whether the legend is true scarcely matters. It is made for these waters and the jagged coasts that frame them. It is made for the myth that at its base seethed the seas of the Underworld, and the River of the Dead, the gateway to Hades. It endures as a testament to the agony of those condemned to years of separation. With the ferry pitching between the islands, I sense both sides of the equation. Gazing down from the rocky heights are those condemned to the waiting, while those at sea are drifting ever further. The gap between them is widening, the umbilical cord stretched to breaking.

I look back at Captain Aristides. His grimace is dissolving. The ferry is in harness to the currents, gathering speed and composure. The mad dervish stops and looks about her, bewildered. Moments later she stumbles to a seat, weeping. A fellow pilgrim tries to console her, but she pushes her away and spits at the heavens. She screams above the dying winds, and the coast of Ithaca is again upon us. The island is implacable. 'To know one place is to know all places,' mutters Andreas.

We round the headland, past the breakwater into the bay of Frikes. Within minutes of berthing, the gypsies are on the road to Kioni, speakers blaring, announcing the arrival of the carpet vendors. Platon has disappeared with his van on the road to Stavros. The ferry quickly reloads, the crowd disperses.

Only Omeros remains. He limps towards us, empty fish trap in hand, as we begin the ascent to the village. 'What is the sea thinking today?' he asks. And, for the first time I sense, beyond the madness, the infernal logic of his question.

BOOK IX
EPILOGUE

The resident tiller of the soil

XANTHE: ITHACA 2002

I LAY down my pen as the first sign of day seeps through the shutters. The walnut table, chest of drawers, the divan and glass-panelled cupboard are intimate companions. I look up at the photo of Stratis and Melita, and the two boys, Andreas and Manoli. Again I am taken by Stratis' disembodied presence. Melita died within months of the photo being taken, and her place was assumed by Irini. The family Stratis presides over is on the verge of disintegration. Only the frame and skilled manipulation hold it together.

I step out on the balcony and look over the strait towards Lefkada. An overnight ferry is moving between the two islands. Afales Bay is a skin of crimson, and the cliffs of Sappho's Leap are tinged with silver. The mountain remains a black presence awaiting the sun's ascent to the heavens. The bus from Kioni can be heard approaching from the lower village. Outside the all-purpose store students are waiting. On an impulse I hurry to the bedroom, wake up Martina, and quickly pack an overnight bag with a change of clothing.

Martina is up and ready to move within minutes. She has become a hardened traveller. We hurry to the road as the bus turns into the village. Martina is taken in hand by girls on their way to high school, and disappears to the rear of the bus. A song blares from the speakers: *Yes, I will wait for you.* We get off in Vathy and eat breakfast by the waterfront before setting out on the steep trek to Perahori, the Far Village.

Within twenty minutes the skies are black, the winds gusting. We unfurl our umbrellas, but they are instantly shredded. We focus our eyes on our feet and follow each step forward. I am *Me ta podia*, the mad one who walks, and Martina is my accomplice.

For an hour the rains continue, until, as abruptly as it had broken, the squall is over, and we are entering the outskirts of Perahori. Paved paths wind towards the thresholds of stone houses, one of which belongs to Irini. She is well into her nineties. No one knows exactly how old. She is one of the last of a dwindling species, women who endured long lives in the mountain villages of the Ionian.

Once upon a time there lived two sisters, Melita and Irini. The younger has outlived the older by more than seven decades. She stands on a ladder in the front garden, pruning an almond tree, unaware of our approach. Her feet are planted on an upper rung, and her thin limbs could be mistaken for an extension of the branches.

When she climbs down Martina gazes at her, fearful and astonished. She has never laid eyes on someone so ancient. Her fears vanish as Irini becomes aware of our presence. Her entire being is alight with recognition. Martina is enfolded in her arms in one seamless movement. I stand back and observe their union.

Irini brushes aside our attempts to assist her and moves with astonishing agility through the front door and into the kitchen.

The television is on, the volume loud, tuned to *The Bold and the Beautiful*. She switches it off, and for our seven-day stay it will remain forgotten.

She brings bread to the table, and bean soup that had been on the stove, simmering. She runs her hands over my face as if feeling for its secrets. She embraces Martina and calls her 'my golden one'. Terms of endearment lie at the core of the Greek language. Perhaps they derive from the deep knowing that the threat of separation is always present.

Martina and Irini are inseparable. Martina trails beside her and I walk in their shadow, drawn by the stubborn will that propels Irini like a wind-driven eddy. Her sight is dimming, but she need only focus on the few metres before her. She moves with ease about her defined sphere, as if enclosed within the arc of a lantern. She has neighbours who help her, but clings fiercely to her independence.

She flits from the kitchen down a flight of steps to the garden and sets to work, pruning, planting. Always moving, from the house to the terraced garden, from the gate through the winding streets of the village, within the territory that sustains her. And Martina moves with her, works beside her, emulates her actions, her slow, steady tending.

Irini knows each tree planted over the years, and names them for Martina: the four almond trees, five orange trees, the three fig trees, the six apple trees, the vines on the trellis, the eleven olive trees beside the house and in the garden. The house is sprouting with potted flowers, geraniums and begonias, hibiscus, frangipani. They line the terrace and stairway, crowd the balcony, and sit on tables by the windows.

On the third day Irini descends to the *katoi*. She has the unexpected gift of two able-bodied assistants and will use them to restore order. Under Irini's directions we drag out termite-ridden trunks filled with blankets, picking bags, rotting sacks, rugs and tablecloths. There are chests lined with Chicago newspapers of the 1920s, and stickers marking journeys through the customs houses of Port Said and Alexandria. New York. London.

We advance deeper into the cobwebbed darkness and extract grape-thrashing tubs, grinding stones, lanterns, bread cauldrons, coils of wire, rotting tables and dressers. We take care in carrying out the loom, and spools of thread packed in wooden boxes. We pause to dust the icons of saints, and photos of Irini's husband with Ithacan compatriots in Chicago.

Our final task is to transfer the rancid olive oil from the ceramic *plithari*. We ladle the oil into smaller containers and find rats preserved in the lower depths. They had eluded poisons and traps only to drown in the thick liquid. I am assigned the task of burying them.

We return to the pile of objects outside the *katoi* in the morning, separate that which Irini wishes to keep, and set fire to the rest. Black smoke billows with the stench of forgotten ancestors. We are three generations entwined, sorting out the accumulated confusion of our forebears. And at the helm of our operation, firmly grasping the tiller, stands Grand Aunt Irini.

She navigates her territory with a steady hand, and spends her days in perpetual motion; but at the core there is an abiding tranquillity. She speaks sparingly, conserving her dwindling energy, but we have begun to comprehend her subtle language.

The rhythm of work is her lyre, and the tales she weaves reside in her silences and tending. They convey nuances that lie beyond the literal telling, wisdom gained in the being and doing. They recall the solace of my childhood walks by the Carrum foreshore and wetlands. They evoke memories of my mother, Sophia, her steadfast tending to my wellbeing, her resolution, despite the incessant rage of Manoli.

And they bring to mind the dignified silences of Fotini; but Irini does not possess the fatalist's shrug, Fotini's sense of resignation. She is fully in command of her confined realm, propelled by the fierce life force in her tiny body. Her entire being has been pared to its essence. She is a tough nurturer and protector of the earth that sustains her. She is a resident tiller of the soil, a mistress of orchards and gardens.

By the fourth day Irini's work rituals have claimed us. We have been absorbed into her realm and voyage beside her. Only when the time of separation is upon us is the spell broken. Irini accompanies us the first fifty metres to the lower edge of the Far Village. Martina is distraught as she recedes behind us. Irini stands on the path, and waves even after she can no longer see us.

Like Fotini, she is a tiny figure growing smaller against the vastness of the mountain. She fades into the landscape like a lizard camouflaged by its scales and stillness. On the slopes above her, the remains of earthquake ruins are crumbling into oblivion between homes that have risen from the debris.

Only as the Far Village disappears do I recognise that, for the first time, I had not interrogated the past with a barrage of questions. Yet I understand that even though she has not once left the island in the ninety years since she set foot on Ithaca, Irini is both voyager and teller, Odysseus and Homer. She is a weaver of work rhythms and silences. So scoured by a lifetime of tending that her tales are embedded in her being.

The thought takes root in my final weeks on the island. Now that the end of our stay is approaching, I am obsessed, as on previous sojourns, with tattooing the landscape on my memory. I have inherited the Ithacan phobia, the fear that I may never return. I am *Me ta podia,* the mad one who walks, and Martina remains my willing accomplice.

We walk the ports of Kioni and Frikes, Polis Bay and Afales. Nets are sprawled in heaps on seawalls and jetties. On the Vathy foreshore, there are Alfa Romeos, Mercedes, BMWs and Volvos, the imported cars of the nouveau riche, waiting like the bare-masted ships that once filled the harbour in winter.

We walk familiar ground and perceive new meanings. The mill that Andreas once tended traps the winds within its hollows. We stray into the lowlands and are lost in gullies thick with wild olives. Dogs burst from timber shacks and stop abruptly, confined by their leashes to ferocious barking. We find our way back onto an overgrown path, and come upon the ruins of churches with cracked walls of faded frescoes.

We stumble towards the heights like drunkards over fields of limestone. In the sea below us, rocks skew the ripples of eddies and currents. The scent of the sea rises to meet the scent of the mountain. The skies are whirling, the earth turning and returning, the sea vanishing, reappearing.

This is not an Ithaca in waiting, an idealised figment of memory, but a living presence. An island that bends labouring breath and muscle to its brute power. The summer is long over, the harvest ended. With each passing day the island is ebbing further into stillness, and with it the old Ithaca returns, that which has outlived the departures of millennia.

We wander hamlets we have rarely set foot in. Goats scatter into the undergrowth. A washing line strung between two pines tilts trousers and vests towards the heavens. A fishing net is spread on the side of the road, like the tentacles of a giant squid. A fisherman disentangles and spreads it further. A spaniel lies in the shade beside him. An elderly woman in widow's black scales the leeside of the mountain.

'This year *tipota*' she says, 'Nothing.'

'And last year?'

'Last year the trees were dripping with olives, but the oil was putrid.'

She screws up her face.

'Next year will be better,' I suggest.

'Why?' she replies with contempt. 'Flies burrow into the fruit to lay their eggs. The eggs hatch, the worms feast, and the olives drop from the trees, sucked dry by parasites.' She spits on the ground.

'And if the olives are good, so what? The middle men will siphon off the profits.' She looks at us for a long time and says: 'Ah, it gives you an appetite being up here, doesn't it?' And in a voice barely stronger than a whisper, she sings:

> *Life has two doors*
> *I opened one,*
> *And came in one morning*
> *And by the time evening arrived*
> *I had left by the other.*

'The last door is open and waiting,' she cackles. We continue up the mountain to a plateau. Again the island is turning on its axis. The path conveys us to a remote enclave where goats graze under the watchful eyes of an elderly couple. A saddled donkey stands beside them. The Ionian eddies below us. And as we walk I know that Martina's is one story that will remain untold. She will be free, soon enough, to come and go as she pleases, free to weave her life as she wishes.

Like Irini she is in command of the moment. She has no time for nostalgia. She is diverted by a praying mantis and jewelled beetles, and startled by red domed mushrooms rising on white stems from rock crevices. She bends down to follow the trek of an ant dragging a fragment of olive skin, many times its size. She stares at a cypress tree split apart by lightning, sending out new growth, and squats to inspect a scattering of minute black orchids and crocuses. She is coming to know the skin of the island, the living fabric. She hums and sings when the mood takes her, and is content to be silent.

On the eve of our departure, we return to the ruins of Homer's School, Mentor's site of healing, and the landscape of his lucid dreaming. We climb the stone steps to the upper rung and sit where he sealed his pact with Stratis. The cliff path to the Marmakas, overlooking the Bay of Afales is a track of silver, the Ionian a rippling skin of crimson. Upon its waters a single caique is returning to the port of Frikes. It is the hour of the homecoming. The crew is within sight of the shepherds' huts on the Marmakas. Somewhere on the island, a hearth is waiting.

I remain seated beside Martina long after the caique has berthed. A breeze flares and leaps like an invisible flame through the ruins. The lights of the villages are appearing. The lighthouse of Lefkada is issuing warnings to strangers. The church on the lower hill tolls the passing of the hours. It is time to resume the weaving. *Arkhe tou paramythiou.* The fairytale begins. *Kalispera sas.* Good evening to you.

AUTHOR'S NOTE

Sea of Many Returns is a work of fiction that has drawn on many personal and historical sources. I owe much to the people of Ithaca for sharing their stories. I am grateful to Andreas Anagnostatis, generous keeper of Ithacan lore, and Dennis Sikiotis, for his knowledge of Ithaca. I thank my partner Dora's extended family in Athens and on the island: Efthimios and Aleka, Yiannis and Dionysia, Makis and Kalliopi, Sevasti and Athanassios, Aunt Agelo, cousin Rigo, Aunt Georghia and the late Dimitri Varvarigos.

I thank Lula Black, Loula Coutsouvelis, Konstandina Dounis, Tony Knight and Helen Nickas for reading the manuscript, and Jim and Melita Vlassopoulos, Tasia Couvara, and Spyridoula Maroulis, generous hosts of many Ithacan gatherings in Melbourne. For their support, I thank George Coutsouvelis, Olga Black, Peter Paxinos, Eustratia and Demetri Pimenides, Effie Detsimas, the late Stathis Raftopoulos, the Ithacan Philanthropic Society, and the editorial board of *Odysseus*.

Michael Heyward is a publisher and editor with an uncanny ability to see the big picture. Jane Pearson edited the book with great skill, care and enthusiasm.

I owe much to Dora: for our many journeys to Ithaca over the past two decades, for family stories, interpreting conversations, advice on the text, and ongoing discussions of its themes. In many ways, it is Dora's book, and Alexander's, our son and travel companion.

While this is a work of fiction, historical events have been carefully researched. In reconstructing the Black Sea voyages, I drew on resources at the Maritime Museum in Vathy, travellers' accounts, and conversations with descendents of Ithacans who traded along the Danube River.

The anti-Greek riots in Perth and Kalgoorlie are based on contemporary reports in *The Kalgoorlie Miner*. I also drew on Reginald Appleyard and John N. Yiannakis, *Greek Pioneers in Western Australia*, University of WA Press, 2002; and Hugh Gilchrist *Australians and Greeks, Vols I & II*, Halstead Press, Rushcutter's Bay, 1992 & 1997. The lyrics for *If I die on the boat* are from Gail Holst's book, *Road to Rembetika*, Anglo-Hellenic Publishing, Athens, 1975. The Gambler is a fictional character inspired by Nikos Kallinikos whose brief biography appears in George Kanarakis, *Greek Voices in Australia*, Australian National University Press, Sydney, 1987.

A State Library of Victoria fellowship provided time and access to the W. G. Alma Conjuring Collection, and to Marion Mahoney Griffin and Walter Burley Griffin's original drawings for the Capitol Theatre. Historian, Donald Leslie Johnson asserts, 'it would be safe to say that modern architecture in Australia began with the Cafe Australia.' I am grateful to Dianne Reilly who administered the fellowship, and to the library staff.

Other books I drew on include: Neal Ascherson's seminal

work, *Black Sea*, Hill and Wang, New York, 1995; Walter Benjamin, *Illuminations*, Harcourt, Brace & World, New York, 1995; Bill Bunbury, *Timber for Gold*, Fremantle Arts Centre Press, 1997; Donald Leslie Johnson, *The Architecture of Walter Burley Griffin*, MacMillan, South Melbourne, 1977; Clive Turnbull, *Frontier, the Story of Paddy Hannan*, Hawthorn Press, Melbourne, 1949; Jeff Turnbull and Peter Y. Navaretti, editors, *The Griffins in Australia and India*, Miegunyah Press, Melbourne, 1998; and Melbourne-based Owl Publishing's Greek Diaspora Literature series.

In memory of Lily Varvarigos, whose house was filled with stories, food and good company, and Babis Varvarigos, a true *levendi* and lover of the sea.